D0441746

Praise for *Worlds Asunder*

Worlds Asunder is a thrill ride that envisions Earth's early colonization of space and the dangers inherent in exploring new frontiers. The superb interweaving of futuristic adventure, political conspiracy, and personal drama will pull you in immediately — be prepared to lose track of time until you reach the riveting and emotional conclusion!

- David J. Corwell, author of "Legacy of the Quedana," which appears in *Cloaked in Shadow: Dark Tales of Elves*

As a kid, I was addicted to science fiction. From Tom Swift to Isaac Asimov, Robert A. Heinlein and Ray Bradbury, I devoured them all. I even took a sci-fi lit course in college. But apart from a brief return to the genre in the '80s for Margaret Atwood's *The Handmaid's Tale,* it's been 30 years since I've read any science fiction. I just wasn't into it.

Kirt Hickman's debut novel, *Worlds Asunder,* may have cured me of my indifference. Or perhaps it's just created a new addiction: to Hickman's storytelling.

The science in *Worlds Asunder* is credible and, given Hickman's engineering background, probably accurate. But it's the fiction side of the "science fiction" label that kept me wanting more. Clean, clear and compelling, Hickman's action-packed story gripped me from the first page and didn't release me until its satisfying conclusion 260 pages later.

- Mark David Gerson
award-winning author of *The MoonQuest: A True Fantasy* and *The Voice of the Muse: Answering the Call to Write*

HARDY

WORLDS ASUNDER

Murder was only the beginning...

Kirt Hickman

2008

Published in the U.S.A. by
Quillrunner Publishing LLC
8423 Los Reyes Ct. NW
Albuquerque, NM USA 87120

Printed in the U.S.A.

Cover art by David A. Hardy

Book design by Michael Dyer, MOCA Book Design
Typeset in Palatino 10/14

This book is a work of fiction. All plots, themes, dates, events, persons, characters, and character descriptions contained in this material are completely fictional. Any resemblance to any events, persons, or characters, real or fictional, living or deceased, is entirely coincidental and unintentional. All locations and organizations are products of the author's imagination or are used fictionally. Kirt Hickman and Quillrunner Publishing LLC, are not responsible for any use of these character names or any resemblance of these character names to actual persons, living or deceased.

Cataloging-in-Publication Data is on file with the Library of Congress.
Library of Congress Control Number: 2008931112

ISBN 978-0-9796330-2-7

For Lisa, who always knew I could.

Acknowledgments

A book like this can't be created by one person alone. It took the tireless effort of many people to make *Worlds Asunder* a reality. My thanks go out to all of you.

First, to Eileen Stanton, who endured the agony of an appalling early draft. Without your honesty and encouragement this book would never have made it into print. Next, to my network of critiquers and test readers: David J. Corwell, Keith Pyeatt, Erle Guillermo, Rick McLaughlin, Gerry Raban, Laura Beltemacchi, Lisa Hickman, and others. Special thanks to Nancy Varian Berberick for catching the things that the rest of us didn't.

To my editor, Susan Grossman, for ensuring that *Worlds Asunder* is the best that it can be.

To all my peers at SouthWest Writers, for your constant moral and technical support. I've learned so much.

To David A. Hardy and Michael Dyer, for exceeding all my expectations for book and cover design.

To my wife, Lisa, for giving me the time and encouragement to begin, to endure, and to finally complete *Worlds Asunder*. I couldn't have done it without you.

And to God for blessing me with all the necessary talents and resources.

Prologue

General Chang reclined in the womb of his stronghold with his feet propped on the conference table.

"It's done." The words, uttered in Chinese, rang clearly through the comm speaker.

"About time." Chang didn't bother to open his eyes, let alone examine the banks of monitors that surrounded him. Alarms would announce anything that required his attention. Besides, he had plenty of men, should a need arise. For now, the stronghold remained at peace.

The man at the other end of the link paused. He offered no excuses or apologies — which Chang would have rejected in any case — for the months that had passed since Chang had hired him.

"I hope you're ready," the man said. "When this thing hits the fan, it's going to get messy."

Chang shifted his cap to cover his eyes and smiled for the first time in a decade. For China's sake, he was counting on it.

CHAPTER 1

"It was really embarrassing." Edward "Chase" Morgan drew the top card from the deck: the queen of diamonds. "We'd just returned from hitting a crack factory and warehouse in Cuba. This was back when President Montros thought he could stop the drug trade with air strikes."

He tapped his cards on the table. Michelle Fairchild, his materials engineering intern from Mars Tech, had won every game that evening. Not this one, though, if he could help it. Chase needed just two cards to win and Michelle hadn't lain down any of hers. Unfortunately, the queen wasn't one of the two. He tossed it onto the discard pile.

Smiling, Michelle picked it up, then placed it and two others on the table.

Chase groaned. That group put her in the lead and, at double or nothing, the credits were starting to add up.

Michelle discarded a ten.

Chase grabbed it, rearranged his hand, and discarded a four. "We had the weekend off before we had to fly back to Nellis, so we went out to celebrate our mission's success.

"We drank most of the night, then went to one of those all-night waffle places. They had this great-looking redheaded waitress. She was..." He stopped, unable to talk about her. Michelle was too much like a daughter to him to get into that kind of story. "Anyway, I was so busy trying to impress her, I didn't realize I'd gotten my syrup all over the place. I kept wiping it off my hands, my fork, the table, you name it. My napkin was shredded, half of it was stuck to my fingers, and no matter what I did, I just managed to make it worse."

With his free hand, he petted Penny, his copper-colored wiener dog, who lolled upside-down in his lap with her ears and tongue dangling toward the floor. "When I got back to my room, I found that I'd wiped my hands all down the front of my flight suit without ever realizing it."

Michelle grinned. "I can't picture you drunk."

"I haven't been drunk since I retired from the air force twenty years ago. It's your turn."

She drew a card and put it into her hand. "Did you ever ask her out?"

"The waitress? No. Whatever chance I might have had, I blew that night. I learned a few months later that the guys poured syrup on my fork handle every time I looked at her."

Michelle laughed so hard she nearly spit her coffee. "That's classic." When she recovered, she laid down a string of cards, discarding the last one. "Rummy."

"Ouch." Chase scooped up the cards and shuffled the deck together. "Sooner or later I'll win one."

"Not tonight. I still have studying to do." She extended her hand, palm-up, across the table. "I believe you owe me."

"Not if I beat you next time."

"Double or nothing again? Are you sure?" She gave him the same look he must have used when one of his real daughters made a bad choice that he knew he couldn't talk her out of. "Sometimes I think you don't know when to quit."

"We'll see." He lowered Penny to the floor. The dog groaned in disappointment. Horribly spoiled, she refused to roll herself over and climb to her feet. "Sorry, girl," he told her.

"All right." Michelle stood and smoothed her plaid flannel shirt, which she wore untucked to conceal the finer elements of her petite figure. In the harsh, solid-state lighting, her skin looked pale, as though it had never seen the sun without the UV protection of a durapane window. "Thanks for dinner."

She lifted Penny and nuzzled the dog's face with her own. "You have a good night, little cupcake." Penny licked her face. "See you in the morning," she told Chase as she set Penny down, then left for the night.

Chase cleared the remnants of dinner and poured himself another cup of coffee. The gold watch that Director Jack Snider had given him at his twentieth employment-anniversary ceremony the previous night was still sitting on the counter. Chase took out the watch and returned to the table.

The NASA inscription across the top offset the Lunar Alpha Base logo beneath the display. Nowhere did it say, "Office of Accident Investigations." Maybe Snider recognized that Chase didn't belong in Investigations. He'd been put there after he lost his flight status four years ago because he was too old to do anything else.

Chase sucked the last of the coffee from his seal-pak mug, then checked the date for probably the fifth time that day. Just two more weeks to retirement. Then he could go home to Earth and what was left of his family.

He'd have to start packing soon. Maybe tomorrow he'd crate up the nonessentials: his drawing table, most of his clothes, even that ridiculous hologram Erin sent him last year, the one that misrepresented Pluto's orbit. Eventually everything would go, except for the framed DeMitri on the far wall. Painted to make use of the base's high-ceilinged lunar architecture, it was too big to take back to Earth. Besides, he'd have little need for an Earthly landscape of the Olympic Range when he could look upon it with his own eyes.

The comm panel buzzed. Chase stretched his lanky frame and got to his feet, then leapt to the terminal against the slight lunar g.

He keyed the link. On the screen, a frown elongated the narrow face of Security Chief Stan Brower, whose sharp eyes were nearly as pale as his graying hair. This wouldn't be good news.

"We've got a ship in trouble," Brower said. "The *Phoenix*. Snider needs you to assemble a team."

"The *Phoenix*?"

"A freighter. Belongs to Stellarfare. She was on her way from here to Montanari when she lost thrust, but it looks like she might come back around toward Alpha ... if they don't regain control."

"You don't sound like you think they will."

"No reason to."

Chase ran an ebony hand through his hair, which had turned gray, along with his mustache and beard, years ago. "Any reason to think they won't?"

"No." Brower hesitated. "Look, Chase. There's more to it than that, but I can't put it on the telnet. You better put a team together and get to Benford's. We'll contact you with coordinates as soon as she comes down."

As he killed the link, Chase tried to imagine what the crew must be going through. During his own deep-space missions, he'd experienced a number of technical glitches. They were nothing short of terrifying, but he had never had a loss of thrust. Usually you had options, but not without thrust. Nothing could make a pilot feel so powerless.

But there was more to it, Brower had said. Chase would find out what before he left the base. He always believed that you have to know what you're up against before you know what to do. So he logged into NASA's data net and scanned the *Phoenix* file. A freighter, the record said. Local, its operations restricted to lunar destinations. Good. That limited the crew size and fuel reserves on board. He scrolled past the physical statistics — size, class, thrust-to-mass ratio — and came to the corporate data.

OWNER: Stellarfare

CREW: Randy Lauback, Phyllis Conway

He read the last line again. His investigations career had come full circle, it seemed. It would end where it had begun. With Randy Lauback.

Chase knew then that he had to take the case, however long it might last, and follow it through to completion. He owed Randy that much.

Then he contacted Benford's, NASA's construction, demolition, and recovery contractor, and told them what he knew of the job. They'd need time to look up the specs and cargo manifest and assemble the gear they'd need for the recovery. "Let's plan on hangar three at midnight," he said.

Chase terminated the link and began his preflight. It was a misnomer because accident investigations rarely required him to fly, but he was used to the term from his younger days. It made him feel like he was somehow still in the game.

He'd told the man at Benford's to assume the worst. That would ensure they brought the right hardware to recover the ship if, God forbid, it became necessary. The rest had to wait until Chase knew more. He couldn't assemble his team until he knew if a recovery would be needed, couldn't pack until he knew how long he'd be gone, and couldn't contemplate strategy until he understood the scenario. He just didn't have enough information. And he wasn't good at waiting.

So he activated the comm. "Morgan to tower."

"Tower. Go ahead, Morgan." Director Snider's face appeared strained. The dark rings beneath his eyes made his close-cropped, blond hair look platinum.

"Tell me about the *Phoenix*."

"Hold on." Snider spoke to someone Chase couldn't see. "Do we have a schematic? … Put it on that monitor." A man with a Stellarfare patch on the sleeve of his jumpsuit stepped into view. Snider made room by the terminal as he spoke to the man. "This smacks of a single-point failure."

"I'm telling you," the Stellarfare man said, "all the essential systems have a backup."

Snider stabbed a finger at the diagram. "Find that failure." He glanced at the holographic display that dominated the front of the small control room, then turned to Chase. "We're losing her."

"She got any thrust at all?" Chase asked.

"Negative." Snider looked past the terminal. "Keep those reporters out of here." Then the screen went dark, disconnected at the other end.

Chase's stomach tightened until it hurt and forced him to sit down. This case was bigger than the landing-field mishaps, taxiway collisions, and forklift accidents he was used to investigating, but it wasn't the scope that knotted his gut. People occupied that ship. If Randy didn't recover thrust before they hit the surface …

Chase couldn't finish the thought. Randy was a good pilot. He would recover thrust. He had to. Nevertheless, Chase must prepare for the worst.

He scrubbed his face and beard with his hands and took a deep breath, then rounded up the people he'd need for a recovery. They'd be gone long enough to complete the job, he told them, anywhere from days to weeks, depending on the location of impact and size of the debris field.

He called Michelle and told her what was happening. "Can you take care of Penny while I'm gone?"

She nodded.

"Take her to your place, if that's okay," Chase said. "I don't want her to be alone."

"Sure."

He thanked her and killed the link. Then he began to gather his things, packing for a recovery when he should be packing for home. He smiled wryly when he thought of his postponed family reunion. He'd planned to stay with his older daughter, Erin, for a couple of weeks, just long enough to find a place of his own nearby. A layover, that's what it was, but he called it a reunion. Now even that would have to wait. At times like these, he realized what his career had cost his family. Was it worth it? Not once during the past four years had he ever thought so.

He recognized the thoughts as self-destructive and forced them back into the dark place they lurked.

Then, his bag packed, he took it down to Benford's. His investigations record was far from stellar, especially where Randy Lauback was concerned, but if the *Phoenix* crashed, this would not only be his last case, it would be the most difficult and important case of his career. This was his last chance to do right by Randy. He wasn't going to waste it.

"Even if we knew where the failure was," the Stellarfare engineer told Snider, "the *Phoenix* isn't airlocked. The crew can't get out to —"

"You can't pinpoint the problem?" a Secret Service man demanded.

"Ships' crews do their own data analysis and navigation. We don't have that kind of telemetry. Or personnel." Snider swept his hand through the air. "Look at my staff. Two traffic controllers and an admin." That was it, not counting the federal agents. Just a few decades ago, a NASA control room could fill an auditorium with data analysts, systems engineers, communication specialists, flight controllers, technicians, administrators, managers, and a host of others. Now all he had was this.

"Chavez," Snider said. "Put the *Phoenix* on the emitter and track her all the way in. I want to know where she comes down, within one meter." The freighter's trajectory replaced the global hologram even before he completed the order. Montanari was on the far side of the Moon, but the *Phoenix* had swept past the mining colony in a ballistic descent shallow enough to bring the ship back around into Alpha control space before it hit the ground.

Snider pulled off his sweater and draped it over a chair back as his mind worked through the next steps in the unfolding crisis. His other controller was bringing in a deep-space transport from the European colony on Mercury. "Robinson, get that bird on the ground. Then give me clear space. Put everyone else in parking orbit.

"Chavez, projection." Ignoring the Secret Service, he took a single, long stride that brought him up behind her terminal, a movement that came naturally after years in lunar g. A yellow line appeared on her display, extending from the *Phoenix* to the Moon's surface, coming down in the middle of nowhere.

Snider buried his head in his hands and tried to think. He always knew something like this would happen someday. Commercial industry had initiated the colonization of space and profits had pushed it recklessly onward — a dozen companies racing to the frontier, never with a sufficient infrastructure to respond to these kinds of emergencies.

Because of this, spaceships had become notably reliable. That was the safeguard. And generally, it worked. Accidents almost always occurred at or near population centers, where the bulk of the people and equipment occupied small, congested settlements. The system simply wasn't designed to handle other types of incidents. As a result, Snider had only ground-based emergency response. He didn't have a single ship that could land at the crash site. "Get Stellarfare for me," he told his admin. "The guy in charge, not the shift manager."

A third controller and several other staff members came in, all part of the emergency-response protocol. The rest of the Secret Service and two base security guards also pressed their way through the reporters milling in the doorway.

Meanwhile, the *Phoenix* followed its projected path until it fell below the radar horizon. It disappeared from the hologram like a flare snuffed by the black of the void. But the marker was just a marker. Hope remained. "Listen up," Snider announced. "We're going to assume those people are alive. Chavez, where are they?"

A three-D surface map appeared on the hologram. The red line changed from solid to dotted where the ship had vanished from radar. "They're on the ground," Chavez said. "I'm picking up their beacon." A flashing red star showed the point of impact. An American flag marked Lunar Alpha, and the flag of Mare Serenitatis — the largest European base — could be seen farther off. "Twelve degrees, thirty-seven point one minutes north. Thirty-one degrees, twelve point four minutes east." Chavez glanced over her shoulder. "Northwest of Sinas Crater."

"Send that to the emergency response team. Tell them to roll."

Brower examined the display. His short, muscular body seemed to radiate confidence.

"What's that marker just north-northwest of the *Phoenix*?" Snider asked.

"Checking on that now, sir," Chavez said.

But Robinson was faster. "That's a geological research base. Chinese. Fairly new. Not much more than a couple habitation tents."

"Chavez, see if you can raise them. They must have a transport of some kind. Tell them to send oxygen and whatever medical aid they can."

"Yes, sir." She switched her transmitter to the Chinese frequencies and began hailing them in their own language.

"Robinson, contact the *Phoenix*."

The young controller made the attempt and reported no reply.

"Keep trying," Snider said. "Transmit our activities thus far. Remember, just because they can't reply doesn't mean they can't hear you."

The third controller took his seat and began to inform the incoming ships of the situation.

"You can start bringing them in now," Snider told him.

The link in Chavez's ear picked up her voice through the vibrations of her jaw and eliminated the need for loud vocalization when communicating with ships. Snider toggled the speaker and Chavez's voice filled the room. She was conducting her conversation in Chinese, but Snider was able to pick out the *Phoenix* coordinates among the chatter. "They'll send help," she reported after several minutes.

"Thanks, Julia," he said, surprising himself by his use of her first name. "Stay in touch and keep me apprised of their progress." Then he turned to Brower. "Where's Morgan?"

"Preparing his team."

"Sir," the admin said, "I have Stellarfare online."

Snider keyed the terminal in front of him. "The *Phoenix* is down," he told the Stellarfare manager.

"What do you mean, the *Phoenix* is down?"

"She lost thrust. Crashed on the surface in the middle of the Mare Tranquillitatis."

"My God." The man bowed his head. "How far from here?"

"Too far for my ERT to reach any time soon. We need a ship to fly out to the site with air, water, and medical supplies."

The man scrubbed his eyes with his thumb and forefinger. When he looked up, his eyes were moist. "You know I can't do that. I haven't got a ship that can launch from there. It'd never make it back."

"We're talking about lives here."

"There're survivors?"

"We're assuming there are."

"'Assuming'?" The Stellarfare manager shook his head. "I understand your problem, but my ships are too expensive. If the *Phoenix* is down, then I've lost one today already. I can't afford another — "

"Now listen — "

"No. What you're asking is absurd. We don't sacrifice ships for rescue operations. That's the protocol. Everyone who boards a ship knows that."

So did Snider. It had been a fundamental understanding as Earth began to populate the worlds. Rescue in space would be impossible. The ships had to be reliable. So all of the development money and effort went into emergency prevention. All the contracts and agreements, even the treaties, were based on that understanding. And maybe once in a lifetime — today, once in Snider's lifetime — it would prove to be folly.

Snider grabbed the monitor as he would have grabbed the man's shoulders, his knuckles white with need. "*Your* ship wasn't reliable. *Your* ship went down. You are morally obligated to — "

"That ship passed every inspection, every safety requirement, that NASA could dream up. If she did break down, Stellarfare's not liable."

"Sir — " Snider began.

"Besides," the man continued, "my insurance policy may cover the *Phoenix*. But it won't cover a deliberate one-way trip."

Snider shook the monitor. "I'll pay for your damned ship."

"With what?"

A federal agent came up next to Snider. "How about the United States government? The Secret Service will buy your ship and pay a crew to fly it."

"Is that so?" The manager's face hardened, on full-defensive now. "I wasn't aware that a field agent had that kind of fiscal authority."

Snider glanced at the agent, who shook his head. "You'll get your ship back," he told the Stellarfare man. "We'll find a way to recover it."

"Right now you look like a man who'll say anything, so you'll forgive me if I don't find your assurances comforting." The manager paused. "Look, Director, I'm just following standard protocol."

"Standard rescue protocol doesn't apply here," Snider said. "This isn't a space rescue. The *Phoenix* is on the ground."

"Then send ground rescue — that's what they're for."

Snider shoved away from the terminal and caught himself on the table behind him, his fist clenched. "They're on their way, but the trip will take more than a day."

"I'm sorry, I can't — "

"I'll revoke your license to fly from Lunar Alpha." Snider's voice shook with forced civility.

"Don't bully me. Revoke our license and it'll be the last thing you do as director. When you're replaced, we'll return."

He was right. Damn it, the manager was right. Stellarfare provided a third of NASA's funding for Lunar Alpha. Snider's threat had only solidified the man's resolve.

"We're under no moral or legal obligation," the manager continued. "And my fiscal responsibilities to our stockholders force me to decline your request. You bring me a contract to buy a ship and rent a crew. Then we'll talk."

The connection went dead.

Out of the corner of his eye, Snider saw another Secret Service man hurrying toward him, flailing in the unfamiliar gravity.

"We can't reach Lederman on the comm."

Snider nodded. Lederman was the agent on board.

"What happens now?" the agent asked after a long moment of silence.

"We wait. We won't know more until we get a response from the ship or until the geologists or emergency response team arrive."

That was the hardest part. The waiting. Snider needed to be in control, needed to have control, but the wreck was simply too far away.

He paced the perimeter of the octagonal control room, covering each side in a single arching step. Occasionally he stopped to peer out a window. He looked past the landing field to the stark line that divided the sunlit landscape from the star-filled sky as though need alone could bring the distant *Phoenix* into view.

Minutes cycled past. Then an hour. The ERT markers in the hologram tracked the locator beacons inside the transports. Chavez updated the progress of the geologists — closer to the wreck than the ERT, but traveling more slowly. At its current rate, the ERT wouldn't arrive for nearly thirty-six hours. The geologists might make it in half the time. Snider rubbed his tired eyes.

"Sir, it'll be hours. If you want to — "

"It's my responsibility, Robinson." Snider didn't mean to sound angry, but the lethargic progression of the markers and the display chronometer wore on his patience.

Another hour passed.

"Sir," Chavez said finally, "the beacon's moving."

The flashing dot drifted away from the crash site and a cheer went up throughout the control tower.

But Snider continued to watch the display. "Wait a minute. They're coming toward us, away from the geologists. The outpost is closer."

"It's only been there for a year, " Brower said. "I doubt the *Phoenix* crew knows it's there."

"They're outpacing the geologists," Snider said. "Hell, they're moving faster than our own ERT. How is that?" Silence bathed the room. "Well, people, let's find out."

Robinson's hands skittered across his panel. "I have it, sir. According to the manifest, the *Phoenix* was carrying a pair of rovers, along with other supplies. But they haven't got much range, and no environmental control." He swiveled the seat of his chair to face Snider. "Sir, they won't last long in the rovers."

When Chase arrived at the control tower, people were loitering everywhere, many of them wearing the black suits and earpieces of the Secret Service. There was more to it, indeed. He knew that US Energy Secretary David Herrera was on the base, but Herrera wasn't supposed to leave until later that evening. Perhaps this business with the *Phoenix* was expected to delay his departure or gave the Secret Service some concern about the safety or security of Herrera's shuttle.

On one side of the room, Snider issued a statement to half a dozen reporters. He looked up before returning his attention to the press.

Chase crossed the room to Brower. "What's going on, Stan? What's with the spooks?"

"Herrera was on board."

"The *Phoenix*? What the hell was he doing there? I thought he wasn't leaving until tonight."

"So did everybody else. We thought it'd be safer this way."

Snider joined them. "You got your team together, Morgan?"

"We're just waiting on Benford's."

The director pulled him as far from eavesdroppers as he could in the crowded room. "You know by now that Herrera's involved?" He kept his voice low. His ice-blue eyes bored into Chase's with an intensity the investigator had rarely seen.

"Stan just told me."

"He may still be alive."

"What about the pilot and the rest of the crew?"

Snider turned his back to the reporters across the room. "We don't know. We're guessing at this point. Somebody left the wreck in a rover, but we don't know who. Even so — "

"How many were on board?"

"Four."

"In a rover?" Chase noted the positions of the wreck and established outposts in the hologram. "They're days from here."

Snider took a deep breath and exhaled slowly. "I know. I don't have to tell you that the shit'll fly if we lose Herrera."

"Jack, there were more people on that ship than Herrera."

Snider pointed to the host of reporters, now taking a statement from Brower. "Do you think they give a damn about the others?" He didn't wait for an answer. "All they care about is a good story. And if Herrera dies, they'll have a doosie. I don't need that kind of press."

Of course the reporters cared; with lives at stake, how could they not? But Chase forgave Snider the callous remark. He was always strung taut anyway. Now he was the first director in Lunar Alpha history to lose a ship.

Snider's tone settled. "We need results on this one. And we need them fast."

"I'll do what I can." Having heard all that he cared to, Chase bounded past the director toward the door. A case of this magnitude wasn't going to be quick.

"That's not good enough," Snider shouted after him. "I want answers. You hear me?"

Three hours later, Chase climbed into the habitation pod with two evidence techs, a data clerk, and four of Benford's crew. He squeezed past the data station, food locker, and sanitary closet to find a bunk – one of four in which they'd sleep in shifts — and stashed his bag beneath it. This tin can, with its scarcity of necessities and complete lack of comforts, would be his home for the next several days. Fortunately, Alpha Base was in the middle of fourteen days of sunlight. That would make the recovery easier, if they could get there and get it done within the week.

While he waited for the rest of the crew to arrive, he composed a message to Erin on his thinpad, which served as either a computer or document as the need arose.

As for his younger daughter, Sarah hadn't spoken to him since Chase's divorce from the girls' mother eight years ago. He was on his second deep-space mission at the time and Linda decided she couldn't be alone anymore. Chase had abandoned the family, she said. And in a way, he had. He'd been gone for three years and wasn't to return to Earth for another two.

Sarah, who'd just turned eighteen, had sided with her mother and neither woman had spoken to him since.

By that time, Erin had been away at college. She'd been more mature and independent than Sarah; she hadn't been around to watch her mother fall apart, and she'd understood better her father's compulsion to push the envelope, to be the first black man to venture past Saturn, and the first human to orbit Pluto and Charon. Erin hadn't forsaken him. She deserved to know that the investigation would likely delay his retirement.

The door of the habitation pod clanged shut with a note of finality and air hissed past the valve to pressurize the seal.

As the hangar pumped down to vacuum, Chase reread his message.

> Dearest Erin,
>
> I'm writing to let you know that my homecoming will be delayed. I know that you and the girls were looking forward to seeing me, and I you, but a case has come up that will delay my departure. I don't know much about it yet — I'm leaving

for the accident site even as I write this letter — but if it's as bad as I believe, you'll see it in the newsblips.

I'll be away from the base for several days. A friend is going to take care of Penny for me while I'm gone. Unfortunately, I'll miss the netcast of Steve's race on Saturday. Wish him well for me.

I'll write as soon as I know how long the case is going to take. After all these years, this may sound hollow coming from me, but I'll come home as soon as the investigation is over. I promise.

Give my best to Steve and the girls.

Love, Dad

Satisfied, he transmitted the file to the Lunar Alpha comm hub with routing from there to Erin's connection code in Seattle. Then he returned the thinpad to his pocket, glad as always that he had it with him.

The hangar door lifted and Benford's procession, including two recovery cranes, two cargo transports, the habitation pod, and a McNeely flatbed began its lumbering crawl toward the site. The unprecedented convoy sapped Benford's of resources normally reserved for construction. Chase couldn't imagine that he'd use it all when he got there.

The following day they received a broken transmission from Snider, crackling through a faulty connection in the comm gear. A pair of geologists had arrived on the scene and found Herrera's bodyguard dead in the cabin. Chase swallowed hard and bowed his head for a moment. People died in space every day, of course. That's the way it was, with so many populating the worlds. They died from mishaps, illness, and age, but deaths in flight were rare.

"Everyone else is missing," Snider finished.

The news was good and bad. It reminded Chase of the fragility of life and the cold ruthlessness of space. And he mourned the loss, even though he hadn't known the man. But according to Snider's report, the rover was still moving. Somehow the others had found the means to endure without the protection of a ship or habitat.

As time wore on, the lunar surface slid beneath the pod, kilometer after bleak kilometer, a vast gray expanse as dead as the man found on the *Phoenix*.

Too much of it lay between Chase and the survivors. He couldn't do anything for them. Besides, the ERT would get there first. So he told the driver to head straight for the crash site.

He disagreed with Snider about focusing only on Herrera's survival, but his boss was right about one thing. The pressure on this case would be high, and if Herrera didn't make it back, Washington would come down on NASA like Thor's hammer. And until Chase found the cause, Snider would be standing on the anvil.

A short time later, Snider's voice came through again, difficult to hear over the rattle of the pod as it crawled its way through the ejecta field of a nearby crater. The speaker crackled over the transmission every time the pod hit a bump. All they got were pieces: "... rover ... David Herrera ..."

And then, "All three are ..."

CHAPTER 2

Chase's first view of the *Phoenix* was a mere glint of sunlight on the horizon. As he drew closer, the fuselage came into view, jutting skyward from the flat terrain like a solitary tombstone in a garden of glittering metal. The effect gave a surreal beauty to the desolate scene.

The pod came to a stop at the boundary of the debris field. The ship was close now. The fuselage, largely intact, rested at an odd angle at the end of a long scar in the landscape. A debris field stretched out to the northwest, away from Chase's vehicle and the direction of the rover tracks. Dents and cracks that marred the hull suggested that the ship had tumbled into its final resting place. The aft section, the cargo hold, was mangled.

As it lay, the evidence was as pristine as Chase would ever see it. From here on out, everything he did would systematically alter the reality of the scene as it had been left by the tragedy. He ordered everyone to stay put while he took an initial look around, then stepped outside into the oppressive heat, 110 degrees centigrade throughout the lunar day. His pressure suit's cooling system pumped its life-sustaining fluid to maintain a safe body temperature, but the heat was evident nonetheless. The profound silence of the scene was broken only by Chase's own breathing, hollow and eerie against the background of the suit's recirculating fan.

For a long time he just stared. Snider's last transmission still ran through his head. *They're dead. They're dead.* Even a day later, the litany played over and over in his mind until the magnitude of his task imposed itself on his consciousness. Benford, with all his trucks, cranes, and other equipment, had underestimated the sheer volume of the debris. Chase scarcely knew where to begin, but that wasn't the problem.

Footprints lay everywhere among the wreckage as though the person who'd left them had sought some special souvenir. He cursed the geologists. They should've known better. Already his objective seemed to be retreating from him, and he'd only just begun.

Chase returned to the habitation pod and requested satellite images of the site. It would take an excruciating six hours, he was told, to allocate an asset to the task. But despite the delay, satellite imaging was the most efficient means to map both the prints and the debris fragments.

When he finally returned to the *Phoenix*, he found the aft cargo door open. The ship lay partially on its roof, rotated about 135 degrees from what he considered to be right-side up. But the cargo remained in place, secured with restraining straps, except for those few pieces that had shaken loose during impact.

Before stepping in, Chase took a vid-scan of the compartment. Despite the damage outside, the interior remained intact, protected by the ship's double-hull construction, which improved vacuum integrity and stabilized the cabin temperature against the harsh extremes of space. The design had done much to extend the lives of the passengers and crew, if only by hours.

Chase stretched his back, tightened by age and the cramped quarters of the habitation pod, then moved past the cargo and into the crew compartment. Agent Lederman lay face-up in a pressure suit near the threshold. His helmet had been removed or had never been donned, and all the moisture had leached out of his body, outgassed into space, leaving a desiccated husk behind.

They're dead. They're dead. Still Chase couldn't silence the mantra. It darkened every thought like a blight and gnawed at his concentration until he wanted to scream at the senselessness. Technical advances and system redundancy were supposed to prevent these things from happening. Randy was a good pilot and a smart guy. Yet despite it all, fate, circumstances, luck, the unforgiving nature of the void — whatever he chose to call it — something had taken the lives of everyone on board.

Professionalism forced his eyes away from the body and focused him on his task. The condition of the cockpit was much like that of the cargo hold. Unsecured items littered what was now the floor. Padded seats hung from the ceiling like stalactites. All the displays were dark, but sunlight filtered through the polarized windshield to illuminate the crew compartment. Again, he took a complete vid-scan, then set down the imager and stepped inside.

The voices of the evidence-recovery teams streamed over his suit's comm as they marked the boundary of the debris field with infrared telemeter pylons. He turned down the volume, reducing the voices to a faint murmur in the background to allow himself to think. Then he stood among the clues and let them tell their story. Some were important. Others were just tossed into place by the random forces of fate.

The first thing that leapt out at him, screaming its presence like an alarm in his mind, was a Lancaster pulse gun lying on a cabinet near Lederman's body. The only person on board who'd have been licensed to carry it was Lederman himself, and his responsibility for Herrera's safety would have required him to do so. So its presence wasn't the surprise. What caught Chase's attention was the fact that it was out of its holster, that Lederman had found the need to wield it. Either Herrera had somehow been threatened with violence or Lederman had used it to threaten another.

Chase looked from the weapon to the items on the floor. He bent to examine a white sheet of paper, its color a contrast to the muted grays of the ship's interior. It was from the *Phoenix* procedures manual, which lay nearby. The page, a portion of the preflight safety checklist, had been ripped from its binding. Chase closed his eyes and took a deep breath of his sterile suit air. He unconsciously closed his fist around the page. Had it been removed prior to liftoff? If so, had that portion of the safety check been missed? Had Randy skipped something on the preflight that would have revealed the problem that later brought the ship down? Had he torn the page out in frustration after realizing that fact? No matter how Chase imagined it, it smacked of pilot error. There must be another answer. If there was, he would find it.

To his left, a length of vacuum tape stretched across a seam in the hull. That pliable metallic strip, with a strong adhesive on one side and the capability of temporarily repairing a minor vacuum leak, raised another question. The ship shouldn't have launched with a pressure leak or with the temporary repair. Had the leak occurred before takeoff, during flight, or upon impact?

Chase smoothed the page and placed it back where he'd found it. In one corner, a toolbox sat open with its contents collected around it. The gathered nature of the pile suggested that the objects been dumped there after the ship came to rest. Repairs? On what? He spotted a wrench and a pair of pliers near an open junction box in the ship's cooling distribution system. If something overheated, that could explain just about any malfunction. Alternatively, the crew may have tapped into the lines as a source of drinking water after the accident.

Too many unanswered questions.

Before allowing the techs inside, Chase made a final inspection. A torn piece of clear tape hung near the co-pilot's console. He went back to the page on the floor, thinking it might have been posted there as a reminder of something. But there was no matching remnant on the page.

After a last look at the body, he left the cabin.

Under Chase's supervision, the techs recorded an inventory of the cargo and personal items on board and removed them to one of the trailers. The data core appeared to be in good condition. This, perhaps the most important piece of evidence they'd recover, was stored in a padded crate and secured separately for the ride home. They also recovered Lederman's body and placed it in a special compartment designed for preserving and transporting human remains. Johnny Benford and his crew loaded the fuselage, ruptured fuel tank, and other large pieces onto the flatbed.

The evidence techs scanned each footprint for size, depth, and tread pattern. If someone had taken evidence, Chase was determined to find out who and what. To some extent, the effort duplicated the data already collected by satellite, but the fact that the accident had happened at all proved that redundancy was necessary, and sometimes insufficient.

Then they went to work on the debris, touching each piece with a marker baton, which measured the distance to the telemeter pylons and laser-scribed a set of coordinates onto the fragment. From then on, the scrap's coordinates became its identification code.

Chase scanned each fragment with the Etherscan, a handheld instrument that analyzed the material density of each object, measured its size and orientation, and estimated the density of the soil in which it was embedded. The data could be used to model the velocity of the fragment at the moment it struck the ground, based on how deeply it was embedded in the soil.

Then the recovery team described each piece and transmitted its coordinate code to a database aboard the habitation pod. They bagged the pieces and packed them in padded crates for transport.

The low angle of impact had caused the *Phoenix* to skip across the Moon's surface like a flat rock on a quiet pond. As a result, the wreckage was scattered across several impact sites separated by, in some cases, dozens of kilometers. By the second day, Chase secured an imaging satellite to locate and photograph the smaller debris fields. Then he split up the team to work two sites at a time, relinquishing some of his control to get the job done before fourteen days of darkness would complicate any further recovery.

The only good news was that there'd been no explosion or fire in either the fuel tank or oxygen canisters, so the pieces were fewer than they might have been and they could be more easily recognized. Nevertheless, the sun had dropped below the horizon before they finally got the last piece categorized, crated, and stowed.

By then, exhaustion pulsed in waves from Chase's tired bones, yet he couldn't sleep. So as Benford turned the convoy toward home, Chase sat at the data terminal. He couldn't get his mind off the Lancaster pistol.

It was out of its holster.

He reviewed the video images of the cockpit.

Technical advances and system redundancy were supposed to keep these things from happening ... Something had taken the lives of everyone on board.

Chase froze the display on a picture of Lederman. The gun lay within easy reach, had Lederman been alive to grasp it.

The only one on board who'd have been licensed to use it was Lederman himself.

Chase stared for a long time, then zoomed in on the man's dead face, seeing him in a different light — with the sunken eyes, shriveled in their sockets, and the parched lips stretched taut over a savage, bony grin.

"You son of a bitch," he said aloud to the mute image. "Did you do this?"

⁂

They retrieved the rover and the remaining bodies and returned to Lunar Alpha two days later. It was midday Universal Coordinated Time, but the base, which sprawled over two square kilometers at the southern tip of the Mare Tranquillitatis, was cast in the black of the Moon's shadow. Flood lamps blazed over the landing field and lights brightened many of the windows. Nevertheless, the base looked small and fragile. Only the spire of the control tower at the northern end broke the flat line of the single-story complex. The array of antennae that bristled like spines across the rooftop was lost in darkness.

The convoy came to rest in Benford's hangar and Chase climbed out of the habitation pod. When he cycled through the airlock, Snider was waiting in a hallway clogged with reporters, vid-scanners, and microphones. The only way out was through the press.

He grabbed Chase by the arm and pulled him into a lavatory adjacent to the airlock. When he secured the door and turned to Chase, his face was stern, his features set. "Tell me what you got."

"Nothing, Jack," Chase said over the hollow sound of suction that streamed from the urinals. "I've got pieces of a broken ship. I won't know anything until I can sort through the evidence and make it make some sort of sense." He'd been out in the desert for the past nine days, sleeping little and working all hours. He reached for the door, too exhausted to face the idealistic demands of his ignorant boss.

"You don't have time on this one," Snider said. "Washington's all over it."

Chase took a deep breath and spread his hands. "I'm not a miracle worker. These things take time. I'll get your answers, but I don't have them yet."

Snider's eyes went cold. But since he didn't seem to recognize the absurdity of his demands, Chase made some of his own. "I need people. Analysts mostly. And administrators to chase paperwork and manage the data. The more I get, the faster the work will proceed."

Snider was a man of action who'd been forced to sit tight and wait for Chase to return. Having something to do seemed to settle him. "Tell me who you need."

Chase handed him a prepared list on a thinpad. It included two Soaring Aerospace engineers, experts on the design and layout of the *Phoenix*, that he'd requested eight days ago via comm link. They'd be invaluable in identifying components and their location during the reconstruction of the ship. He listed the administrators and analysts that he'd need to commandeer backup copies of the relevant data from both Lunar Alpha and Montanari, including the ship's cargo manifest, telemetry, communications transcripts, security vid-files from the control rooms, procedures documentation, and so forth. Others would contact the Soaring assembly site and component part manufacturers. As the serial number of each part was determined during the reassembly, he'd request the manufacturer's production and quality-control records for the specific component in question. He also planned to engage his intern, Michelle, and assign a round-the-clock security team to protect the evidence. The request was unprecedented, but then again so was the case. And Chase could use the director's angst to secure the help he needed.

Snider reviewed the list and nodded. "You'll have to talk to the reporters."

"I have nothing to say."

"Morgan. Talk to them." He sounded as tired as Chase felt. "You've seen the site. Tell them what you know, or what you think. You've got to have theories. Speculate if you have to, but talk to them. If nothing else, it'll give you some breathing room for a couple of days."

Speculate? Had Snider forgotten the *North Star* case? Chase would have to speculate, of course; it was part of the process. But not publicly. Not this time. "I won't speculate, Jack."

"Then tell them what you don't know — I don't care. Just talk to them." Snider turned to usher him into the hallway.

Chase didn't budge. "No, Jack."

Snider wheeled on him.

"I won't run this investigation like a three-screen vid-circus. I'll talk to the press when I have something to say." He softened his voice and tried to keep his words from sounding like a threat. "You can force me into the corridor, but I'll have no comment. You can accept that, or you can go out there and promise them a statement that they're not going to get." He met Snider's glare until the pause grew palpable between them.

Finally, Snider nodded once and opened the door. Without a word, the two men pressed their way past the gauntlet of reporters.

"This way," Snider said as they escaped the corridor. He led Chase down a hallway to their left and into a small conference room.

Inside, a tall man in a stock suit turned to face them. He had to be a Fed, the way he clung to the out-of-date fashion and wore it like armor. His skin hung from his face in folds like those of a bulldog. His eyes, sunken but alert, harbored no threat.

"This is Special Agent Forsythe, from the FBI," Snider said.

Chase stiffened. "I didn't know Alpha was in your jurisdiction."

"It's an American base. By treaty, it's American soil." His voice wheezed from breathing the toxic atmosphere that shrouded Earth's cities.

"You here to take over the case?" Chase felt his authority erode as he spoke.

"Not unless there's evidence of murder."

"There's evidence of a lot of things." He struggled to keep his emotions from his voice. They'd only serve to increase Forsythe's control. "But I'll draw any conclusions of fault or culpability objectively. And only with definitive proof."

The agent pulled his hands from his pockets and motioned to a chair at the conference table. Chase glanced at Snider and sat down. When everyone was seated, Forsythe continued. "To be honest with you, Mr. Morgan, the FBI has never exercised its jurisdiction beyond America's Earthly borders. And, frankly, that's a precedent the president's not prepared to set. At least, not yet. I'm here to observe your investigation, not interfere with it." He sat back in his chair as if to relax his authority along with his body.

But for how long?

⁂

Chase had planned to stop by his apartment and take a shower while the others unloaded the cargo. That would put him back in hangar three before any of the crates were opened. He hadn't had a shower since he'd left the base, and even he was beginning to notice. But now that he'd seen the level of public scrutiny that the investigation would receive, he went straight to the hangar to supervise the unload.

The rest of his team began to arrive within the first thirty minutes. As they did, he sent them away with tasks commensurate with their skills.

Michelle showed up. Her large sapphire eyes, usually filled with wonder and enthusiasm, expressed only apprehension as she worked her way past the crowd of reporters hovering in the corridor.

She had worked for Chase for just over six months. As a materials engineer, she'd been grossly underchallenged in the investigations department, but that's where NASA had put her. Chase was glad to give her something technical, rather than administrative, to do for a change. He handed her a crate.

"What is it?" She eyed both him and the box with apprehension.

With all the fanfare the case was getting, she must have been petrified. So Chase added a reassuring smile. "Samples. They're all labeled. Take them to the materials lab and work with the techs. I need to know the complete chemical makeup of each." It was the first technical assignment he'd given her, something to cut her teeth on that actually related to her education. "The techs'll run the equipment and show you the ropes. But I need a representative in the lab. I'll tell you what I need, which samples are most important. See that they run those first. And help out with the analysis as necessary. Can you do that?"

She breathed a sigh. "Sure."

Of that, Chase had no doubt. She was a smart girl, but she didn't give herself enough credit. This would stoke her confidence, show her that she could use the skills she'd learned in school. After all, that's what the intern program was all about.

It was two A.M. before Chase finally got to sleep, and he woke four hours later to bad news. He rushed to the electronics evaluation and simulation laboratory and quickly oriented himself in the chaos. Four rows of terminals packed the small room, each linked to Alpha's substantial computing core. The place buzzed with programmers and analysts sifting through the available data and using every technical means to acquire or generate the information they lacked.

Chase addressed the woman working on the data core. "What are we missing?"

"Everything after impact," she said with an apologetic look.

"Voice or data?"

"Both. There was no electrical feedback after the ship lost power."

"What about voice? It should've picked up something on battery power."

"It should've, but look at this." She pulled the top off the core, plucked one wire from the spaghetti of leads, and displayed the end. The battery cable was corroded through.

Chapter 3

Chase took several slow breaths to maintain his calm. There was no telling what the corroded cable would cost the investigation. If the crew had identified the cause after landing, they'd have discussed it. Now, unless they had mentioned the problem between the onset of trouble and the moment of impact, conclusions would be slow to come.

Furthermore, he'd expected cockpit conversations to tell him when the crew had donned their pressure suits, why Lederman drew his gun, and whether the vacuum leak had occurred before or after liftoff. Now all that would likely be speculative. The data core had been his best chance for a quick resolution to the *Phoenix* conundrum.

But he still had everything else: the rest of the ship and a wealth of records. The problem was that Snider had given him only a third of the personnel he'd asked for, and only a fifth of what he needed.

The room quieted as the techs became aware of his arrival. Some stopped to hear anything that he might say about the data core. Others continued their work quietly, their fingers clicking on their keyboards. Electronics-cooling fans thrummed in harmony with the air-handling system, and the smell of coffee filled the air from cups sitting at nearly every station. More than one tech was bleary-eyed from the late night followed by an early-morning start.

Chase approached a young man working on the footprint map. "What've you got?"

"Well, you see — " the boy cleared his throat and sat up in his chair. "I've taken the satellite photos and mapped each footprint to a grid. Now I'm going through the scan data. Fortunately, each person had a distinct print. Though Lauback and Secretary Herrera both had the same boot size, Herrera was heavier. His prints are deeper. Conway's are smaller. The geologist — " he glanced at Chase — "it looks like only one left the truck. His tread pattern is different from ours."

"And Agent Lederman?"

The tech shook his head. "I don't think he ever left the ship."

"And I can tell you which prints are mine," Chase finished.

The remainder of the terminals displayed text, so what the rest of the techs were working on was less obvious. "Do we have the communications transcripts and data capture files from the Montanari and Alpha control rooms?" he asked everyone in general.

"Yes, sir," one man answered. "They came in yesterday afternoon."

"Excellent." He turned back to the woman working with the data core. "How long to go through what we've got, starting at preflight?"

He expected it'd take a while. Even with the data truncated, there were still several hours to go through. And those hours contained continuous feeds of data from thousands of sensors — voltages, currents, temperatures, pressures, flow rates, velocities, and more. All would be compared, microsecond by microsecond, with the expected values at the time.

The woman hesitated before answering. She looked around as though considering what drag the other simulations might have on the collective computing resources. "Forty-eight hours. Maybe."

"You have twenty-four." Chase turned to the footprint analyst. "Twenty-four hours?"

The boy nodded.

"Okay." Maybe it would take too long for them to piece the ship back together, but they might be able to put everything else together more quickly. "At this time tomorrow, we'll convene in hangar three with all the available data. We're going to recreate the accident. We'll also need a mechanical and ballistic model of the impact."

A tech in the back of the room stood up. "I'll take that. I can get the ship's position and velocity from the radar data."

"Good," Chase said. "Soaring should have a computer model of the ship's mechanical response. Simulations are required for safety certification of any new design. With that, you should even be able to simulate the ship's damage profile. You may have to assume the ship's attitude, but you can compare your results with the actual damage and debris pattern to validate your assumptions." He paused. "Twenty-four hours?"

The tech shrugged. "I'll bring what I got."

"Okay. In the meantime, I'll prepare the hangar and round up a team for the reenactment."

He grabbed a coffee from a dispenser by the door, took a sip, and savored the flavor before stepping out into the broad hallway.

"Morgan!" Snider's voice boomed from behind him before he'd taken three steps.

Chase reluctantly faced the director.

Snider launched himself up the corridor in a flat arc that brought him to Chase in a single leap. "Tell me you got something."

"I've got a broken voice recorder. Does that count?"

"Damn it, this is serious."

"I am serious. We've got nothing from the cockpit after impact."

Snider froze for several seconds. He just stared back at Chase. Either Snider didn't believe him or — well, it looked like he didn't believe him.

"Damn it." Snider lashed out at the air like an arthritic pitcher launching a phantom spitball. He thrust an index finger at Chase's face. "I want answers. You hear me?"

"Jesus, Jack, it's only day two. We'll find answers."

Snider backed off and took a settling breath. Then he pointed down the corridor. "Walk with me."

"I'm going that way." Chase indicated a different hall. He wasn't, of course, but if he held up the director, it might shorten the man's lecture.

"You may see this as day two," Snider said. "But that ship went down ten days ago, and Washington's been on me ever since. Not to mention the press, the public, NASA, you name it. You can't imagine the heat I'm feeling."

"I'm on my way to the hangar now," Chase said finally. "We'll put this thing together." It was all he could offer.

"I've scheduled a press conference at nine. You're giving the briefing."

"Jack, no."

"Just hear me out."

"No."

Snider leaned into him, his face mere centimeters away. "They'll ask questions. And you better have answers, or by God, I'll put somebody on the case who will. You hear me?"

What a thought, to be free of this business shortly after nine. Maybe he'd retire on time after all.

Then Chase's stomach soured. That would be a fine sum to his career, removed from his last case because he couldn't cut it. He'd lost his flight status the same way. Though he'd been spared the debilitating stresses that a lifetime of Earth's gravity could inflict upon a body his age, Chase had failed his cardiac stress test. Ever since then, he'd worked mostly behind a desk. He'd spent the time living with the stigma of a washed-out pilot, hearing whispers in the hall from those still in the program. "Couldn't cut it." "Washed up." "Over the hill."

"Wasted."

After a while it gets to you. And somewhere along the way, he'd started to believe it.

Nevertheless, something about leaving the job undone didn't sit right with him. So as an acknowledgment of the stress that Snider was under, Chase acceded to the press conference, but he'd worry about it when he got there. He had things to do first.

Snider disappeared around the corner and Chase made his way down the hall. The base was just waking up. Facilities workers, clerks, and administrators would soon filter into the operations and commercial sectors. The Common, the social center of Lunar Alpha, wouldn't come alive for a few more hours. Off-duty security guards and custodial robots had already gone home to rest up or recharge for the next night's shift. The emptiness, combined with the pewter tint of the aluminite walls, gave the corridors a look as sterile as a surgical berth.

He went straight to Michelle's apartment.

"Good morning, Ed," she said.

Few people called him that anymore. Most used "Chase," the call sign he'd earned as a fighter pilot for his ability to stay on anyone's tail.

"Coffee? Breakfast?" she asked.

"No time. We lost the data core and Snider's pushing for a press conference at nine."

"What do you mean, we lost the core?"

"It's crap. Battery cable was bad. There's no data after impact."

"Oh, man. What are you going to do?"

Chase shrugged. "Piece events together as best as I can without it."

"Not by nine."

"No." Chase looked at his watch. "I just came for Penny." He scooped her up and scratched her ears.

"It doesn't sound like you'll have much time for her for the next couple of days. If you want to leave her here..."

"Thanks, but I need her with me. Sometimes I think she grounds my sanity." He chuckled. "She may be lazy, but she reminds me that there's more to life than working. Besides, I plan to keep you just as busy. Speaking of which, anything from the lab? I've got to give the press something."

"Not yet. But we prepped a few samples last night. We should have data this afternoon." She pursed her lips. "Sorry." Her reply underscored the point Chase had made to Snider. It was just too early to expect results.

"I'm planning a reenactment of the accident," Chase said. "So far, the most likely causes are contaminated fuel or overheated electronics. So I need analyses of the fuel sample and cooling water. Everything else is secondary."

"You got it." When she smiled, her whole face lit, her girlish enthusiasm a balm for his abraded nerves.

He took a long pull on his coffee and tossed the cup into reclaim, then recovered Penny's purple blanket and food bowl from the floor. When he dropped her off at home, she dragged her blanket into a corner, circled twice, and lay down.

From there, Chase hurried to the hangar.

Once there, he cleared the bay and told the crew to remove the empty cargo trucks and bring in the *Phoenix* fuselage. "Set it down exactly as we found it, rolled over on its back, and block it into place. When you're done, we'll begin the reassembly."

He left the recovery team to their task and arrived at the press room at 9:02. Snider stood in the doorway with his arms crossed over his chest, looking more annoyed that Chase was two minutes late than pleased that he'd shown up at all. Chase ignored the director's glare and squeezed past. As he did, Snider pressed a thinpad into his hand.

The press room was packed with at least two dozen reporters, twice the number for which the room was designed. A few were local correspondents.

Several more had arrived as part of Herrera's retinue. The rest, standing on the periphery, steadying themselves and their equipment in the unfamiliar gravity, were the new arrivals from Earth, sent by networks rich enough to afford shuttle seats at last-minute prices.

The room quieted when Chase entered. Voices died away into a shuffle of bodies and the clamor of equipment and key clicks as the audience set their thinpads and other devices to record his statement. Within seconds, even those noises faded, leaving a pall of anticipation by the time he reached the podium.

Chase was never comfortable speaking in public, though he'd sent several public-relations messages back to Earth from his deep-space missions. Then, his audience was at the far end of a comm link, beyond his sight and too distant to affect him. Even when he repeated the performances before a live crowd, he was expected only to tell a few anecdotes and respond to questions about his experience — questions for which he had answers.

As an accident investigator, he was on a changed playing field. He was poised before a veritable firing squad of officials and reporters who demanded information that he more often than not didn't have. Questions could come from anywhere. Some reporters were realistic in their expectations. Others could become belligerent at any perceived attempts at evasion. But all would be relentless in their pursuit of the facts.

Chase didn't look up when he reached the podium. Instead, he laid the thinpad on the stand and opened the only file on it, as though it was a prepared statement or perhaps a set of notes. The contents must be pertinent or Snider would've waited until after the conference to deliver it. But more than that, Chase needed time to collect his thoughts and fortify his composure.

The file contained four pages, each a preliminary coroner's report for one of the victims. He scanned them quickly, scowled at the last one, and lifted his head to face the press.

"Ten days ago," he began, forming his statement as he went, "the Stellarfare freighter *Phoenix*, on a routine flight to the Montanari mining colony, reported a loss of thruster control at 6:14 P.M., Universal Coordinated Time. Shortly after that announcement, the *Phoenix* crashed on the Moon's surface. Three of the occupants, Randy Lauback, Phyllis Conway, and Secretary David Herrera, tried to return to Lunar Alpha in a short-range Moon rover.

Unfortunately, they only made it halfway. The fourth passenger, Agent Samuel Lederman, was found dead at the crash site." A general shuffling ensued from the audience. What Chase had presented was already well known. They craved something new.

He continued. "The recovery operation took place over the next nine days and returned to Alpha yesterday afternoon. Since then, the investigation team, under my direction, has pooled every available resource to sift through the evidence, both material and documentary."

He cleared his throat. No one had thought to leave him a glass of water. "As we speak, the wreckage is being prepared for the reassembly and inspection of every system, component, and piece for signs of distress or malfunction. As you can imagine, the process is extensive, tedious, and time-consuming, but it's also thorough and effective. I'm confident that we'll find the cause."

The reporters grumbled, many making offhand remarks to those around them. Chase had just implied the thing they least wanted to hear — he didn't have the answers they sought.

Chase didn't deign to look at Snider, who'd be even less pleased. "In the meantime, we're compiling an enormous amount of electronic and communications data, which we'll use to recreate, to any extent possible, the events as they occurred on board. This exercise may yield information much more quickly than the reassembly will."

Chase went silent. He knew more, of course, but he didn't want to expose any avenues for questioning that he didn't have to. The reporters would find plenty to explore on their own. Finally he said, "I'll take your questions."

Every hand in the room went up. Chase selected a young reporter in the back, hoping that youth implied inexperience and would lead to an easy question.

"What can you say of the cause of the accident?"

The heat of the lights and the electronic eyes of the vid-scanners made Chase's body warm and his skin itchy with perspiration. On the surface, the question was easy. In fact, he'd already answered it. But it marked the beginning of a process. It was hard to stand on a pedestal, in a spotlight, in front of the nation and the worlds; hard to stand before millions of Americans who were angry at the needless deaths of four of their countrymen; hard to stand up and say, I don't know. The reporters knew that. They would ask the question again.

"It's too early in the investigation to answer that." He said the words quickly and selected another reporter.

"Can you tell us the cause of the victims' deaths?" the second reporter asked.

"Yes," Chase assured with some measure of relief. He held up the thinpad. "I was handed the preliminary coroner's report just a few minutes ago. Lauback, Conway, and Herrera died from asphyxiation. Their O_2 tanks were empty when we found them. They ran out of air."

"And Agent Lederman?" the reporter asked.

The report on Lederman also said asphyxiation, but listed the determination as speculative. According to an appended comment, the condition of the body made the evaluation "problematic."

But to Chase, it didn't make sense. Lederman's air tank was full when they found him. Could he have been a victim of his own gun? Chase made a mental note to discuss it with the coroner. "The cause of Lederman's death is still undetermined. His body was exposed to space. That complicates the autopsy."

Chase selected a reporter in the front row.

"Is it true that the data core was damaged?"

"Yes, but it still contains valuable information." He acknowledged another reporter.

"Obviously the investigation's just getting started, and you've yet to draw your conclusions, but can you name any possible contributors to the incident, based on the evidence you've seen?"

There it was again. They'd push a little further each time they asked until they forced him into a corner that he couldn't talk himself out of. *I don't know. I don't know. I don't know.* The mantra wailed like a siren in his mind. He searched for the courage to say it out loud.

His thoughts went back to his first case. He'd been unable to say it then, so he'd speculated. The *North Star* fire had started somewhere in the cockpit before liftoff, during preflight.

"Could the pilot have performed the preflight checks incorrectly?" a reporter had asked.

"Yes," Chase had answered. He didn't know whether he had or not, but he *could* have.

The reporter mistook the response as a finding of blame against the pilot.

That pilot was Randy Lauback.

Chase had realized his blunder only after the newsblips filled with accusations of guilt against Randy, whose flight license was immediately revoked. Chase hadn't wanted to correct the statement until he was sure it was wrong. It shouldn't have taken more than a few days to prove one way or the other. But it was weeks later when he discovered the faulty wiring that had sparked the flames, which had spread rapidly in the oxygen-rich cockpit. Randy was innocent.

In the meantime, the press had repeated the original accusation with damning regularity. And although Randy regained his license, his reputation never recovered.

Chase still hadn't forgiven himself for that mistake, but he had no way to make it right. He'd even tried to persuade the networks to run a retraction and apology. But the public didn't care, so neither did the press. Now, with the *Phoenix* case, he might make some small form or recompense.

In the room before him, the reporters became restless as they waited for Chase to respond.

"It would be inappropriate for me to speculate at this time." He'd learned much about the media in the last four years.

"Can you describe the circumstances on board at the time of the accident?" Another push toward the corner.

I don't know. I don't know. "The investigation is still in its infancy. We know very little at this point. Next."

"What did you find at the site?"

Chase described the scene. He detailed the state of the ship, the distribution of debris, and the profusion of footprints without mentioning the interior of the crew compartment. He didn't want the reporters speculating on their own any more than he wanted them to hear his speculations.

"Is there any indication of pilot error or inadequate preflight procedures?"

Chase paused. The question probably stemmed from that very accusation he'd made against the same pilot in the *North Star* fire. It was the brand that Chase had put on the man. But there was another, more ominous possibility. The reporter might've found out about the cooling-water problems or vacuum repair that may have existed before takeoff. Or she might have discovered that a piece of the preflight procedures had been separated from the ops manual. But Chase didn't think so. "No. There's no evidence of that."

"Will we be allowed to attend the reenactment?" one reporter asked.

"No," Chase said, though he could see Snider nodding at the edge of his vision. It'd be too disruptive to have myriad reporters in the bay clambering for a clear camera angle. "But we'll record the event and make the vid-file available."

"What was the secretary of energy doing on a freight ship?" an impatient woman shouted.

Good question. Chase hadn't even considered it. But it was odd, to say the least, and it belied his initial statement. The *Phoenix* flight had been anything but routine.

"That's all the time I have." With that, Chase abandoned the podium, ignoring the voices that rose behind him. He hadn't provided the answers that Snider had promised them. To do so would have required him to speculate irresponsibly or lie. He wasn't willing to do either.

Chapter 4

Chase had more work than his team could do in twenty-four hours, but he couldn't wait for answers, so he set his people to the tasks that mattered most: analyzing the transcripts, telemetry logs, and vid-files. Quality data from the hardware manufacturers would have to wait until he had a better handle on which components were important. Right now, everything was suspect. With luck, the following morning's activities would narrow the list.

In the meantime, he selected his "actors" for the reenactment. Chase himself would play Randy, but the decision to do so hadn't been easy. On one hand, he'd flown as a NASA pilot for sixteen years and understood the hazards of space, the systems of the spacecraft, and the required procedures and protocols. Nobody could question his qualifications. But because of his history with the pilot and his need to draw a fair conclusion on Randy's behalf, he wasn't sure he could remain unbiased in his participation. He might overlook some degree of fault or negligence that Randy may have committed, but he must defend Randy to the point of absolute proof against him. On a personal level, that was important.

Then he chose a copilot. He could've recruited another qualified pilot, but he didn't want to expand the group beyond the current investigation team if he could help it. His techs and analysts would focus more on the data than on the crew's likely response to it, so he offered the role to Michelle, who readily accepted.

For Lederman's role, Chase went looking for the Secret Service. Only an agent would think like an agent under any given set of circumstances.

"What the hell did they do that for?" he asked Brower when he found out they'd gone back to Earth.

"Herrera was dead. There was nobody left to protect."

"They're witnesses — "

"No shit. I took a statement from — "

"A statement?" Chase glared at Brower with his hands on his hips. "That wasn't your call to make."

"Snider disagreed. You were in the field, and I'm in charge of security here. I couldn't justify keeping them."

Whatever the rationale, whether Chase agreed with it or not, they were gone. He had to find somebody else. So he turned to Forsythe, who said he'd been through some of the same training and could probably adopt the necessary mindset.

Chase gave the role of Herrera to Snider, mostly because Snider had insisted on being present and because Chase didn't want an extra body taking up space in the cabin.

But Snider had been against the reenactment from the beginning. "Waste of time," he'd said. In the end, though, he allowed Chase to proceed in spite of his reservations. If it turned out that Snider was too close-minded to give his enthusiastic support, Chase would deal with that when the time came.

Brower offered to run a vid-scanner for the press file. "I want to observe the exercise anyway. If it reveals evidence of a security breech, I want to see it firsthand. Besides, we'll want to control any information we release to the media."

Then Chase returned to the *Phoenix* and prepared the cockpit. On a thinpad, he kept a list of clues — the vacuum repair, the gun, the torn page, the tools, the apparent cooling-system work. One of these would lead him to the cause. He replaced all articles exactly as they had been when he'd found them at the site, going through his video images once to place the items and again to confirm that he'd placed everything correctly.

When he was done, the cockpit looked the same as it had when he'd found it. But it felt different, no longer morbid and depressing. With the body gone and nothing beyond the windshield but the corrugated panels of the hangar door, the *Phoenix* had the inert feel of a training simulator.

Nevertheless, the process answered one of his key questions. As he placed the roll of vacuum tape, he realized that he'd found it sitting on a horizontal surface — horizontal in the ship's odd crash-site orientation — and near the location of the repair. The leak had occurred during impact. But his other questions remained unanswered.

At seven the next morning, the participants and analysts arrived, along with the coroner. Chase reviewed his expectations and the analysts checked out their equipment.

"Okay," he said when everyone was ready. "We'll start with the assumption that Randy did the preflight checks correctly." Snider gave him a skeptical look, so Chase added, "If we have any reason to question that assumption later, we'll come back to it."

He turned to the data-core analyst. The core had been relocated, along with the analysis and simulation terminals, to the cargo compartment of the *Phoenix*. Moving the equipment into the ship, in place of the actual cargo, represented a compromise in the fidelity of the recreation, but Chase couldn't do the reenactment without the data. "You've had time to complete your analysis?"

She nodded.

"And?"

"The first anomaly occurred just before they drifted off course."

"Okay, start there. Overlay the communications and control-tower logs."

The analyst brought up a graph labeled CONTROLLER OUTPUT. Another terminal showed the trajectory curve that had been visible in the tower at the time. "Before the anomaly, the ship was on autopilot, executing a preprogrammed series of burns to bring it down on a prescribed trajectory." She paused, watching a mission chronometer in the top corner of the screen. Her finger hovered over the keyboard. "The next burn should occur in a few seconds.

"There." She punched a key to stop the display, which showed a momentary spike in the graph, followed by a drop to zero. "The thrusters failed to fire and the malfunction light came on." She restarted the clock and changed the display to show several data traces at once, then pointed out the relevant aspects of each. "The pilot switched to manual and engaged the thrusters by hand. Nothing."

A speaker beside the data core came alive. The recorded voices sounded distant and hollow. "Shit," Randy said under his breath, but if the data core heard it, so did everyone in the passenger compartment.

"What's happening, pilot?" Herrera asked.

Lederman mumbled in the background, but Chase couldn't make out the words.

"We'll know more in a few minutes," Randy said.

"They had no warning prior to failure," the analyst explained without stopping the playback. "Only minutes before, the autopilot made several burns, each in turn and on time." She pointed to the screen. "The pilot cycled the manual/automatic switch twice and tried the thrusters again. No change."

"Wait," Snider said. Both Chase and the analyst looked up before he continued. "You said there was no warning?"

"That's right."

"Nothing in the data showed a problem before the thrusters quit? No indication of cause?"

"Not yet."

"Whatever killed the thrusters did so by this point in the flight. If there's nothing in the data by now, then there won't be later." He took a step toward the hatch. "I'd say we're done here."

"Not necessarily." Chase grabbed Snider's arm. "The crew had more information than we do: the feel of the ship, any sounds too faint for the data core to hear, visual clues – smoke, fire – smells. They may have learned something and will tell us what it is."

The analyst gave him a sympathetic look. "If it were that simple, I'd have mentioned it the first time I heard it."

"Nevertheless," Chase said, "a lot of things went on in this cabin that I don't understand. If we explain one of them, it'll be worth our time."

Snider resumed his place. "Make it quick. I'm a busy man."

According to the data core, there was no discussion in the cabin for some time. Chase heard a shuffling of paper as the crew opened their procedures manuals. He listened carefully for the sound of a page being torn out. There was none.

Then he heard Phyllis's conversation with Montanari Tower for the first time.

"*Phoenix*, Montanari Tower. You're off your vector. Abort your landing and try again. Repeat, abort your landing. Acknowledge."

"Acknowledged, Montanari." The voice from the *Phoenix*, that of a mature woman, was calm and resolute. "But we've lost thrust. We're a dead stick. Please stand by."

"Roger, *Phoenix*. Standing by."

"According to the data," the analyst said after the exchange, "the crew did a rapid shutdown and a flawless restart of the thrusters."

"Flawless?" Chase asked.

"Yes."

"Absolutely according to procedures?" He wanted to make this point clear in Snider's presence. The director had been pressing him for a statement of blame for the past two days and this would help to defer a "pilot error" conclusion. If the cause eventually boiled down to some mistake, so be it. But until then, Chase would work to dispel any such suspicions.

The analyst nodded. She pointed out each relevant shift in the log traces while the audio recording continued in the background.

"What's happening?" Herrera asked again, much more agitated now. Randy didn't respond.

"You listen up, pilot." The voice was Lederman's. "The secretary asked you a question. We demand to know what's happening and what you're doing about it. I'm responsible for the secretary's safety, and let me make something perfectly clear. If anything happens to him because of your ship, I'll hold you personally responsible."

"You heard her," Randy said. "We've lost control. We're going down and we're going down fast. Now it's my turn to make something clear. If you don't sit down and buckle in, you won't survive the impact. And what's more, I may be able to stop it, but not if I spend the next few minutes pacifying you."

Phyllis gasped. The clear sound came through the data core and echoed Chase's own thought. Lederman didn't seem like the kind of man to piss off. But Randy was right.

Then Herrera intervened. "Sit down, for Christ's sake, and let the man work."

Lederman must have done so because Chase heard the click of a flight harness.

"Play that again," Chase asked the analyst. Had Lederman drawn his gun?

Forsythe had no reaction to the replay.

No, Chase decided. Anxiety had risen in Lederman's voice, but the confrontation wasn't strong enough to suggest a threat of violence. And Herrera, though clearly unsettled, had effectively defused the conflict.

"Okay," he said. "Let's move on."

The analyst restarted the record. "They completed their checklists and engaged the thrusters. Still nothing."

A tech in the back chimed in. "The tower just lost the *Phoenix* from radar."

"Hold on," Randy said. "Here we go."

Chase craned his neck to see into the cargo hold. "Do we have a simulation of impact?"

"Yes, sir," a tech announced. "I folded in a contour map of the lunar surface, using the debris fields for reference."

They all gathered around the monitor and watched the simulated *Phoenix* scrape the ridge top at the trailing edge of a large crater. That slowed the ship and started a gradual end-over-end somersault. Kilometers swept beneath it.

The tail came over the top of the nose and struck the ground with a loud crunch. Then the recorder went silent. The mechanical-impact model showed a shower of debris as the ship bounced in the low gravity, doing several more somersaults before coming down again. Eventually, it tumbled to a stop on the large, flat expanse of the Mare Tranquillitatis.

The work would get harder now without the data core.

Chase moved the actors back into the cockpit and tried to put himself into the moment. "If I were Randy, I'd make sure everyone was okay." He turned to the coroner. "Injuries?"

The man frowned and shook his head. "Bumps and bruises."

"Okay," Chase continued. "At this point there's a vacuum leak in the cabin."

"How do you know?" Forsythe asked.

Chase pointed to the vacuum tape on the bulkhead.

"No," Forsythe said. "How do you, as Randy Lauback, know the cabin's leaking?"

"Good question." Chase looked around before pointing to the console. "The pressure gauge."

"There's no power." Forsythe's hands never left his pockets.

"It's a manometer gauge. It doesn't use power. And there's light coming through the window to see by."

Michelle eyed the repair skeptically. "That's a pretty small leak. In a chamber this size they wouldn't see the gauge move for," she paused, "ten or fifteen minutes."

"So they didn't discover it right away."

"Maybe they heard it," she said.

"Either way, they know there's a leak, but they don't know where it is. How do they find it?"

"The air's escaping," Michelle said. "Use the air flow."

"How?"

After a moment, Forsythe put a forefinger into his mouth and held the wet digit in the air.

Chase shook his head. "Even if the flow was strong enough to feel, that'd be too crude. They're looking for the exact location of a tiny fracture."

The team stared at one another. Forsythe buried his hands in his pockets and waited. Snider's expression said he was about ten seconds from canceling the whole exercise.

"Release something into the air and follow it?" The inflection in Michelle's voice made the statement a question.

"Okay. What?" Chase scanned the cabin for something light enough to float in an air current. A handful of lunar dust would stay suspended, but Randy wouldn't have vented the cabin for a handful of sand. The silence lengthened and Chase began to doubt the proposal until his eyes fell upon the discarded procedures manual and the torn page. "There." He pointed.

Forsythe's cocked brow pulled at the folds of skin beneath his eye. "Would it float?"

"We're at one-sixth gravity. In a reasonable current, it'd float." The realization belayed Snider's objections and explained the most troubling bit of evidence against the pilot. But it concerned Chase as well. As each clue was explained away, it narrowed the possibility of a lead coming from the reenactment. He'd learned much — but thus far, nothing pointing to cause.

"Okay. There're no serious injuries and they've stabilized the ship. Nobody's touched their EVA yet. Agreed?" He stared at the pressure suit he'd placed on the floor to represent Lederman's body and resisted the urge to review his list again.

"Now Randy's looking for options," he continued. "With the repair completed, he had time to consider their situation. His first priority was oxygen. Only one tank remained that wasn't ruptured during the crash, a little more than twelve hours' worth, plus a couple of hours in the cabin and whatever they had in the EVA suit tanks." He stroked his beard thoughtfully. "Food and water weren't a problem. They could bleed water from the cooling system, if necessary. As for food, they'd suffocate long before they'd starve to death. All electrical systems were out. The only thing still operating was their emergency locator beacon, which ran off its own lithium cell."

The idea of extracting water from the cooling system had occurred to him earlier. It might have been the reason for the apparent repair, but he'd ruled that out when he found that a bleeder valve had been provided for the purpose. They wouldn't have needed tools.

A cooling problem, then. But why repair it after impact?

"How long before they could expect rescue?" Forsythe asked Chase.

"They might not have known, but they had navigation capability until impact, so they probably had a good idea of where they were." He was thinking out loud, working his way through the problem as Randy would have. "They thought Lunar Alpha was the closest base, but it was a long ways off ... days, they'd figure."

"Were you en route already?" Forsythe asked.

"ERT was," Snider said.

"The recovery effort left a couple hours later," Chase added.

"What about a ship? Could you send a lander?"

"No," Snider said. "Deep-space vessels and Earth-return shuttles aren't suited for this sort of thing. Stellarfare had a couple of crater jumpers, but they can take off only once without refueling, so they'll land only at an established facility."

"That left them with the rover," Michelle concluded. "They tried to meet the rescue team halfway."

Chase nodded. "They strapped the remaining oxygen tank to the buggy and plumbed it to their pressure suits with flexible tubing salvaged from the wreck. Flexible tubing," he realized suddenly, "that they took from the cooling line." That explained the tools and open access panel and ruled out a cooling problem. One more lead vanished.

"Their other problem was fuel. They had several drums in the cargo hold, but rovers have only a small tank. They're not designed for long distances.

So they took a drum with them and a pump to siphon what they needed to refuel. They also took the emergency beacon."

"I don't like their chances," Forsythe announced.

Chase's brow creased. They'd been pretty thorough in the analysis. "I think that's what we've got." Then he addressed everyone, including the analysts in the cargo hold. "Does anybody see anything we're missing?"

Silence.

The rasp in Forsythe's tone turned icy and his face took on a severe cast. "Lederman would've considered the odds unacceptable." Forsythe was adept at playing the roll, but his seriousness was beyond that warranted by the reenactment. His statement had an ultimatum-like quality.

"So … what would he do?" Chase asked.

"Based on your evaluation, it boils down to air. The more air, the greater the odds. Is that right?"

Chase nodded. He saw where Forsythe was headed.

"And the fewer the people," Forsythe continued, "the more the air."

"So what would he do?"

"Well, if twelve hours of air gets four people halfway back, then the same air will get the secretary and one other person all the way back. That's what Lederman would propose."

"Would he use his weapon to make it happen?"

"Yes. If he thought he had to." Forsythe sounded certain.

"It's not that simple," Michelle said. "An oxygen tank and fuel drum were discarded along the rover's path. Both were empty. They went on with the fuel in the rover's tank and the air in their pressure suits. Even with three of them, the fuel ran out first. Two people would've had more air, but they wouldn't have made it much farther on foot."

"That's true," Chase said. "If they'd run out of air first, the rover would've still had fuel. As it was, we had to scrape the bottom to get a sample for analysis."

"Then reducing their number to three gives Secretary Herrera the best chance of survival," Forsythe said. "That's what I'd do."

"Even if it meant murder?" Chase pressed. He wanted him to think of it in those terms.

Forsythe met his gaze, the skin of his face tightening. "Even if it meant murder … or sacrifice."

"You're suggesting that Lederman committed suicide?"

"He may have." Forsythe addressed the coroner, hands back in his pockets. "Did you find anything on him? A small capsule or pill in his possession?"

The coroner shook his head. "We found his ID, but that's it. Did he have a suicide pill when he left the base?"

"He should've. Cyanide."

The coroner chewed the back of his lip. "Cyanide prevents oxygen from getting into the blood cells. It could give the appearance of asphyxiation. I'll go back and do a trace analysis. If it's there, I'll find it."

"So Lederman does the math, as you did." Chase motioned to Forsythe. "And comes to the same conclusion. He argues the point with the crew, finds resistance, and pulls his gun to force the issue. Then Randy brings up the fuel problem — "

"Or Phyllis does," Michelle said.

"Or Phyllis does, and Lederman decides to pop the pill instead." One by one, Chase's leads fell like dominoes before the logic of circumstance — explained away as direct effects of the situation, rather than contributors to it — and left his case devoid of leads.

With nothing left, the reenactment became academic and, like himself, a failure, but he was one to finish what he started. So he forged ahead before Snider could sense his disappointment and call it quits. "The survivors prepare the rover for departure, load as much fuel and oxygen as possible, and give the rescue team a head start until the cabin air is consumed. They don their pressure suits, pop the hatch, and wrestle the rover through the opening. Then what?" He turned to the footprint analyst.

"I coded each person's tracks in a different color," the boy said. "The cluster by the door had too many overlapping prints to analyze, but everything else was workable."

"Let's see it."

At the outset, each footprint was black with a colored outline. The analyst started the program and two sets of tracks sequentially illuminated, one red, one blue, each print lighting up as the foot fell to make the track. "Once they got the rover into position, Herrera and the pilot climbed in. The pilot in the front passenger's seat, Herrera in the back." He pointed to the string of light green prints leading back to the *Phoenix*. "The copilot went back inside."

"For what?" Forsythe asked.

Chase remembered something he'd forgotten. He pulled a photograph from the pocket of his jumpsuit and displayed the picture. "This. The coroner found it in the sleeve pocket of her suit." He moved the picture to the torn remnant of tape stuck to the copilot's console. The vestige of tape on the photograph matched perfectly.

"Who's in the picture?" Michelle asked.

In the photo, a young couple smiled back at Chase. The woman bore a resemblance to Phyllis, but Chase didn't know the relation. Text on the back read, "Ralph and Karen Porter," with a date. He put the photograph back into his pocket. "I think it's her daughter."

Footprints tracked again on the display and the analyst continued. "Then she walked out among the debris."

Chase scowled as he watched her path unfold. It seemed to meander from one side of the site to the other.

"What's she looking for?" Forsythe demanded.

After several minutes, Chase began to recognize the pattern. "She's scouting the debris field, finding its edges." All the tracks were Phyllis's. The geologists hadn't wandered among evidence after all.

"She's consuming the air that Lederman died to give them."

"Relax," Chase said. "She's getting a bearing on Alpha Base. They need to know which way to go before they — "

"By looking at the ground?"

"Sure. They were headed toward Alpha when they hit the ground, so the debris field's like an arrow pointing the way. Once she has a bearing, she can use landmarks on the horizon to maintain her course."

"Is that good enough?"

"They had the beacon. If they were off by a few degrees, it'd delay the rendezvous by only a few minutes."

"Minutes they ultimately needed. You can't tell me they didn't have a compass."

"Wouldn't have helped if they did. The Moon has no magnetic field."

"What about GPS?" Forsythe asked.

Snider shook his head. "Like a rescue lander, it's not worth the expense. They're only useful in cases like these, which happen only about once a decade."

"Besides," Chase said, "they didn't need a compass. Their route was direct and on target."

"The copilot returned to the buggy and climbed into the driver's seat," the footprint analyst said. "That leaves two more sets." He pointed to a trail highlighted in orange that went straight to the *Phoenix* and back. "The geologist made these." Then he looked up at Chase. "The yellow prints are yours."

When the others began to file out at the end of the reenactment, Chase replayed the beginning of it in his mind. It had started with a spike in the controller output. He'd almost missed its significance because he couldn't tie it to anything on his list, but it was the most important clue he had. It told him that the cause was not contaminated fuel. The problem wasn't in the engines, valves, or injectors. Those things could respond to the controller output, but they couldn't influence it. Helm control, autopilot, navigation, and the communication lines to the thrust controller could also be ruled out. The controller had gotten the signal to fire. If it hadn't, the voltage wouldn't have spiked before the output went dead.

Chase found a Soaring engineer sorting through fragments in one of the crates. "Find the thrust controller," he told her. "That's where our problem is."

Snider pulled Chase aside. "That was a lovely exercise," he spat, "but you haven't answered the basic question: why?" Veins bulged in his forehead as he said the last word. His eyes, crazed as though he was on the verge of a breakdown, spoke of the unbelievable pressure that he must be under. Chase had thought he'd understood, but matters were apparently worse than he'd imagined.

"Look, Morgan." Snider dropped his voice. "You must answer that question. And soon. I'm getting to the point where I don't even care if it's the right answer." He looked Chase in the eye. "You hear what I'm saying?"

Chase nodded, speechless. It wasn't his shock at Snider's comment, but the implications of it, that made him hesitant to speak. What was Snider afraid of? Was he afraid that Chase wouldn't find the answer? Or was he afraid he'd find the right one?

Chapter 5

That afternoon, Chase finally got Erin on the comm for the first time since the *Phoenix* had crashed.

"I saw the press conference," she said. "When I got your letter I had no idea..."

"We still don't know what really happened, but I think we may be nearing something. I hope to be home soon."

Erin's face stretched into a skeptical frown, as though she'd heard it all before. "Just promise me you'll come home when this is over. No more cases. The girls want to see their Gramp."

Chase chuckled. "Is that what they call me? Gramp?"

Erin nodded.

"It sounds like 'Cramp.'"

Erin laughed. "It's your own fault. The last time you were home, that's the only way Laura could pronounce it."

"I remember."

"She calls you that every time you show up on the newsblips. Katie's picked it up too. And since you aren't here to correct them, it's stuck."

"I'll fix that when I get there."

"Promises, promises." She smiled through the admonition, but she wasn't wholly joking.

"Promise."

"You better."

"I have to go."

Her eyes turned sad. "I know."

He cut the transmission and vowed to himself, again, that he would keep the promise this time.

The next morning, the coroner confirmed the presence of cyanide in Lederman's blood, a finding that struck the agent's name from the suspect list. Chase got the news while he was coordinating the reconstruction of the wrecked ship.

By then, he'd accessed Phyllis's record and determined that she'd indeed had a daughter named Karen — the woman in the photograph. He thought of his own daughter, and his mind drifted to one of his fondest memories of her childhood.

It was late one evening, when Erin was about a year-and-a-half old and Chase had had a particularly rough day. He could no longer remember what had upset him, but when he and Erin got home, his nerves were frayed and his patience was depleted. He pulled into the garage, well past Erin's bedtime, turned off the engine, and climbed out, looking forward to putting her to bed and shutting down for the night.

Erin, wide awake despite the hour, gabbed to herself and to him as he reached into the back seat to release her.

Before the restraint clicked open, she said, "Erin's turn drive car?"

He often let her sit and pretend to drive. When he didn't, he gave her a reason. "No, honey, it's bedtime." She'd either accept it or cry. But this night, he said only, "No," firm and final, and reached in to pull her from her seat. There were better ways he might have handled it, but at the time, he couldn't seem to find them. God, that night of all nights, he didn't want a fight.

The girl's brow creased as she processed the reply. It took only a second for her to look up, her face bright and inquisitive. "Well, why?"

The remark was so unexpected that it got him to laughing. It was the first of many times she'd ask that question, but at the time it showed a level of reason and sophistication that he wouldn't have credited to a child her age. And with those two words, she smashed through his anger and frustration with hammers of pride and amusement.

Ironically, those were the same words that were causing him such trouble now.

One of the Soaring engineers interrupted his musings. "Mr. Morgan? We've found something I think you'll want to see."

He shifted his gaze. "What is it?"

"The thrust controller. You were right." The woman led him in long strides through the carefully-arrayed ship fragments to an electronics compartment. She pointed to a small circuit board, about five centimeters square. "It's this. It doesn't belong in here. In fact, it doesn't belong at all. It's not part of the original design."

Chase studied the installation. "Have one of the techs scan the whole cabinet for fingerprints."

"You got it." She flashed him a smile, obviously pleased with the importance of her discovery.

But to Chase, the implications were seriously troubling.

"Sabotage? Are you sure?" Snider said when Chase reported later that day.

"I just came from Stellarfare, who's been the sole owner of the *Phoenix* since it was built three years ago. They didn't put it there, which means it was planted without their knowledge. And it was wired into the thrust controller." Chase tossed the images onto Snider's desk and stabbed a finger at them. "I don't believe in coincidence. That board's responsible for the crash."

Snider chewed his lips, anger building in his expression. "Damn it!" He came to his feet. "Have you told Forsythe?"

"What? And deny you the pleasure?"

"He'll take over the case."

"Probably."

"He'll yank it out from under us like a tablecloth. And we won't all be standing when he's done. He'll audit everything — security, safety, maintenance, records, you name it. Hell, he'll climb down our shorts if he thinks he'll find something damning."

So would Chase if he thought it would solve the case. "We can't keep this buried."

Snider took a deep breath and released it with a loud sigh. "I know. I'll contact Forsythe."

An emptiness settled over Chase when he left Snider's office. Technically, he'd done his job, and in remarkable time. He'd discovered the cause and cleared Randy of any wrongdoing or negligence. The question of who sabotaged the ship would become a criminal inquiry, beyond the charter of Accident Investigations. But he hadn't proven anything yet. The presence of the board was strong evidence, but until someone analyzed its functionality, it remained circumstantial. As such, if he lost the case to Forsythe now, Chase would feel like he'd left the job unfinished.

~(O)~

The following morning, Chase started his day in the materials lab, where he'd taken the circuit board for analysis. When he entered, the smell of chemicals stung his nose. Michelle was there among the clutter of the prep area with the discarded box of samples, two microscopes, a mechanical polisher, a handheld coring drill, and an acid workstation. A blue antistatic lab coat was draped on her shoulders, and a schematic was displayed on a screen in front of her.

Michelle smiled when she saw him. Though the gesture seemed genuine, it lacked her usual zeal. Dark bags hung beneath her eyes, making her look as tired as Chase felt. The long days were taking their toll on everyone.

"You get any sleep at all last night?" he asked.

"Not much."

He gestured to her work. "What do you know?"

"This is the layout of the primary chip, as best as I can determine from a top-down inspection. The remaining chips are commercial components that can be bought anywhere — a timer, several current and voltage sensors, and an analog-to-digital converter. I think the board was designed to cut the signal from the thrust controls to the propellant valves when a specific series of events was sensed, or at a specific time."

"But you don't know what series of signals it was looking for?"

Michelle waved a hand over the diagram and several educational thinpads. She picked one, pressed the icon, and showed him the title, *Contemporary Electronic Circuit Analysis.* "That's what I'm working on now. The catch is, I'm not convinced I've got the circuit right."

"Why's that?"

"Looking at it top-down, I can see all the leads and connections, but the active devices are built into the substrate. The doping changes can't be observed optically, so I'm trying to infer them from the geometry of the connections."

Standing there listening to the difficulties of the task, Chase was struck by the thought that this must be quite unlike the typical college homework problem. "Enjoying the challenge?"

"I keep looking for the answers section in the main menu."

"Sometimes life's problems don't have answers." He wasn't alluding to the circuit.

She set the thinpad down, sighing. "It wouldn't be so bad if I was good at it. I've taken courses in chip manufacturing, but they focused on processing and materials. This is beyond my basic circuit analysis."

"Where's the chip now?"

"There." She pointed to a nearby microscope.

Chase peered into the eyepiece and saw the complexity of the circuit. The top of the chip's package had been removed to reveal the electronics within. It looked like a poorly-laid network of streets in some bizarre city.

"It's a fairly simple part, as nanoelectronics go," Michelle said, "with only one layer of interconnects. I think it was made in Japan." She handed him a thinpad with a picture displayed. "This is the chip before we took it apart." The enlarged image showed Asian text on the top of the package.

"What about the materials?"

"That's today's project for the techs."

Chase glanced past her to the bank of analysis machines. "Where is everyone?"

"They won't be in 'til eight. I came in early to get another look at the chip. The next phase of tests will be destructive."

"Get a picture."

"Already have. But it's easier to see the vertical geometry under the scope by playing with the focal plane of the lens. That information's lost in the pictures."

"Can't you take a three-D image?"

"The imager's down, waiting for parts. We'd have to send it to an Earthside lab."

Chase shook his head. "We can't afford the delay."

"I know. That's why we're proceeding with what we have."

He picked up the thinpad containing the images. "May I keep this?"

"Sure."

"Thanks," he said, and left the lab.

Next, he canceled the day's meeting. If Forsythe planned to commandeer the team, he'd do it at the meeting. This would put the agent off for at least a day. Besides, everything that could be done was being done — the techs continuing the reassembly, the lab analyzing the sabotage device, Brower investigating Stellarfare. Somehow, pulling people from their work to attend a meeting seemed a poor use of time.

That done, he went back to his apartment and spent the rest of the morning and most of the afternoon on the telnet with NASA's Earthbound investigations branch.

Almost immediately, they determined that the chip was Chinese, not Japanese, and that the text on the package translated into a product code and serial number. That was promising. If they could determine who made the chip, they might be able to track it to a customer, and from there, to the person who planted it. They sifted through the data from China's many nanoelectronics manufacturers, but by mid-afternoon, they'd gotten nowhere.

"Keep trying," Chase told his colleagues. "Somebody made that chip."

CHAPTER 6

When Chase entered the conference room the following day, he felt tension in the air. Everyone was there — Snider, Brower, Forsythe, the techs, analysts, and administrators — all silent and brooding amid the sterile décor of aluminite paneling. The excitement of the device discovery had worn off and everyone seemed to sense a change in the course of the investigation.

He moved to the head of the table and pressed a button on the control panel. The wall display came to life with a default image, that of a US flag flying over Alpha Base, the same image NASA used for its publicity brochures.

He began by reviewing what they knew. It wasn't much, but it was clear that the chip was their strongest lead. At his request, Michelle slipped a data card into a slot in the aluminite table, then rose to present. She displayed several images, including the chip package, a top-down view of the circuit layout, and the circuit board. After describing the peripheral chips, she put up her own schematic of the primary component, as well as she'd been able to determine, and admitted that she wasn't sure of its accuracy.

Snider sat up in his chair. "If it's not accurate, why are we discussing it?"

Michelle froze. "I — We can discern its general function without — "

Snider waved a dismissive hand. "Morgan, I expect your people to be prepared for their briefings."

Chase understood Snider's foul humor. Forsythe was a sword dangling over his domain, a sword that would likely rip through his organization with ruthless precision. The result would lay bare any weakness in his leadership or authority. But he was out of line to take it out on Michelle.

Part of the purpose of her internship was to further her own education and experience. Snider couldn't expect her to contribute at the level of a degreed engineer.

Chase had to stop the attack before Snider crumbled her confidence, but he didn't think the inexperience argument would strike a chord in the director this morning. "Jack, this circuit is foreign to all of us. We're not working from a published product schematic. Michelle put this together by visual inspection, a painstaking and tedious task. And, quite frankly, an impossible one with our in-house capability."

Michelle stood beside the display with wide eyes and flushed complexion, waiting to see what would become of her work.

"Do you have a block diagram of the circuit?" Chase asked.

She nodded and advanced to the next image. From there, she identified several of the circuit's modules — electrostatic protection on the inputs and outputs, voltage comparators, amplifiers and switches. Snider held his tongue for a time and Michelle's voice grew stronger. But her analysis fell short when it came to the details of the chip's core functionality. Snider picked up on this and began asking pointed questions.

Brower, who'd spent the entire discussion gazing through a small window into the void beyond, turned his attention to Michelle and contributed to the belittling of her report.

Again, Chase intervened. "The data core shows well enough what the circuit accomplished. Any more time spent on functionality would've delayed or prevented the physical analysis, which is much more interesting, and perhaps the key to the whole case. Michelle, why don't you move on to the metallurgy results."

Both men seemed intrigued enough to hear what Michelle would say next. Chase had set her up to drop a major lead into the lap of the investigators. She'd discovered the significance of the metallurgy and she deserved the credit. But Chase had another, more personal and long-term, agenda.

As her mentor, it was his responsibility to help further her professional development. She wanted a career with NASA after she graduated. The best way to assure that was for her to make substantial, visible contributions now.

She gave Chase a look of gratitude and advanced her presentation by two slides. "This is a spectrograph of the metal used in the primary component."

The graph showed two lines. The green line, labeled "Baseline," had two peaks — one marked "Cu," for copper, and a smaller peak, marked "Sn," for tin. The red line, labeled "Sample," showed the same copper peak but included two smaller peaks, "Ni" and "Pd."

"The baseline," Michelle explained, "is the standard used throughout the nanochip industry for metal interconnects. Our sample contains both nickel and palladium. This is not only unusual, it's unique."

Several observers sat straighter in their chairs. Snider stiffened, Forsythe's eyebrows shot up, and Brower's attention was again pulled from the window.

Michelle continued. "I did a literature search for any metallurgical research in the past ten years related to nanochip fabrication. Many alloys have been explored, but none perform better than the baseline for mainstream applications. And there were no references to either nickel or palladium doping. Whoever developed this process has kept it from the public record."

"What about the other materials in the component?" Forsythe asked.

"All normal." Michelle went back to the image she'd skipped. "The industry uses a much wider variety of insulating materials than they do metals. And different materials perform better for different applications. But the dielectrics we found here appear in parts from many suppliers."

"You said the chip was Chinese in origin." It didn't sound like a question, but Brower leaned forward, elbows on the table, and awaited her reply.

She faced him squarely. "It appears to be. The markings on the package were Chinese."

"What do you have left of the component?" Brower asked.

"We have half the chip intact. The rest was destroyed during the analysis."

"I suggest we send it and the data to the Intelligence Agency," Brower said. "If this is a government chip, they may know more about it. It'd also explain why you didn't find it in the literature. Governments tend to be more tight-lipped about technological improvements than commercial businesses are."

Chase's brow creased. A government chip? Governments weren't in the manufacturing business, except for military applications. But that would explain why the product code hadn't come up in his commercial search. "Let's send the data, but I want to hang on to the chip. We may need it again."

"You said you've already done everything you can in-house. So if you want anything else, you'll have to send it Earthside anyway." Brower's manner was casual, but his voice held a sharp edge. "Send it through the CIA. And from there to wherever you want."

"We can't take a three-D image to map the circuit, but we have plenty of materials-analysis capability."

"More than you could get on Earth?"

Chase stiffened like a cur with raised hackles. Brower was throwing down the gauntlet in front of Snider and Forsythe. What did he have to gain from challenging Chase's authority? The security department would come under fire whether Forsythe stole the case or not. But Chase had never been on a criminal investigation. Maybe Brower had the credentials to put himself in charge. "Our lab will be faster."

"If you can get someone who knows what they're doing."

Chase winced inwardly at the undeserved insult. "Michelle is our liaison to the lab, and she's helping out there, but she's not in charge of the analysis." He hated to downplay her contribution now, but he had to divert Brower's attack before the man could undermine the credibility of the data.

Snider said nothing during the exchange, probably evaluating Chase's performance as a leader or weighing the merits of Brower's remarks. Chase decided he'd had enough, so he played his trump card. "The chip stays here. Michelle, summarize the data you have. Work with Forsythe on who to send it to." End of discussion. Chase was still in charge.

Snider came to his feet. "Now that that's settled, I have an announcement to make. The FBI has exercised its jurisdiction over Lunar Alpha." He flashed Chase an apologetic look, incongruous coming from a man with the hard-nosed reputation of Jack Snider. But Snider didn't have a choice. "Effective immediately, Special Agent Forsythe owns the case." He motioned to the agent and sat down.

Forsythe stood and moved to the head of the table, forcing Chase to turn his seat around to face him. The gesture was subtle but effective. Not only could Chase no longer lead his team, he couldn't even see it.

The agent stuffed his hands into his pockets, rocked back on his heels, and addressed his audience. "We need to start looking at opportunity. We have no motive, but sometimes if you can identify the 'who,' then the 'why' becomes more obvious. We need to talk to Stellarfare and compile the names of everyone who worked on the *Phoenix* between the time it was selected for Herrera's flight and the time it took off. That device was put there during that interval."

Chase's mind reeled. Like the loss of his marriage and flight status, losing control of the case was another blow to his dignity's shaky foundation, yet he was still on the team. That in itself was a vote of confidence from Snider — an indication that Chase still had a contribution to make and that he could make it without destabilizing the ship. Maybe Snider thought he'd take his retirement. Not a chance. After Chase had lost his flight status, ruined Randy Lauback's career, destroyed his own marriage, and alienated his family, this last assignment had become too integral to his own measure of self-worth. If he walked away now, with the job undone, then he walked away a failure. And what's worse, he'd see himself as such for the rest of his life. The *Phoenix* was the capstone of his career. If he couldn't own it, he'd at least make his contribution count.

Forsythe continued speaking. "We need to find out who knew that Herrera would be on that ship."

"You're assuming the attack was directed at Herrera," Chase said.

"Do you believe otherwise?" Snider gave him a hard look.

"Who knows? Maybe Randy Lauback had an enemy."

"It's possible," Forsythe said. "We can't rule it out."

When Chase left the meeting an hour later, he felt a hollow ache inside. He wandered the tall corridors of the base, sifting through his feelings. He'd been in charge of his own activities for decades. The autonomy of the Office of Accident Investigations, like that of deep-space flight, had allowed him a freedom of action that he'd miss under Forsythe's direction. As his loss of flight status had been four years before, this was one more step toward the inadequacy and dependence that defined old age.

Chase woke to a muffled boom that shook the whole of Alpha Base. He squinted at the clock, then grunted at the complaint of his joints as he rolled to his feet. 3:09 A.M. Only half-conscious, he keyed the terminal and checked the newsblips. They were reporting the latest numbers in the presidential campaign polls. Whatever had caused the disturbance, the local press hadn't responded yet. Then he tuned to the ERT alert channel. The screen flashed white letters over a red background.

ALERT: FIRE IN HANGAR BAY #3
EVACUATE DELTA WING WEST OF CORRIDOR J

Hangar Three. The *Phoenix*!

CHAPTER 7

Suddenly wide awake, Chase scrambled into his jumpsuit, then into the corridors of the base. Adrenaline pumped through his veins as he raced along the broad passageways, leaping in the meager gravity. When he reached the main corridor, he grabbed the railing along the wall and propelled himself forward, hand-over-hand, a technique much faster than trying to run in lunar g.

As he approached Delta wing, the fire alarm wailed. People gathered in groups in the halls, as if for comfort. One stocky man grabbed his arm. Chase suppressed a curse.

"What's going on? What's happened?" the man shouted.

"That's what I'm going to find out if you let go of me." He pried the man's fingers loose and bounded away.

In Delta wing, the crowd thickened. Chase forced his way through the throng until he reached the ERT barricade at corridor J. Only emergency personnel were allowed to pass. Impatient, he thrust his credentials at one of the guards and raced into the empty passageway beyond.

A man with a red vest and comm link stopped him at the next intersection. By then, Chase could feel heat radiating down the passage. He waved his pass again and launched himself forward.

But the man grabbed Chase's sleeve. "I'm sorry, sir. ERT only." He waved down a pair of security guards.

This is where the distinction between emergency response and accident investigation rankled Chase. Officially, he'd be shut out until the danger was past. To these guards, he was just an old man with the wrong

ID. He turned back to the guy in the vest.

The man loosened his grip. "It's too dangerous."

Chase recognized the voice of the incident commander directing fire-suppressions activities down the hall. In a sudden flash of movement, he yanked his arm free and bounded past. The guards yelled after him and rushed to intercede, but he managed to reach the commander.

She rolled her eyes inside her pressure suit. "He can stay," she said to the guards. Then she grabbed a fishbowl helmet from the rack and tossed it to Chase. "If he suits up."

Chase pulled on a pressure suit and helmet as the guards retreated. When he walked down the hall to the hangar, the reason for their caution became obvious. Ripples in the softening durapane between the corridor and the bay distorted everything beyond the window.

Smoke swirled in an eerie shroud over the massive bulk of the *Phoenix*, huddled amid the ruins of the hangar. But there was something else too, a dark form where there'd been none yesterday. Ignoring the commotion around him, Chase moved to another window for a better look. From there, he could identify the object — a forklift, and affixed to its tines was a solid-fuel rocket.

Arson. Not only that, but arson designed to defeat the fire-suppression system, which wasn't intended for solid fuels. The devastation was too complete, the ramifications too severe for Chase's tired mind to grasp. The image was like the fading vestiges of a nightmare viewed through a haze of waxing consciousness. Yet everything else around him was vivid with colors and shapes too authentic to be a dream.

Normally, the ERT would've opened the bay doors and sucked the air into space. That would've put out an ordinary fire. But unlike liquid fuel, solid propellants contain their own oxygen supply and burn until the propellant is spent. If they'd let it outside, the fire might have spread to the ships parked on the blacktop.

But the fuel was spent now, and only secondary fires remained. Chase punched his code into a nearby panel. DEVICE ERROR, the screen displayed.

He slammed his fist against the bulkhead.

"We tried that already," the commander said through the speaker in his helmet. "The door's expanded in the heat. It's jammed. We're evacuating the hangar through the vent valve. It'll take another twenty minutes."

He spun on her, a retort on his lips, but nothing he could say would make him feel any better. Their miscreant was out there and had just taken the upper hand. There'd be nothing left of the evidence by the time the fire burned itself out.

Chase pointed to a discarded chair lying on its side in the hall. "Was there a guard on duty when you got here?"

She followed his gaze to the abandoned seat. "No. That was by the door, but the hall was empty."

Chase's gaze returned to the hangar. He could see little through the haze, but one thing was clear — between the heat, smoke, and partially-evacuated atmosphere, nobody could survive inside. He wouldn't get in to see more until the fire died and everything cooled. So he commandeered a small conference room and moved in a pair of terminals to monitor the newsblips and ERT channel. It was going to be a long day for everyone.

"Where's Stan?" Chase asked when Snider arrived.

"Coordinating security for the area."

"And Forsythe?"

"Haven't seen him."

The incident commander came in an hour later. "We're giving you the okay to go inside. There're two bodies. Security's cordoned off the area and we're handing control of the scene to you. Unless you need them, I'll send my team home."

Chase shook his head. "They can go."

Next, he turned to Michelle. "Track down Forsythe. The rest of us will see what's left inside. " He told Snider, "We'll need the coroner."

"You'll have him."

Chase entered the bay and examined the rocket booster that had been used to ignite the fire. For safety reasons, solid fuels were stored in a detached bunker, without a propulsion nozzle, and no nozzle had been attached to this one. The open end of the tank was aimed at the *Phoenix*. There was no doubt. This was a deliberate destruction of evidence.

The ship itself was a charred mess. Most of the outer hull, a durable carbon composite designed to withstand the temperature extremes of space, was relatively undamaged, though it was blackened and in some places softened to the point of deformation by the blaze. But all exterior wires, cables, insulation, fasteners, labeling, paint, and instrumentation had been completely consumed. Even the interior of the ship, some of which had been untouched by the flames, had reached a temperature high enough to melt almost everything.

Chase waded through the thick layer of soot and ash that gave the hangar an air of desolation matching the landscape outside.

The cargo stacked at the far end of the bay had fared better. The flames there had come from secondary ignition of the excess drums of rover fuel, and the fire-suppression system had saved some of the supplies.

The bodies, when he found them, were nothing more than a partial set of scorched bones and ash, incompletely cremated, with a few melted personal effects. Bile filled Chase's throat and forced him to turn away. Damn it! Nobody was supposed to be in there. The death count was now at six, and Chase had known some of those people. He swallowed the vomit that rose in him, fortified his resolve, and looked again upon the victims. Both skulls remained intact, their bony grins mocking him from the ruins of his investigation. He imagined the perpetrator doing the same from somewhere nearby.

At the meeting the following morning, Brower and Snider came in late together. Brower paused at the door while the director moved to the head of the table. "The bodies," Snider said without preamble, "have been identified as Arthur McDaniel, the guard on duty at the time, and Agent Forsythe." He paused to let the information sink in, but for Chase it was no surprise. They'd spent the previous day searching for the two men, and by evening, he'd suspected the worst.

"Their families have been notified," Snider continued, "and arrangements have been made to return their remains to Earth for burial. My secretary is coordinating a memorial collection. See her if you'd like to contribute. We don't have any information about services yet, but as soon as we do, she'll let everybody know. Right now, the best thing we can do for McDaniel and Forsythe is to find their killer."

Brower sat in his usual seat across from the window. "Any reason Forsythe might have been in the hangar at that time of the morning?"

"None I'm aware of," Snider said, "but that'll be part of the investigation, which I'm turning over to you, Brower."

Chase choked on his coffee, nearly spewing it onto the table. "What?" He coughed again, trying to expel the inhaled liquid. "Jack, it's my case."

"Not any more." Snider's tone left no room for debate. He turned to the others as if to make another announcement.

With the pall of McDaniel's and Forsythe's deaths hanging over the meeting, this was no place for the argument that Chase was about to start, but he didn't care. When the feds took over, nobody'd had a choice in the matter, but now it was Snider's call. And Snider was someone Chase might influence. "Jack, I brought this case to where we are now — "

"'Now'?" Snider wheeled on him, raising his voice. "The case is in ashes now, and two more men are dead."

That was unfair. Snider couldn't hold Chase responsible for the deaths, especially since Forsythe had commandeered the case, but it would only make Chase sound petty to say so. "We know a lot more than we did when we started."

Snider took a slow breath and calmed visibly. "Listen, Morgan, this isn't about performance."

"Bullshit." Chase shot to his feet. He knew Snider. Everything was about performance.

"You're my accident investigator," Snider continued. "But this was no accident. It was sabotage, arson, and murder — all criminal, security matters."

The confident demeanor Snider had learned in the control room grated on Chase now. Snider had made his decision. Still, once Chase had set his own mind, he didn't know how to give up. "Organizational weaknesses provided an opportunity for sabotage. Those weaknesses will likely be in Stan's department. He lacks the independence he needs to lead the team."

"He hasn't been here long enough to have shaped the organization or its procedures," Snider said. "That makes him independent. He'll be responsible for any future changes, so I'll let him recommend those changes."

Brower acknowledged the commitment.

"Damn it, Jack. You can't take this away from me." Didn't he see that this was all Chase had left?

"It's not yours. It wasn't an accident. It's not even appropriate — "

"Fuck appropriate!"

The room fell silent. Michelle's eyes went wide and she glanced fearfully from Chase to Snider and back.

Snider's face became a stone carving of fury, immutable and silent. When he finally spoke, his voice carried the weight of his position. He clipped each word as though truncating a diatribe. "Sit. Down. Now." He waited for Chase to comply, then leaned over the table. "Brower's my security chief. He gets the case. Furthermore, I'm taking you off it. Given your language, I question whether your contributions under Brower's leadership will be constructive."

"You're firing me?"

Snider's declaration had come out of nowhere. Brower's appointment as team lead was unexpected, but if Chase was honest with himself, he'd admit that it made sense. The man had hired in as the security chief, so his experience must be more applicable to criminal matters than Chase's own. On the other hand, taking Chase off the case entirely made no sense at all.

"You've put in for retirement, and I suggest you take it. But that's up to you." Snider rubbed the back of his neck with one hand and then smoothed his hair. "Either way, this is your last meeting on the *Phoenix* case."

Brower stared out the window as if he had no interest in the dispute's outcome, apparently mesmerized by something he saw there. Chase glanced through the portal to see what had captured the man's attention. It was dark outside and he saw only the reflection of the indoor lights.

Chase opened his mouth again, but Snider silenced him in a cold tone of suppressed fury. "Enough. One more word and I'll have you escorted from the meeting. You hear me?"

Chase stood, shoved his chair into the wall, and stormed from the room. When he got home, he poured himself a cognac.

❧☾O☽☙

The meeting continued for another grueling hour, during which Brower stumbled through a variety of topics, groping for a path forward. When it finally broke up, Michelle went straight to Chase's apartment. "Give me one of those," she said when she saw the drink in his hand. She'd never seen him drink before and wasn't about to let him do it alone. "You need company."

Chase hiked his eyebrows in a suit-yourself manner and poured her a glass.

Michelle took a sip, winced at the pungent taste, and set the drink aside. She stared at him for a long time, trying to read in his expression the best way to reach him. "You know why he did it, don't you?"

He shrugged.

"It's not your performance or the case, your language, or anything else he brought up in the meeting."

Chase dragged out a chair and slumped into it. "Does it matter?"

"Yes, it does. You think you can hide what this is doing to you, but you can't."

"Okay." He waved his drink noncommittally. "Why?"

"Because you don't know when to quit. You never did. And every time somebody tries to make you, you take it personally."

Chase raised his drink like a toast, then downed it in one gulp.

"Don't you see?" She grabbed his wrist to keep him from getting up for a refill. "He did it for you."

"Ha!"

"He knows you won't go home otherwise. He's letting you retire."

"That's what he thinks." Chase stared at her hand on his wrist and said nothing more.

"Stan's a good guy," Michelle continued. "You don't have to stay just to make sure this thing gets done." Moisture gathered in her eyes. "*I'll* miss you, though."

Chase looked up.

"You've done a lot for me, and I'm not just talking about fostering my career." She smiled. "As pathetic as it sounds, you're the only real friend I have on base."

"I *have* been working you too hard."

"That's nothing a deck of cards and a bottle of brandy won't fix. What do you say? Double or nothing?"

He took her up on the cards—and lost again—but Michelle's drink was the last one he poured all afternoon. And that, she left half-full.

Despite Snider's instructions, Chase had no intention of leaving. Before Michelle went home, she gave him the name of her CIA contact, Tom O'Leary. Then Chase spent the evening playing telnet-tag within the agency before he finally got hold of the man.

"Yes, we got the data," O'Leary said with a remnant of his hometown brogue. A separate comm link hung from his ear, nearly hidden by his red hair and matching Abe Lincoln beard.

"Have you had a chance to look at it?"

"Of course."

"And?"

"There's nothing I can tell you."

Chase pursed his lips. O'Leary couldn't have heard already that Chase had been pulled from the case. "Even preliminary information — "

"Look. I'd like to help you, Mr. Morgan." O'Leary glanced at his watch. "I have a meeting. I'll contact you later."

Then the screen went blank.

Chase sat back and sipped his booze. As he pondered O'Leary's peculiar response, three things became clear. One, the investigation was, in fact, a CIA priority. Two, O'Leary knew something significant to the case. Three, he was keeping that information from the investigation team.

Chapter 8

At nine P.M. Eastern Time, the United States president, Victoria Powers, appeared on every monitor in the station. Because Universal Coordinated Time ran five hours ahead of the East Coast, Chase didn't see the announcement until the following morning's newsblips.

Wrinkles at the corners of the president's eyes and across her brow added dignity and wisdom to the square shape of her face. She hunched slightly over the podium with a backdrop of American flags. "My fellow Americans," she began, her tone somber. "As many of you know, United States Secretary of Energy, David Herrera, was killed when the Stellarfare *Phoenix* went down on its way to Montanari base. It has been brought to my attention that this event was not an accident. It was, in fact, a deliberate attack against the United States, an act of sabotage directed specifically at Secretary Herrera."

Chase's cup froze midway to his mouth, his attention rapt on the monitor.

"Evidence recovered from the spacecraft reveals that the technology used in the attack is one owned exclusively by the People's Republic of China. A second attack, made early yesterday morning, destroyed the remaining physical evidence in the case in an attempt to conceal China's involvement. Six American lives were lost in these two attacks.

"I have come before you this evening to issue a warning to China's president, Li Muyou, and to assure the American people that the United States will not tolerate this or any other form of attack against our military, government, or civilian personnel. The investigators continue their work to locate the individual or individuals who perpetrated these acts of war. Once they're identified, we will bring upon them every form of justice allowable for spies and terrorists under international law."

The statement hit Chase like a sucker-punch. He reeled with questions he couldn't begin to answer. How could a leak of this magnitude have happened? Was the evidence against China real? Apparently. Had Forsythe or the Secret Service initiated a separate investigation on Earth?

"For the past five decades," the president continued, "the international community has enjoyed the benefits of the space demilitarization provisions set forth in the Third Outer Space Treaty. Although we have no direct evidence at this time that the People's Republic of China has violated any specific requirements of the treaty, these attacks are clearly provocative and contrary to the spirit and intention of the treaty, and will not be allowed to continue. The United States will defend its interests, its property, and the lives and liberties of the American people."

The last statement arrested Chase's train of thought. The president's record on foreign affairs was that of a staunch supporter of democratic freedom, but she'd never before threatened military action. The statement spoke of the seriousness with which Washington took the attacks.

The address lasted no more than four minutes. Then the networks settled in for hours of debate and analysis over the wording of the speech. To Chase, at least, the message seemed clear.

He leaned back in his seat, turned the volume down, and considered what had prompted the announcement. Since the investigation had become a criminal inquiry, the investigators hadn't shared their findings with anyone beyond the team. Furthermore, the president had reported information that the team didn't have. And it was obvious where she'd gotten it — the Central Intelligence Agency, and specifically, Tom O'Leary.

Chase activated the comm and keyed O'Leary's connection. Of course nobody was there, it being four A.M. on the East Coast. Chase got an automated mailbox.

"O'Leary. This is Ed Morgan." He always used his real name when introducing himself in an official capacity to a relative stranger. "I saw the president's address this morning. It sounds like you owe me some data. And an explanation. Contact me." He added his connection code and severed the transmission.

He tried O'Leary again at eight Eastern Time. Still no answer. An hour later, O'Leary called him.

"O'Leary," Chase said, ready to read him the riot act.

The agent held up his hands and preempted Chase. "Before you say anything, let me explain." Chase gave him a cold stare but said nothing, which O'Leary took as leave to continue. "The metal alloy is used only by the Chinese government."

Chase had surmised that much from the president's message. He opened his mouth but O'Leary cut him off again. "A spy working for the agency reported the technology some time ago."

Chase leaned forward. "That was privileged information in a criminal investiga — "

"Are you suggesting that the President of the United States isn't privileged?"

Chase slammed his fist on the table. "Damn it! By letting this out, you've risked an international incident."

Unperturbed, O'Leary continued. "This was a calculated attack upon the United States of America. We don't keep things like this from the president."

"But there's no proof. We don't know who's responsible — "

"We don't know who did it," O'Leary said, "but that doesn't change who's responsible. It's a government technology."

Damn. O'Leary obviously thought his actions justified, and Chase held no sway over him. And the fact that Chase couldn't finish a sentence with this man only served to increase his frustration. "Okay." He pinched the bridge of his nose and forced himself to remain calm. "At least you can feed us information to help out on our end."

"Of course."

Chase looked up. He felt tired — impotent. "Are there any other applications of the technology?"

"None that I can discuss."

Chase punched the disconnect and stormed from the room. Every time he took a step forward, somebody kicked his feet out from under him. If it wasn't Snider, it was Forsythe. If it wasn't Forsythe, it was Brower. If it wasn't Brower, it was O'Leary. To say nothing of the enemy.

He couldn't go to Snider or Brower because Snider had shut him out of the case. Instead, he went to Michelle. The information was related to the materials analysis, so he'd let her report it to the team.

While he was there, the newsblips showed several excerpts from an announcement made by President Li to his own people. Li, a prune of a man with more years on him than he ought to have lived through, also directed his address at the US president. His voice shook violently, but he looked directly into the vid-scanner as he denied Powers' accusations and urged restraint in American threats against the People's Republic. He challenged Powers to disclose any evidence against China, and specifically, the nature of this unique and exclusive technology.

When he got home, Chase had time to consider Li's address. The network had shown only portions of it, but something about it struck him as peculiar. Something didn't make sense, but he couldn't put a finger on it. He sat at the terminal to download the complete broadcast and was distracted by an incoming transmission.

He keyed the link. "Sarah?" He hadn't seen his younger daughter in years. How old was she now? Twenty-five? No, twenty-six.

"Hi, Dad."

The sight of her, and the sound of her voice ... He gripped the edge of the table to steady his hands. She looked well, though troubled. "Sw — sweetie, how are you?"

Her features betrayed a moment of emotional softness so subtle that Chase might have imagined it. Then they hardened. "This isn't a social call. Have you spoken to Erin?"

"No." Chase's heart leapt into his throat. It was two A.M. in Liverpool, where Sarah lived. "What's happened?"

Bits of Erin's life flashed through Chase's mind like single-frame images plucked from a vid-file of her childhood: Erin, staggering toward him as she learned to walk, her arms splayed for balance, with a bottle of milk in one hand and a stuffed otter in the other; Erin, sitting in her sandbox in second grade with a red-headed girlfriend whose name Chase couldn't remember; Erin, playing tag a few years later on a slide with a boy she liked. The images stopped there, shortly after the point in her life when Chase had joined NASA.

Nothing mattered more than his little girls, regardless of how old they got, yet somehow life's urgent matters had lured Chase away. Somehow he thought there would always be time... *Oh, God, tell me it's not too late.*

Erin was the only family he had left.

"Steve's been in an accident," Sarah said.

Steve. Not Erin. Thank God it wasn't Erin. But his selfish relief lasted only an instant. "Is he okay?"

"He died this afternoon."

For a moment, Chase couldn't reply. His heart reeled in denial. Finally, he said, "I've got to call her."

"You've got to do a hell of a lot more than that. You've got to go to her."

"I know." His mind was numb. He was four-hundred thousand kilometers away and transports to Earth ran only about once a week.

"I'm booked on a flight to Seattle in the morning," Sarah said. "But she needs you too. When can you come home?"

Chase put his elbow on the table and pressed his forehead into his palm. "I don't know, sweetie."

When he looked up, Sarah's eyes were cold.

"She needs you. Call her." She severed the connection.

Chase clenched his fist. It was always like this with her. He hadn't meant that he wouldn't go, only that he didn't know when the next shuttle left for Earth.

He logged into the telnet to book his flight. His need to comfort Erin was so great, even that task proved too much for him, but he couldn't call her until it was done. Erin would ask when he was coming home. He needed to be able to give her an answer.

Finally the schedule came up. Five days, it said, plus two days' flight time. When he tried to make payment to secure his reservation, the word BOOKING... scrolled across the screen for longer than his patience could stand.

Screw it. He killed the connection and keyed Erin's code. His leg bounced in agitation as he waited for the system to establish the link. For a long time, there was no answer.

Finally, a woman who Chase didn't recognize appeared. "Hold on."

Chase waited. In the background he heard her say, "It's your father." The compassion in her voice nearly broke his heart. It confirmed the news that Sarah had given him.

When Erin came to the terminal, her eyes were swollen and red. Blotches discolored the dark skin of her face. She sniffed, and wiped her nose with a tissue in her hand.

"I just heard." Now that he had her on the comm, he didn't know what to say. "How did it happen?" It sounded like a reasonable question in his head, but as soon as he said it, he knew he shouldn't have.

New tears welled in Erin's eyes. "He was working on the speeder..." She shook her head and looked away.

"Oh, honey." Chase had lost people in his life, but never before had he experienced a death that had such a personal impact on someone about whom he cared so much yet knew so poorly. He wanted to reach through the terminal and hold her. What words would comfort her?

After a moment, Erin regained her voice. "The speeder exploded. If it had been in the garage, it probably would've taken the whole house with it."

"Is everybody else okay?" His own voice began to crack. "The girls?"

She sniffed and nodded.

"Thank God for that. I hope to be there for the services."

Just then Erin's doorbell rang. Distraught, she just walked away to answer it.

The other woman returned to the comm. "Sorry. She didn't mean to do that."

"It's okay. I'll talk to her later."

The woman smiled weakly. "She'd like that. She loves you, you know."

"Tell her I'll be home on the first shuttle."

"I will."

At some point, Penny had climbed into Chase's lap. As soon as the link went dead, she sat up and started licking his cheeks. Chase brushed them with his hand. He hadn't realized he'd been crying.

He sat in his chair, numb to everything around him, for a long time before he finished booking his flight. Perhaps he'd lost the *Phoenix* case for a reason — to prevent him from staying when his family needed him on Earth.

Nevertheless, he was stuck at Alpha for the next five days. He could spend the time fidgeting around his apartment, twisting his gut over his absence from Erin, or he could apply himself to something constructive.

Despite anything Snider might have to say about it, Chase still had five days in which to solve the case.

~(O)~

Chase arrived at the Stellarfare operations wing just as Brower was leaving. The security chief intercepted him in the hall. "Hey, I heard you decided to take your retirement after all."

Chase had told Snider yesterday, so he wasn't surprised that Brower knew. "I leave on Tuesday." His reason for going drained his enthusiasm for what he had to do before he left.

A look of consternation crossed Brower's face. He glanced back at the Stellarfare complex, then at Chase. "What are you doing here?"

Chase couldn't tell the chief that he was working on the *Phoenix* case. He'd see it as interference. Someone chasing leads independently could tip off suspects, taint evidence, leak information, and cause no end of problems. Reporters did that to Chase all the time. And he hated it.

When he hesitated, Brower continued. "Look, man, I don't know what you're up to, and frankly, I don't want to know. But let me give you a piece of advice." He glanced both ways down the hall. "I don't know what's up Snider's ass, but he's been irrational since this whole thing started. I'd hate to see what he'd do if he found you poking around where you shouldn't." He put a hand on Chase's shoulder. "If you're working on the *Phoenix*, don't."

Chase's brow creased.

"At a minimum, Snider'll have your badge. He could charge you for interfering with a criminal investigation. I'd let it go if I were you." With that, he bounded away.

Brower's last threat was extreme, but theoretically possible. And he was right about Snider's recent behavior. Still, Chase didn't think it would go that far.

Maybe he should leave it alone, but he knew he wouldn't do that. On the other hand, he couldn't afford to lose his badge. With it went his security codes, his only way to access certain kinds of information.

After a moment, he moved down the hall away from the Stellarfare complex. He had a better idea.

CHAPTER 9

When the end-of-shift tone came over the speaker, Horace Greenburg lifted the nine-meter blade of the immense bulldozer he drove at the Montanari strip mine and turned his rig toward the grid-seven transport stop, where he'd catch the overland shuttle back to the colony. He could see the lights of the refueling tankers already arriving.

Just before he passed refinery four, one of the fueling trucks broke away from the convoy and veered in his direction. That was odd. Usually the tankers stayed at the rendezvous, where they spent the night transferring their load to the mining rigs. He slowed to see what it would do.

The tanker flew toward the new reactor. With the sun down, Horace couldn't see its number until it moved through the light of his floods. When it did, he picked up the link. "T-nineteen, this is D-four. Do you need help? Over."

No response. After a pause, the comm came alive with a dozen others hailing the runaway vehicle.

The tanker picked up speed as it barreled into the open maw of the reactor's truck ramp. An explosion erupted inside, blowing rock, sand, and bits of building material high into the air. Instinctively, Horace wrapped his arms around his face-plate as shrapnel from the blast showered his 'dozer. He held his breath and waited to see if the windshield would shatter. Then the tumult subsided.

Shaken, he peered out the durapane and squinted through the swirling debris. Though construction was drawing to a close and the reactor was still offline, there might be workers inside. God, he hoped not.

He pulled closer and hit the structure with his floods. The damage seemed contained and the absence of flames made a secondary blast unlikely, so he drove his 'dozer up the ramp. The fuel truck had careened into the soil collection pit and the concrete sides of the hole had channeled the force of the blast. As a result, the damaged superstructure above teetered drunkenly. Suddenly, the hairs on the back of his neck rose as he saw one, no, two men trapped on a catwalk twenty-five meters off the ground, one of the men obviously injured.

He hurriedly turned the 'dozer and nosed it forward until he could reach a walkway below the workers. If the damaged structure would support him, he could climb up from there to help lower the injured man.

Once in place, he depressurized the compartment and climbed out. His heart sank when he saw the distance that he'd have to jump.

The men called to him through the comm, urging him to hurry. Suddenly, a support buckled and the whole catwalk began to give under their weight.

Horace took a deep breath and leapt the four-story drop, sailing gracelessly across the gap to the trusswork with centimeters to spare. The structure sagged beneath him and he crashed to the grid-metal floor of the walk. With few handholds and gloves too bulky to find purchase, he slid off the edge. At the last instant his hand found a loose railing, and his weight caused that, too, to bend. But he managed to retain his grip.

The railing swayed alarmingly and the rivets stretched beyond their tolerance. He dropped another three meters and prayed that the next set of anchors would hold. Heaving with all his might, he worked his way hand-over-hand to a more stable portion of the structure, then climbed the additional two floors to the trapped workers.

Both men were injured, one with a broken arm. The other had a piece of refinery shrapnel piercing the pressure suit into his leg. A stout ring clamp, designed to seal twenty-centimeter flexible pipe joints, squeezed the man's suit against his thigh.

Horace helped the worker with the broken arm to cross the trusswork to an access ladder. Then, hefting the other man across his shoulders, Horace followed the worker to the ground and then up a ladder to the 'dozer's cabin.

By then, four other men had emerged from farther inside the building.

One of the men was limping. Another had a patch of vacuum tape on the sleeve of his pressure suit. "Climb aboard," Horace shouted through the comm.

Then he peered into the pit one last time. Little was left of the tanker and even less of the driver. Horace shook his head at the senselessness and carried the injured man into the cabin.

Once it was pressurized, he removed the clamp to allow blood flow back into the lacerated leg. "Anyone else inside?"

The man gazed through him.

Horace shook him. "Is there anyone else?"

Dazed, the man looked around slowly. Then he shook his head. "No. No, just six of us... performing the final inspections."

Horace confirmed the count before backing his tractor out of the building. They were lucky. If this had happened after the plant had opened, there'd have been at least two hundred people inside.

⁂

Zhang Mingzu, China's ambassador to the United States, keyed the terminal for his contact in the State Department and made his way through the bureaucratic protocols to speak directly with Secretary of State Tony Mariano. Zhang peered at the screen through a cloud of nicotine. "I have information of which your government must be made aware. This is not something within my authority to disclose — "

"Then perhaps you — "

" — but my conscience ... I could not look my children in the eye if I did not say something."

Mariano's face turned grave. "What is it?"

"The attack on the Montanari mine." Zhang sucked on his cigarette, drawing courage from it. "I know who's responsible."

He crushed his cigarette in the tray before it could fall from his trembling fingers. "My people." He couldn't meet the American's eyes. "My government. Li Muyou. He wants to discredit your country, to prove to the international community that it has neither the strength nor the influence to stop the attacks."

Now he faced Mariano squarely. "It is impossible, I know. A fool's mission. He has not lived in America. He cannot understand what I know of the spirit and courage of your people."

"Why are you telling me this?"

The question wasn't as simple as it seemed. Mariano was trying to gauge the credibility of the information.

"During my years of service in your country, I have come to love and respect your people. Your way of life. It brings me sorrow to see my own leaders, whom I have supported in the past, commit political and economic suicide in an endeavor that must ultimately fail. I hope that by making you aware of this, you will take proper measures to discourage these attacks."

"Do you know where he plans to strike next?"

Zhang lowered his gaze to the table. "I'm sorry. I'm not privileged to such information. And I have said too much already. I must go. There are things I must do." He killed the link before Mariano could reply, then keyed the computer's voice input and dictated his resignation.

Obviously, after what he'd just done, he must resign, but not because he'd betrayed his country. In fact, he hadn't, though some would argue the point. No, he must resign to maintain the illusion of that betrayal and to disrupt communication between America and China. That would delay any diplomatic response that the Americans might make.

Besides, he no longer worked for the People's Republic. He worked now for the China Dominion.

~(O)~

President Powers flew back from a campaign drive at the Midwest conference of the National Education Association as soon as she heard of the Montanari bombing. She arrived in the Oval Office a full eight minutes before an emergency staff meeting on the subject.

While she waited, she stared down at the carpet, which depicted the Presidential Seal — an eagle with a fist of arrows grasped in one talon and an olive branch in the other. A change made during the Truman administration had turned the head of the eagle so that it faced in the direction of the olive branch, the direction of peace, rather than in the direction of the arrows of war. It seemed ironic that she'd notice the seal now and remember the story. Perhaps it was a warning to practice caution and restraint in this time of crisis.

The United States must clearly respond to the latest attack, but how?

Just then her chief of staff, Warren Parker, walked in. Bald and clean-shaven, with broad shoulders and immense girth, he was a steadfast anchor in the vortex of executive activity. "What do you think?"

"I'm worried." The president drummed her fingers on a walnut cane that she held more as a status symbol or object of succor than as a walking aid. "China seems hell-bent on war. If this continues, we won't have much of a choice."

"We already don't have a choice." Secretary of Defense Dan Norton, whose features remained those of a man in his prime through the artifice of hair dye and dermal regeneration, marched into the office with Tony Mariano and half a dozen military experts and analysts. "We've got to strike back."

Norton appeared to have more to say, but the president raised her hand to intercede. "Save it for the meeting. You'll just have to repeat yourself when everyone arrives."

Norton looked around as though he believed no one else would be necessary. "Who are we waiting on?"

"Tom O'Leary, Anne Portman, Rick Newhart, and a few others. Let's move to the Situation Room." She lifted her cane and led the procession into the hall.

Once everyone had arrived, the president banged her cane on the hardwood floor and called the meeting to order. "I trust that you're all aware of yesterday's attack at the Montanari mine?" She took the assorted nods and grumbling to be responses in the affirmative. "Just to make sure we have a common understanding of the events to date, I've asked Secretary Mariano to prepare a short presentation. Tony."

Mariano motioned to one of his aides, a man of maybe twenty-five years. The aide slipped a data card into a slot in the table and keyed the first image. A hologram of Lunar Alpha Base appeared over the emitter in the center of the table. "Ladies and gentlemen." The speaker shifted his weight from one foot to the other. "The People's Republic of China has made a series of deliberate and successful attacks on several United States interests located on the Moon. First, the Stellarfare freighter *Phoenix* and the US energy secretary. Second, NASA's Lunar Alpha Base and the federal agent investigating the first attack. And yesterday, the Fusion Resource Corporation and the new helium plant at the Montanari mine."

He spent the next ten minutes cycling through a series of holograms related to each attack. The images of the first two events, he said, had been provided by Stan Brower at Mariano's request. Those of the third attack appeared to be converted screen captures from the afternoon newsblips. "Shortly after the latest attack, Secretary Mariano received an encrypted comm from Ambassador Zhang, who reported that China was responsible for the attacks." The young analyst played a vid-file of the telnet transmission on one of several two-D displays that lined the east wall.

"Madam President." Mariano signaled the aide to take a seat. "We could take Zhang's report at face value, but I think we'd be wise to consider other possibilities. The first strike was against an individual, a high-ranking, US government official. China had nothing to gain from the death of Secretary Herrera. His policies and programs were in no way detrimental to China or its bid for energy resources, either on Earth or in space. He was selected as a target of opportunity, a strike against the US government, and specifically the executive branch of that government."

The president sat up in her seat. Mariano had just labeled her a potential target if China thought they could get to her. She felt a momentary stab of guilt that Herrera might have died in her stead. But the feeling yielded quickly to anger, anger that she couldn't afford. Fingers drumming on the cane across her lap, she returned her attention to the speaker.

"Second, the hangar fire." Mariano's mustache wagged on his upper lip as though he chewed his words before he spat them out. "This may have been to destroy the evidence of the first attack."

Anne Portman, Powers' political advisor, leaned forward. "Madam President. That hangar, because of the activities taking place there, was a high-profile target. It was already in the news and could induce an emotional response of outrage on the part of the American people, a response that would have them demanding action from you."

"An action Li hopes I'll be unwilling to take," the president said.

"Damn straight," Norton mumbled from across the table.

"Dan?"

Norton cleared his throat. "Li Muyou did the same thing to the United Nations over his sterilization crusade."

"That's right," President Powers acknowledged. When tax incentives had failed to stem the rising population in China, the economic and environmental pressures of overpopulation drove Li into a policy of forced sterilization. He began using his military to abduct women with one or more children. Millions were permanently sterilized against their will by chemical injection. It was the worst human-rights disaster since the Holocaust.

The result was an uprising of the Chinese people known as the Fertility Riots, which Li's army suppressed through violence and bloodshed. Thousands of civilians died.

The UN tried to impose economic sanctions or threat of military force to stop the mass sterilization, but that required the approval of the Security Council. And China used its veto authority as a permanent member of the council to block the resolution.

Nevertheless, something had to be done. So the United States, backed by the European Union, introduced a resolution in the General Assembly to revoke China's permanent membership in the Security Council, thereby rescinding its veto power. The measure was controversial because neither the US nor the EU offered to give up their own permanent membership. An opposition group, led by the Middle East block, even tried to use the fertility crisis as leverage to remove all permanent-member and veto privileges from the Security Council charter.

In the end, the United States and its allies mustered enough support for the US resolution to pass. Then, the night before the vote, three of its supporters were assassinated. The resolution failed — the General Assembly deadlocked, the Security Council remained cuffed by China's veto, and the mass sterilizations continued. The worlds' perception of UN authority and efficacy plummeted.

Over the next several years, forty-two countries withdrew their membership. They and many others formed alternative venues, such as the African Hegemony, with less bureaucratic inertia to resolve matters of pressing interest to their countries, leaving the United Nations all but impotent.

"On the surface," the president said, "this is different from the fertility crisis, but it fits a pattern. Li's provoking a greater political power in a way that prohibits reprisal. He also opposed giving the International Space Consortium, which would have formed a single, international government for space, legislative authority over extraterrestrial affairs."

"So did we," Mariano replied.

"My point is," the president continued, "that China has systematically attacked any political power greater than itself. We're the only one left. " She surveyed the room to gauge the attitudes of the others. No one disputed her conclusions.

Powers had had presidential ambitions at the time the UN broke down, so she'd studied the political fallout. The United States had threatened unilateral military action against China to stop the sterilization and was joined by Europe and Russia. Under such pressure, Li Muyou returned to economic incentives for single-child families to keep the population in check.

Later, Li Muyou's minister of state security, Chang Lei, released a vid-file taking full responsibility for the UN assassinations, which he claimed to have done without Li's knowledge or consent. Then he disappeared. It was enough to save President Li the personal repercussions of that particular crime. Of course, nobody believed in Li Muyou's innocence, but with the end of the sterilization campaign and Fertility Riots, there wasn't enough international support to oust him from power.

"So what are you going to do?" Anne Portman asked the president. "We've got to stop the attacks. According to the polls, most Americans believe that some response is appropriate, but if we respond, we'll give China the moral high ground."

"They've already drawn first blood," Norton said. "That gives the moral high ground to us."

"Not necessarily," Anne replied. "They've denied the first attack. The others were done in such a way that they could credibly deny those as well. What we're talking about here is a direct attack by the United States military."

"Maybe we could make a covert strike, as they've done," O'Leary offered.

"At what target?" Mariano asked.

"If all of this is coming from President Li, maybe we could try to take him out."

"Too risky," Norton said.

"Probably. But it's an option."

"What we need," President Powers said to the assembly as a whole, "is a measured response. Let's ratchet up our level of defense, particularly at our lunar bases. I want an obvious show of force and a meaningful threat of immediate and devastating retaliation if China strikes again.

"We'll precede the move by a public warning. If the whole world knows beforehand that we'll strike back without additional provocation, we'll pull the rug out from under their precious moral high ground."

"If we can convince China that we're in a position of superior military strength, the warning may be sufficient," Norton suggested. "That's what stopped the sterilization campaign."

"What do you recommend, Dan?"

"Chinese military troops outnumber ours five to one. Hell, their population outnumbers ours ten to one, if it comes down to a draft. But we have superior tactics and superior equipment and technology. Put the active military on full alert and call up the reserves. The early warning and anti-missile defense systems will make any long-range attack of little strategic value. If they want to attack us, they'll have to come here to do it. We still have the finest navy in the world. Display it. And finally, launch the stealth space fleet. Station it at Lunar Alpha as a defensive measure to protect our interests there."

"How many CATS have we got?" The President knew it'd be a small number. Funding for the Covert Armed Tactical Spacecraft program had been a hot budget-debate topic three years before and had continued to come up during the past two. As a space technology, the CATS represented thirty years of development for a weapon system with no practical application. But military contingency-planning demanded that the country be ready to confront any conceivable threat, including those in space, in the event of a foreign treaty violation.

"Four ready to fly."

The president stifled an impulse to cringe. There should have been more, but she knew as well as anyone that they weren't talking about fighter jets. The CATS symbolized a marriage of the worlds' most advanced military technology with the worlds' most advanced space-flight technology. And in a budgetary context, the word *advanced* meant *expensive*.

But development and proof-of-concept had been completed, along with the first two ships, before Powers had taken office. From a military-contingency standpoint, demonstration of capability was the most important phase. Then it became a question of quantity.

"We have two more in production," Norton was saying. "They're supposed to be completed in six months, but we can probably pull that in to two."

The president was only half-listening. It'd been her decision that had largely killed the program. Republicans argued for funding to create a stockpile of CATS warships — anywhere from a few dozen to several hundred units, depending on what version of the appropriations bill you looked at. But Democrats, backed by President Powers, calculated a cost of several hundred billion dollars in manufacturing capability and covert transportation as well as storage and maintenance facilities — much too high for a system labeled, "not likely to find use in the near future."

"Eventually, somebody'll break the treaty and we'll need the CATS," the house minority leader told her during a private meeting one day.

"Eventually new technologies will emerge and the CATS will be obsolete," the president had replied sarcastically and somewhat naively.

In the end, she'd signed a budget that included a manufacturing schedule of two per year, just enough to maintain the technical knowledge and facilities. Manufacturing was behind schedule, it seemed.

"Madam President," Parker said, bringing her back to the meeting, "if we launch the CATS, that'll constitute a violation of the conventional-weapons clause of the Third Outer Space Treaty. We'll open the door for a proliferation of Earth's military into the heavens. China will do the same."

"Followed by Russia and the EU," Mariano added.

"If we, or anybody else, violate that treaty," Parker finished, "it could tear all of the colonized worlds asunder."

"I don't think China's left us a choice in the matter," Mariano said.

The president nodded. "I agree with Tony. Dan, put all branches of the military on standby. Have everyone ready to move, but don't deploy the forces yet. There's been no overt move by the Chinese military here on Earth, and I don't want to be the first to take that step. But our forces must be prepared to respond when the time comes. Launch the CATS. Deploy them to Lunar Alpha. Expedite the completion of the two in production." She stared at each person around the table.

"Anne and Tony, you two prepare a statement. I'll need to address the worlds as soon as the CATS launch. Any questions?"

"I'll contact Russia and the EU to see where they stand on matters," Mariano offered. "If this thing escalates, we'll need to know who our friends are."

"Let's hope it doesn't come to that. But by all means, make the contacts.

Is there anything else?" No one spoke as the president's gaze swept the assembly. "Thank you all for coming."

She waited until she was alone before climbing to her feet. The hologram of the bombed-out reactor still hovered over the table. *Not this time,* she vowed silently to herself and to the Chinese president. *Not the United States.*

Chapter 10

Major Bill Ryan tossed his duffel bag into the back seat of his cherry Calypso convertible and checked his watch. Damn. He pulled his tall, well-honed body into the driver's seat and turned the key even before he was fully settled behind the wheel. Tires chirped on the pavement as he pulled away from the curb.

He could have punched in Dana McCaughey's address and engaged the autodrive, but it would abide by the speed limit and other traffic laws. Bill needed to make up time. So he sped through the operation sector of MacDill Air Base, past the array of F87 Raptors in the air field, and toward the housing annex. Overhead, a CATS trainer, identical to the real thing except for the lack of stealth cladding and armaments, glided in for a landing.

As he drove, he imagined Dana standing in the window watching the street, eagerly awaiting his arrival. You'd think that sixteen years in the air force would've taught him punctuality.

He arrived at Dana's just after noon, a strategically selected time that would make lunch their first stop. Her window was vacant. She probably didn't realize he was late, probably didn't care. That squeezed his heart a little. But in truth, he should be grateful that she'd agreed to go with him at all.

Dana had captured his attention the moment he first saw her in a crowd of hopefuls sweating through the CATS tryouts six years before, but he wasn't allowed near her until she'd been accepted into the program. By then, he'd idolized her distant beauty to such an extent that his normal confidence had crumbled into a fumbling series of crude passes that he hoped were more charming than oafish.

But despite some apparent interest, she'd repeatedly refused. Now, his heart ached whenever he was with her and sobbed when he wasn't.

He ought to give up. But he couldn't, even if it meant condemning himself to a life of meaningless flings among the many groupies his uniform attracted, a life of shallow sexual satisfaction in his times of frustration, or even a life alone. He was addicted, addicted to hope.

He checked his appearance in the rearview mirror, found a single gray hair hiding among his dark brown bangs, and plucked it out. It was the third one this month. Sooner or later he'd have to decide between gray hair and baldness. But not today; he was only thirty-seven, for Christ's sake. He combed his fingers through his hair, twisted the mirror back into place, and climbed out.

Dana opened the door just before Bill reached the buzzer.

His heart stopped, as it always did, when he saw her, with her dark brows and eyes the color of the clear sky — not the sky you could see from the ground, but the sky you could see from above the industrial haze that engulfed the globe. Her face was framed to the shoulder by a mane of straight blond hair and she had a blue comm link jacked into her ear. Though the links were military issue, she had them in several colors and wore them like jewelry.

He spread his arms and enveloped her hard, athletic body. For a moment, time froze as he savored her closeness. He bent his head next to hers and inhaled her scent. A soft moan escaped his lips.

She released him quickly and stepped back. "We'd better go."

When they got to the car, he opened the door for Dana before getting in on the driver's side. "Had lunch?"

"No, not yet."

"Stuffy's?"

"Sounds good."

They arrived with the lunch crowd and made their way to the order line. Bill bought a hamburger — he never ate anything else at Stuffy's — and offered to buy Dana lunch "... for helping me out today," he said.

He took their number card to a table against the wall and slid it into the slot to tell the system where they were seated.

The food was delivered by a robotic waiter, little more than a motorized cart with pattern recognition and proximity sensors to navigate the ever-changing map of guests moving about the dining room. They sat in silence while Bill dressed his burger. Then he met her gaze.

Dana held his for a time before her mouth twisted into that sweet, quirky smile she got whenever she was self-conscious. She speared a slice of cucumber from her salad. "So, Major, what are your plans for me?"

"It's Lisa's birthday next week. I want to buy her an outfit. But I don't trust my taste in women's clothes."

She pointed her fork at him and spoke around her second mouthful. "I've seen your taste in women's clothes."

"Not appropriate for a little sister?"

Dana burst into laughter. "Not unless she's a hooker."

Bill's face flushed as it always did when she teased, and he hoped it didn't show. He gestured with a French fry. "Hence your input."

"Oh, it's not so bad." She tried without success to stifle a giggle. "I've worn stuff like that myself every now and again. I've even worn it for you."

His brows shot up.

"In some of my sleazier moments," she added.

He'd had enough. "How're your folks?" Anything to change the subject.

Dana's mood sobered instantly. "I don't want to get depressed. Let's talk about something else."

He stared at her mouth. Her eyes, if he met them, would distract him from the conversation and remind her of his ardent feelings. But even her mouth was dangerous. Her lips, sensual in their nakedness, showed every expression as clearly as her eyes.

The two had fallen into a platonic relationship. Yet even while he longed for more, his determined proximity had fostered a closeness he'd never experienced with any other woman. He smiled, but his throat constricted with sadness. At least she let him share some part of her life.

The conversation migrated to the latest rumors around the base and stayed there for the remainder of the meal, after which they climbed into the car and headed for the mall.

The outing consumed most of the afternoon, and they spent more time than necessary sifting through rack after rack of clothing, searching for the perfect outfit. For this he relied entirely on her judgment. But she enjoyed the shopping and wouldn't commit to a selection until they'd covered the six-story mall from top to bottom. Craving her company, he let her take her time.

The two were standing in the warren of the women's clothing department at Macy's when a succinct transmission came over both their links. Dana ran back to the dressing room to change out of the outfit she'd just modeled, one more revealing and suggestive than he'd even consider buying for his sister, though he wouldn't disapprove of it as long as someone else bought it for her. He chuckled. As if Lisa had ever sought his approval for anything.

"It figures," he said when Dana returned, alluding to the comm they'd both received.

"That's all right, we have an hour to report." She placed a hand on his arm, just above the elbow, and squeezed gently. Her hand felt warm against his bare skin and caused a tightening in his groin. "Come on." She led him away. "I'll show you which one you should buy."

⁂

They got back to the base with no time to spare, so Bill left the car parked illegally by the command building and they ran inside. He'd rather have his car towed and pay the fine than to be late for a drill. They rounded the corner into the classroom-style briefing area. All eight crews were there, except the three members who'd been granted leave.

"Nice of you to join us." The commander, usually tolerant of Bill's antics as long as he didn't cross the line into tardiness, showed no sign of forbearance today. With his strained features camouflaged behind glasses that gave him an academic look, he spoke with a voice that commanded attention. "All right, people, take a seat and listen up."

Bill found a chair and planted himself. A dead silence descended as they all waited for the commander to speak.

The commander stood behind a podium decorated with the air force seal, flanked on either side by twin American flags. "This is not a drill, people. I repeat, this is no drill." He held up a sheaf of hardcopy. "This is an executive order, a deployment of all operational Covert Armed Tactical Spacecraft. You'll be armed with live munitions. The countdown is now at — " he looked at his watch — "five hours and forty-three minutes."

Bill's heart resounded so loudly in his own ears that he barely heard the rest of the commander's speech. Launching the CATS? They were so top-secret that they'd never been out of their underground bunker before. With live ammunition? Did he hear that right? It was a violation of international law. An act of war.

Dana stared at the commander, her mouth open and jaw slack. Some of the others looked around uncertainly. Most just listened.

Bill returned his attention to the front of the room. "... Lunar Alpha Base. You will attain a readiness posture and await further orders. I repeat, you will remain on alert status at all times. A complete briefing will be available on board.

"This is a covert mission, people. Do not discuss it with anyone outside this room. While on board, you will use only secure, short-range communications.

"The following teams will be deployed: Ryan in the *Puma,* Gabaldon in the *Cougar*, Etre in the *Jaguar,* and McCaughey in the *Snow Leopard*. All other crews will remain on standby."

He paused and swept the assembly with his harsh glare. "I suggest you hurry. You have five hours and — " he glanced at his watch again — "thirty-two minutes until launch.

"Dismissed."

There was a loud shuffling as twenty-one crewmen rose and filed out of the briefing room to congregate in the hall. Bill looked for Ted Branson, the mission specialist of one of the standby teams. "Ted, let me see your thinpad a second."

"Sure." He pulled the device from a pocket of his flight suit.

Bill typed a few short lines and handed it back. "This is my sister's address. I just bought her a gift for her birthday next week. It's in the back seat of my car. Can you see that she gets it by the twenty-ninth?"

"Sure, man." Ted placed a hand on Bill's shoulder. "Wish I was going with you."

"Your turn'll come. Don't you worry."

"It's the real thing, man. And you're the wing leader. You'll be the first person to ever fly a real CATS."

Bill smiled now, the biggest, dumbest, most genuinely happy grin ever to cross his face. "I'm going up," he said finally, his head bobbing as if attached to a spring. He'd gone up many times, of course. Space flight was no big deal anymore, even to many civilians. But this was the real thing, the machine that he'd been trained to fly. "I sure hope the things actually work."

They both laughed.

Then Ted's expression sobered. "You think we're going to war?"

Bill's smile faded. "I don't know. I hope not." His crew waited in the clearing corridor. "I've got to go." He joined his men and led them away.

⁂

At T–minus-two hours, Bill strode into the CATS' underground hangar with his pilot, Cory Abrams, and mission specialist Duane Townsend. The latter's title had been adapted from NASA terminology because "weapons specialist" was both politically unpalatable and too telling.

Four warships stood majestically before him, towering twenty meters from tail to nose. Each clung to a solid-fuel booster that would assist in the escape from Earth's gravity. He nodded his appreciation for their design. Huge wings, meant to support the craft in thin atmosphere, would allow the CATS to land on any inhabited world in the solar system. The sharp, awkward angles helped to achieve a low radar cross-section. But as Bill understood it, it'd taken decades to develop a composite that combined the desired stealth-radar properties with adequate heat shielding for atmospheric reentry. The matte black exterior would make the craft difficult to spot optically against the star-filled darkness of space.

He moved down one of the rows of ships, arranged two wide and two deep, giving a wide berth to the men loading missiles into the munitions compartments, and located the one with the name PUMA stenciled in white block letters. The silhouette of a jungle cat and the fifty–four-star American flag completed the logo. That was his baby.

He stepped onto the hydraulic lift to the cockpit with his pilot and mission specialist.

With the preflight startup sequence completed, the bird was ready to fly. But, through superstition or extreme care, protocol required the crew to double-check several critical systems. They, of course, had the most at stake if something went wrong. Bill, for one, liked the policy. He had more faith in the abilities of his crew than he did in anyone else.

At T–minus-thirty minutes, yellow lights flashed in the hangar. The ground crews counted their tools to make sure they had left nothing in the maintenance compartments of the ships and secured their equipment carts and rolled them from the bay. Missile lifts were removed. Fueling hoses, water, air, data, and power umbilicals were rolled into their repositories. The inspection crews performed their final checklists and secured the access panels. Bill did the same for the cockpit door.

The hangar was clear.

Minutes later, a tremendous pop reverberated through the cavernous hangar from the huge doors in front of the cockpit window. The squeal of the unused rollers filtered into the cabin like a scream of protest against this change in military posture and set Bill's teeth on edge. Then he initiated the automated launch sequence.

"Take care of me, baby," he said aloud, just before the rockets fired, "and I'll take care of you."

Four fireballs lit the sky as the CATS fleet launched into space for the first time in American history.

The launch, momentous as it was, wouldn't likely attract undue attention from the enemy. Training launches from the base were as routine as NASA shuttles from nearby Cape Canaveral. And if the CATS were tracked, the radar would note only the solid boosters as they returned to Earth. With the ships running stealth, anything else they did would be lost in the noise of the commercial traffic that supported the orbiting ports and stations.

Early the next morning, the CATS were followed by two fully-loaded Soaring 1067 military troop transports.

◦(O)◦

Chase made the last few entries and fired his report off to the director. He'd titled it, "Final Report." By content, it was a summation of his independent work over the past week on the *Phoenix* case. But to Chase, it represented the culmination of his life's work. A meager contribution, by his own assessment, but there was no mistaking the finality of it. So, in a bow to his own melancholy mood, he left any reference to the *Phoenix* out of the title, giving it a more suitable timbre.

After he'd run into Brower outside Stellarfare, Chase had realized that he couldn't solve the *Phoenix* case single-handedly in the time he had left. Any attempt to delve into the heart of the evidence would have been met with resistance and perhaps termination by Snider. Instead, he decided to work the case periphery.

He spoke with Michelle daily to learn what angle the team was pursuing and the nature of Brower's plans. This allowed Chase to contribute to the team's information without duplicating its efforts. But because of the ethics issues involved he was careful to omit any reference to Michelle in his report. And the facts were generic enough to avoid raising any eyebrows, at least to the extent that retribution or reprimand was likely, even if her involvement was discovered. The resulting report allowed Chase to inform the team of his findings after it was too late to take his badge.

He stood and took a final look around the place. All of his belongings were boxed and labeled with Erin's Seattle address, ready to follow him in a day or two.

Beyond the durapane, a crescent Earth topped the horizon. It was funny; he'd spent most of the last two decades in space and he still thought of Earth as home. And despite the ugly turn that the case had taken and the grim circumstances of his return, Chase felt oddly at peace.

He transferred the money he owed Michelle from their card games, turned his badge in to Snider's secretary, and made his rounds to say goodbye. When he got back, he lifted Penny off her blanket and eased her into a rented travel carrier, which wasn't much larger than his carry-on bag. She went in easily enough, but as soon as he closed the door, she began to whimper.

He stuck his fingers through the bars and let her lick them. "I know, girl. I know. It's only for a little while, and I'll be with you all the way." After a few minutes of her crying, Chase grabbed her blanket. He opened the door to put it in with her, but the blanket was too big.

When he tried to pull it out, Penny grabbed it with her teeth and started a tug-of-war. Chase laughed and Penny growled playfully, shaking her end of the blanket from side to side. He indulged himself in the moment before reaching in to grasp Penny's jaw. "Okay, girl, we don't want to tear it."

Reluctantly Penny let go. She whined again when Chase closed the door.

"It's okay. I'll be right back." It took him twenty minutes to locate and unpack one of his kitchen knives. Then he left the room, cut the edge of Penny's blanket, and ripped off a quarter of its length, though not enough for her to miss, he hoped, when he gave her the larger piece later. After replacing the knife and packing most of the blanket, he put the small piece into the carrier with Penny.

She quieted instantly, tugged the purple scrap to the back of the carrier, and lay down.

Chase closed the door and stuck his fingers through again. "Who loves you, girl?"

Penny licked them twice and set her head on her paws, apparently content.

∽(O)∼

All Chase had with him when he got to the Trans Worlds Aerospace dock was Penny, his carry-on bag, and a ticket for Shuttle 7991 to Earth, leaving at 2:18 P.M. When he arrived, he stepped into the pipe for a security scan. A moving floor controlled his speed as soft X-rays probed his body, Penny's carrier, and the bag. Sniffers and scanners examined him for explosives, drugs, weapons, and biotoxins. Infectious diseases could be serious in the enclosed environments of space, so every effort was made to prevent their spread from base to base.

At the end of the pipe, two guards armed with Lancaster pistols patted him down and inspected the bag and carrier for other illegal contraband, anything that the pipe might have missed. Only then was he allowed to enter the dock.

An information kiosk displayed a hologram showing the position and trajectory of each incoming shuttle along with its designation and estimated time of arrival. A two-D display nearby listed TWA 7991 as in dock and on time. Chase had arrived an hour and a half early, so he settled into a booth at the café to watch the news and enjoy a leisurely lunch. He couldn't let Penny out of her carrier in the restaurant, so he fed her bits of his cutlet through the bars.

At 1:30, President Powers interrupted the newsblips to address the nation and the worlds. Her message, brief and clear, denounced the attack on the Montanari mine, described it as provocative, and called it an act of war. She announced the launch of an undisclosed number of US military spacecraft to a tactical deployment on the Moon, "in order to protect American interests and citizens against Chinese aggression. No more attacks will be tolerated," she said, adding that they would "result in a swift and decisive response against Chinese military, political, and economic targets on Earth and abroad." She left no margin for misunderstanding.

Immediately after the announcement, Peter Hunt, the president of the European Union, pledged his support to the United States should a military conflict arise.

Chase sat in his booth while the media analyzed the latest developments, but he was no longer listening. He was doing an analysis of his own.

Recent events had initiated a chain of dangerous political overreactions. How could a single attack, even on a US dignitary, escalate so alarmingly? He thought back to the Chinese president's message several days before. Something about it had bothered him then. Even now, he didn't think circumstances were quite as they appeared.

Some of the evidence pointed to China, that was true, but it was all circumstantial. China had developed the alloy, but somebody else could have found out about it, as the CIA had. Somebody could have copied it.

Did President Powers have evidence that Chase wasn't privy to? Even if she did, why had President Li challenged her to publicly reveal a secret Chinese state technology?

Was Chase naive or blind? Or was he the only one seeing things clearly? The longer he thought about it, the less it made sense that China was guilty. And Powers' pronouncement of Chinese involvement was the sole basis of Brower's investigative strategy.

The worlds were headed for war, it seemed. And if Chase was right, proving China's innocence was the only way to stop it. Perhaps he should stay at Alpha. He might learn something important and somehow mitigate the crisis, or he might convince Brower to broaden his efforts — but only if Snider permitted it.

So far, all Chase had was a hunch.

And what of Erin and Sarah? Although he'd missed the funeral, the tragedy of Steve's death would bring the family together, at least physically, like no other event could. And unfortunate though it was, Chase hoped that some good might come of it. By being there with Sarah in her sister's time of need, both working to ease Erin's pain, he might make the first steps toward reconciliation.

Of course, he'd spoken with Erin several times since Steve's death, but there was no substitute for physical presence to show love and support. And if Chase stayed at Alpha, Sarah would use the opportunity to poison Erin's attitude against him.

He couldn't afford that.

He tried to tell himself that political events would subside as Brower discovered more about the perpetrators. But what could Brower learn without changing his underlying assumptions? No wonder his team was floundering.

Chase had to do something.

He took a difficult breath, like he'd taken just before saying, "I do" — the best decision he'd ever made — and before signing his deep-space papers, an act that had ultimately cost him everything. Then, ten minutes before his scheduled departure, he threw his bag over his shoulder, grabbed Penny, and walked away from TWA shuttle 7991.

Chapter 11

Chase didn't go home. He went instead to the War Room — the name Brower had given to the *Phoenix* team's conference room. As he approached, Chase heard the muted sounds of a meeting in session. Unsure of what he'd say, he pushed open the door and barged in.

He came up short in the doorway. Before him sat Brower, Snider, Michelle, and two security guards. No one else. After a moment of speechlessness, "This is it?" was all he could manage.

Snider rose as if to challenge Chase or perhaps head off any scene he might make. Brower's expression hardened and his eyes narrowed in an adversarial manner. On the other hand, Michelle beamed, a single bright spot amid the grim company.

Chase set Penny down, dropped his bag by the door, and stepped inside. "Where is everybody?"

"What do you mean?" Brower sat in his customary seat across from the window.

Chase moved toward the head of the table, where he'd command more authority. "The techs? The analysts? The Soaring engineers? The admins?"

"I sent the Soaring people home," Brower said. "It didn't make sense for them to stick around once the wreck was gone. Same thing with the techs and analysts. We're fresh out of physical evidence and they finished the data analysis a week ago. So I've replaced them with two of my best men.

"This is Mike Penick." Brower indicated a young man with dark hair, freckles, a round face, and a thick neck. "And Frank Lesperance." The other boy, with the arms and chest of a bodybuilder, drummed his fingers on the table as though nervous or impatient. "They can chase down the suspects faster than those forensics geeks."

Chase frowned. Brower probably knew that Chase was there to challenge his command and Chase understood his defensiveness. But that wasn't license to be disrespectful.

Brower continued. "We still have all the administrative support we can use, but I didn't see the need for them to attend every meeting."

"What are you doing here?" Snider asked when Chase came up beside him. "I thought you'd be gone already."

"I'm not going."

An annoyed look crossed the director's face.

"Did you see the president's address this afternoon?" Chase asked.

Now Snider's brow creased in concern. "When did she make an address?"

"Just a few minutes ago, followed by one from the president of Europe." Chase quickly summarized the content of the two presidential statements. "I suspect China will make a formal response within the next twenty-four hours."

"Military spacecraft? Armed?" Snider said.

"That's what she said."

"Headed here?"

Chase nodded. "To the Moon somewhere. I imagine that means here."

"My God."

Chase remained quiet for several moments to let him absorb the news.

"In over a hundred years, there's never been a weapon in space." Snider spoke more to himself than to the others. Then he looked back at Chase. "Why'd you decide to stay? This doesn't have anything to do with you."

"Because it doesn't make sense. Think about it. The Chinese attack a freighter with a minor government official on board. A hangar fire destroys a ship that was already scrap, whose only relevance was to the investigation. And now, a bombing at the Montanari mine that causes no fatalities other than the bomber himself. These are small targets with no military importance, a long way from Earth. Another thing: Li challenged Powers to reveal the technology she cited as evidence against China. Why would Li prompt anyone to publicly reveal his own government's secrets? It just doesn't make sense."

Brower came to his feet. "I'm sure they see your point. But frankly, your opinion of military policy, though interesting, is irrelevant." His tone was edged with mock patience and sarcasm. "And you're disrupting my meeting."

"Hold on. He's got a point." Political developments had pulled the media's attention away from the local investigation and Snider had recovered his old confidence. "These are terrorist attacks. I've never heard anything about China sponsoring terrorism."

"Neither have I," Chase agreed. "There's got to be another answer, Jack. And I'm going to find out what it is."

Snider paused. "I've already given the case to Brower."

"Then give it back to me."

"Now wait a minute — " Brower began.

But Chase wheeled on him. "What have you learned in the past week?" From his conversations with Michelle, Chase knew the answer. "Nothing." And he knew why.

"That's crap." Brower reached for a thinpad as if collecting evidence.

"Okay, crap then." Vehemence filled Chase as a week of suppressed frustration poured out. He closed the space between himself and the security chief. "You're chasing a mirage. You've formulated a list of suspects based solely on race, hoping that one of them will lead you to evidence. And we've just established that the perp might not be Chinese."

Brower clamped his hands on his hips and matched Chase's glare. "The ship's gone, along with the evidence. How else am I supposed to generate leads?"

"You don't. You follow the ones we've already got. Let the evidence point you to a suspect. Not vice versa."

"All we have are the access lists and maintenance records." Brower handed Chase a thinpad from a stack on the table. "I checked out Stellarfare a few days ago. There's nothing there."

"There must be. Look harder. Dig deeper." Chase turned back to Snider. "I'm convinced the fire was set to destroy evidence, but the motive for the bombing is unclear. Montanari was the *Phoenix*'s destination." Because he knew Snider hadn't yet read his final report, Chase braced himself before adding, "So I've been looking into their operation."

Snider was silent — pensive and observant. Good. Chase had begun to weaken the legs upon which Brower's credibility stood. He couldn't have done it a week ago. He had to give Brower a chance to fail.

In truth, it pained him to do this. He respected Brower, but the investigation was stalled and there was more at stake than the others realized. Perhaps, if Brower had made better progress ...

Nevertheless, Chase's conviction remained strong. He was only doing what he must.

"The mine is owned by Fusion Resource Corporation." When he spoke, he spoke to the assembly, but it was Snider he must convince. "It's a strip-mining operation, the largest in the worlds, larger even than the ice mines of Europa. They tear up vast stretches of lunar topsoil and crust, dump it into a processor, and extract the helium." Because he'd tied the bombing into the *Phoenix*, he'd bought himself a small measure of patience. "The Montanari site is unique because of the age of the surface there and the fact that the Moon is the only sizable world without an atmosphere or magnetic field. That leaves it exposed to the solar wind, which deposits traces of helium and other gasses."

"Who cares?" Brower said.

Chase's analysis was only peripherally relevant and might not be important to the case, but it was information that he knew Brower didn't have — and he hoped that the depth of his research would impress Snider.

"Who uses the helium?" Mike asked.

"Everybody. It's a power source."

"They're extracting the helium-3 isotope," Michelle added. "When it's fused with ordinary hydrogen, it releases a tremendous amount of energy." Helium fusion was the standard of power throughout the solar system — especially around the outer planets, where the drop in the Sun's intensity made solar power impractical, or in bases like Alpha that spent long periods of time in the shadow of their planetoid.

"Sounds like a hell of a military target to me," Frank said.

"Got that right," Brower agreed.

"The question is — " Chase leaned over the table — "why was Secretary Herrera going there?"

"I looked into that," Brower said defensively. "Fusion Resource was ready to bring their new processor online, which was supposed to increase their output by thirty-three percent. Herrera had planned to meet with the management and congratulate them on the expansion. He also had a speech scheduled for the employees. Shake some hands, win some votes, that sort of thing."

"The secretary of energy is a cabinet position," Michelle said. "It's appointed, not elected."

"You know what I mean." Brower waved the point away. "Anyway, it was largely a public relations visit."

"What isn't widely known," Chase continued, debunking yet another one of Brower's facts, "is that they don't have enough manpower to realize the gain. The company's trying to keep it under wraps to bolster their stock values — possibly a financial motive for the recent crimes." He turned back to Snider. "I don't know if this has anything to do with the *Phoenix* murders, but my point is that there's much more to this than any of us understands."

Snider heaved a sigh and stepped between the men. "Morgan's right." He held up his hand to keep Brower from interrupting. "No offense. This has become far too important to not have my senior man in charge. Morgan will lead the team."

Chase was supposed to be happy, yet he felt like he'd just signed his deep-space papers all over again.

Unable to dispute Chase's experience, Brower changed tacks. "I've led this case ever since it became a criminal inquiry, and I have collected a lot of evidence in the past week. Chase hasn't been around at all in that time. He'll have to come up to speed before he'll know where to go next."

"Then see that he catches up quickly."

"Sir." Brower led Snider into a corner of the room and continued in a low voice, but Chase was close enough to make out the words. "This is an opportunity for me to demonstrate that I can do this kind of work, that I can handle this project. It's a step up for me. I think I deserve a chance to show you what I can do."

"You'll get that chance," Snider assured him. "Morgan's still retiring after this thing is over."

Brower sat down with a clenched jaw and a cold stare while Snider also took a seat.

Chase remained standing. "Okay, let's see what we're up against. Why the subterfuge with the *Phoenix*? Why didn't Herrera use the chartered shuttle that had been arranged?"

Brower leaned forward and blew out a loud breath before speaking. "According to the Secret Service, a threat was made on Herrera's life during his speech the day before. So they requested an earlier liftoff. We picked the *Phoenix* because it was already scheduled to make the trip. Nobody'd be able to catch a change in its flight plans."

"When did they decide to change flights? And who knew about it?"

"The plans were finalized about eight o'clock in the evening before his departure. We started looking at options a couple of hours earlier, right after the threat was made."

"What time was that?"

Brower pursed his lips. "Between five and six."

"Where did the threat come from?"

"The telnet."

"From within Lunar Alpha?"

"We don't know."

Chase typed it into his thinpad as a lead to pursue. "What time did the *Phoenix* launch?"

"Eleven o'clock the following morning."

"Who had access to the *Phoenix* between eight the previous evening and eleven the day of the crash?"

Brower motioned to the thinpad he'd handed Chase earlier. "As soon as the decision was made, the Secret Service requested a safety inspection, a mechanical test of all flight-critical systems — anything that could be tested without actually flying the ship. Stellarfare pulled five guys off other duties for the inspection. That maintenance log shows who worked on it and when."

Now they were getting somewhere. "Who ordered the inspection?"

"The head of Herrera's security detail — I've got his name here somewhere." He began searching through the notes on his own thinpad.

Chase continued before he could find the information. "Who contacted Stellarfare?" This didn't seem too different from accident investigation, he thought. You find out what happened, and when, and then add the question, "by whom?"

"I did," Snider said.

"You made the request yourself?"

"I wanted prompt cooperation."

Chase examined the maintenance log for a few moments. It listed five names over a period of six hours.

"The problem is," Brower said, "the record doesn't have enough detail. Several hours of work are given only a few lines in the log. And some procedures list two names without indicating who did which portion of the work."

Chase scanned a few pages back. This seemed typical of other entries as well.

"We needed more specifics," Brower continued. "So I spent a couple of days interviewing everybody on that list, and everybody they saw in the hangar or on the launch pad between eight P.M. and eleven A.M. It's all right here." He tapped the screen of his own pad.

Chase paused. He'd exhausted that line of questioning, so he changed topics. "Who knew that the *Phoenix* was selected for Herrera's flight?"

"I'm tracking that down. The list is longer than I expected." Frank keyed his thinpad and found the desired document. "Everyone in Herrera's security detail, a total of nine people." He named them. "Also on the list are David Herrera; Jack Snider; Stan Brower; Randy Lauback and Phyllis Conway, the *Phoenix* crew; Julie Chavez and Avery Robinson, the traffic controllers on duty; and anybody who had access to the online passenger list." He looked up. "I was surprised to find that it reflected the change."

"It's required to be accurate before the ship leaves the launch pad," Chase explained. "If there's an incident like this, we need to know who's on board. The lists aren't accessible by the public."

"They're accessible by anyone in Stellarfare ticketing, boarding, billing, telnet administration, or management."

"Do we have a list of those people?"

"Not yet. I've made the request, but I haven't gotten anything back."

Chase added that to his notes, then turned to Michelle. "Anything new from the lab?"

She shook her head. "We've done all we can with the chip."

"Okay. Let's talk about the hangar fire. What do we know about that?"

Brower started with the obvious. "Somebody hauled a solid-fuel booster into the hangar with a forklift, lined it up with the *Phoenix,* and ignited it."

"What time did that occur?"

"Three in the morning."

That matched what Chase remembered. "Anybody see it happen?"

"We haven't found any witnesses," Mike said. "It was dark that night." He motioned to the small portal in the conference-room wall. The Sun was still down, and the reflection of the inside lights obscured any view of the outdoor landscape. "Unless its flood lights were on, the forklift would've been nearly impossible to see from inside."

"What about people outside?"

"It was three in the morning. There was nobody outside."

"Do we know why Agent Forsythe was in the bay at three A.M.?"

"No. He was quartered alone and hadn't said anything to anybody about working that night."

"Have you searched his quarters?"

"No," Brower said. "Why?"

Chase shrugged. "Something might turn up." He stood silent for a few moments. "Sounds like we don't know much about the fire. What about Montanari?"

"All we know is what we saw on the newsblips," Brower said. "A mine employee, a Chinese national named Zhou Zheming, climbed into a fuel tanker with a case of mining explosives, drove it into the new helium plant, and blew it up." He still spoke in a belligerent tone. "Structural damage was significant but repairable. Reports indicate anywhere from three to eight people injured. Zhou Zheming was the only fatality."

Michelle spoke quietly, almost to herself. "Even if the three crimes are connected, they may not have been committed by the same person."

"That's possible," Chase agreed. "In fact, if there haven't been any shuttles from here to the mine since the fire, the bombing must have been committed by a second person."

"I'll check it out," Brower said.

"Good." Chase looked around the table. "Frank, I'd like that list of people with access to the Stellarfare information by five, along with the list of those who knew about Herrera's flight change. Mike, see if you can run down any additional witnesses related to the fire. Maybe someone saw Forsythe on his way there. And search his quarters. Stan, find out where the threat was made from. See if there've been any flights to Montanari since the fire and contact the authorities at the mine. Get any additional details on the bomber. Oh, and send me a copy of this maintenance log and your related notes. I'll put the lists together. If we're lucky, there'll be a common name."

"What about me?" Michelle asked.

"Looks like you get the night off. We'll meet back here at this time tomorrow."

Now Chase had to contact his daughters and try to explain, in some meaningful way, why he was putting his career before his family.

"Why shouldn't he?" Sarah would say. "He always has."

But to Chase there was more to it. Much more. It was a chance to stop a war before it got off the Moon. To save countless lives. To make a difference.

Sarah would see only that he'd put his family last.

CHAPTER 12

President Powers glanced up from the latest version of the Transatlantic Mass Transit Proposal when her administrator walked into the Oval Office.

"Pardon the interruption, Madam President, but you'll want to see this." She activated the wall terminal.

Li Muyou, the president of China, was talking. An interpreter spoke over Li's voice, translating into English. "... categorically deny all accusations made by the American president."

Powers stared intently, as if she could read Li's mind.

"Furthermore," Li continued, "the Americans have launched armed ships into space. This is expressly forbidden by the Outer Space Treaty. This is an act of war. Should the United States choose to attack China or Chinese assets on Earth, in space, or on any other world, we are prepared to protect those assets. We will not bow before American intimidation."

Thirty minutes after the Chinese declaration, another aired in which Russia pledged its support to China in its stand against "American aggression."

Tit for tat. But the next move was still Li's. "Choose wisely," Powers said out loud, as though her adversary were there in the room. She prayed that Li would.

⁂

Bill Ryan and his crew made their way to the Armstrong Lounge, a popular hangout for the fliers whenever they found themselves at Lunar Alpha. As they stopped in the doorway, Bill instinctively noted the number of single females in the bar. Something about flight uniforms brought the ladies out by the dozen.

"Water, water everywhere," Abrams said. He tapped Bill on the shoulder as he passed. "Come on, I'm thirsty."

But despite the lively banter, flashing lights, and canned music that filled the place, Bill recognized it for what it really was, an emotional minefield to be traversed carefully if he wished to emerge whole on the other side. He stepped over the threshold, crossed the crowded lounge, past a fair representation of the Crab Nebula on the south wall, and squeezed up to the bar. "Beer," he said to the man behind the counter.

"Beer?" Townsend said. "Screw that. Make mine a moonshine."

Bill had forgotten about the local blend — forgotten almost everything about the night he'd been introduced to it, in fact. Better to play it safe and steer clear of the strong stuff. He pressed his thumb to the scanner, grabbed his beer, and made his way to the table.

He joined Abrams near a row of floor-to-ceiling windows, beyond which stood a life-size statue of Neil Armstrong and Buzz Aldrin planting the first American flag in the lunar soil in the same spot it had originally stood. A plaque hung nearby, inscribed with the famous words, "Tranquility Base here. The Eagle has landed."

It wasn't long before Bill caught the eye of a young lady across the room — radiant blond hair, big eyes with thick lashes. He smiled but didn't otherwise encourage her. Then again, why shouldn't he? Of course, Dana would be in later, but it wasn't like they were a couple. She wouldn't keep him company overnight and there was no reason he should spend his time alone.

Bill was still debating the question when the other crews began to file in. He was on his second drink by then and was remembering that when it came to alcohol, the oxygen-rich atmosphere didn't make up for the reduced air pressure maintained in the habitat. He'd better slow down if he wanted to be conscious when Dana arrived.

George Gabaldon walked up and nudged him with a closed fist. "Hey Ryan, your girlfriend show up yet?"

"Who? Dana?"

"Yeah, Dana."

"She's not my girlfriend." Bill didn't mean to sound brusque.

"Make your move," Gabaldon suggested. "She's a piece. She'll let you."

"I wish." Bill studied his glass for a long time, until the silence began to drag.

"Hey, man, I'll see ya. I'm gonna get a drink." Gabaldon turned and vanished into the crowd.

Why wouldn't she? Bill wondered. Dana was a fun-loving girl. She'd flirted with him often enough. Hell, she'd flirted with the other guys too, when she was in one of her more ornery moods. But she seemed to date only civilians.

Why couldn't he share *that* part of her life? Whenever he tried, she was just responsive enough to make him think he had a chance. But in the end, she always kept him at arm's length.

But Bill had resolved years ago not to psychoanalyze her behavior. He reminded himself of that pledge now to prevent his mind from slipping into that self-destructive mire of a woman's emotional logic. Women's prerogative, he repeated over and over again to make himself believe it. Some days it got to him more than others.

"Fuck it." Bill downed his beer, slammed the glass on the table, and headed for the bar.

He introduced himself to the local girl.

"Michelle Fairchild," she said without shaking his hand.

"What brings you to Lunar Alpha?"

She brushed her hair over one ear. "I work in the materials lab."

"Really?" He tried to sound interested. "What do you do there?"

"Materials science. I'm an intern. Mars Tech." Her expressive eyes shone with adoration or alcohol.

Bill cocked his brow in an effort to look impressed. "What does that mean, materials science?"

She shrugged. "I work with materials, try to understand their technology. What's in them. How they're made."

"What they're good for?" She'd have a heyday with the *Puma*'s stealth cladding, but that was a topic Bill couldn't discuss.

"Yeah, what they're good for." She seemed to lose herself in her thoughts for a moment. When she continued, she spoke as if the idea was new to her. "It seems like every technology ought to be good for something. Doesn't it?"

Bill ordered another round for himself and the girl. He was still there when Dana came in and saw them together. It made him feel guilty somehow, like he was cheating or something. But Dana either didn't notice the girl or she didn't care, having reacted not at all to her presence.

No. She'd seen her and she didn't care. That hurt most of all.

God, he'd missed her these past two days.

Finally, he shoved his frustration into the pit of his heart and buried it. How had it escaped? He looked at the glass in his hand and knew the answer. Then he tucked away his guilt too, for good measure. "Excuse me," he said. It was time to see how Dana's flight had gone.

The CATS crews lingered into the early morning hours, long past the time that the national guardsmen showed up from the troop transports with their commander, Lieutenant Cottington. The crowd began to thin. Most of the single guys, and a couple of married ones, left the bar with some of the local attractions.

"I think I'll turn in," Dana said finally.

Bill stood, palm flat on the table. "I'll walk wissh you." The low g confused his balance.

"I think *I'll* walk with *you*. You look like you could use the help. See you tomorrow, guys," Dana said to the men at the table. She took Bill by the arm and helped him from the bar.

Her hand felt warm and, as they walked the corridors with only the custodial robots as witness, the pressure of her fingers stirred things better left dormant. Though still light-headed, he'd regained his balance and thought he could probably walk on his own. Instead he stumbled into Dana. She staggered and they both laughed. Then she slipped her arm around him and took more of his slight lunar weight.

"Don't do that," she said, giggling, when he leaned into her again. And neither stopped laughing until they reached his doorway.

He just hoped she didn't notice the stiffness that rose in his pants as she helped him across his apartment to the bed.

By the time they reached Bill's quarters, Dana was breathing heavily, but not from exertion. She eased him down on the bed, sat beside him, and told herself it was the low gravity and alcohol that made her lightheaded. Not his physical presence. Not his hand resting on her leg. Or his eyes. But he was gorgeous; she'd noticed that immediately. And in six years his attractiveness hadn't diminished. At times like these, it threatened to overwhelm her.

Seeing him as he was now, floundering and in need of physical assistance, excited her more than she could describe. This man, as self-confident and capable a man as she'd ever known, needed her. She could easily take advantage of his condition, and he would welcome every thundering heartbeat of it... Her skin felt suddenly warm and tingly. Her tongue moistened her lips.

But she couldn't.

She forced calm into her voice and prayed that he was too drunk to perceive her desire. "Feel better now?"

"Much. Thanks."

She surveyed his quarters. "Looks like mine."

"They all look the same."

The silence stretched for five, six, seven heartbeats. His thumb caressed her thigh.

"That's a nice Raptor." She pointed to an aluminum-framed picture of the fighter plane.

He didn't reply. When she looked back, he was staring. The conversation died away and they just gazed at one another.

"Well ..." She started to rise. He put his hand on hers and she sat back down, realizing too late that she'd done so. By then, she'd lost herself in his chocolate, come-with-me eyes.

Bill leaned forward and pressed his lips to hers in a light, tentative kiss. It'd been too long since she'd had someone. It was that and the drinks, she told herself, that made her stay.

He kissed her again, still light kisses, but each lasted longer than the one before. She returned them now, refusing to admit that it was a weakness to do so. Stop him, her mind cried, but her body didn't hear.

He placed a hand behind her head and pressed his lips hard against hers. Dana let him in and their tongues began to play. The embrace consumed her for several minutes before something inside finally registered the alarm. Every fiber of her being vibrated with warnings as well as passion. She gasped for breath and composure, placed a hand on his chest, and pushed him away. "Bill ..."

"I know," he said in resignation but without obvious disappointment. He seemed lucid, more sober than he'd been a moment ago.

"I'm sorry. It's just that — "

"No really, it's all right." He sounded sincere.

She'd done this to him before. The first time had been a few months after they'd begun working together. It had gone too far then, though not much further than it had gone this time. She'd have to be more careful.

She'd have given herself to him then if it hadn't been for one thing. Bill was her commanding officer. And she was unwilling to give him that much control that kind of control — over her.

They'd been awkward together for a long time after that but had eventually settled into a tacit understanding. Friendship. Flirting. Nothing more.

But Bill was no stranger to women. He could read the signs, and he understood — he must understand — that she wasn't strong enough to resist if he carried on. But he seemed to sense also that the night of passion he'd receive would cost them their friendship. Dana couldn't possibly maintain a relationship that she felt was inappropriate, and once she'd gone that far, his friendship would never be enough.

"I should go," she said, standing. This time he rose with her and walked her to the door.

So he stopped. She kept her head down to hide the disappointment that must show in her eyes. He always stopped, like he did now, unwilling to lose her friendship for a brief moment of lust. That, more than anything, told her that he loved her.

"Good night, Bill. I'll see you in the morning." She kissed him lightly on the cheek and left, letting the door slide shut behind her.

Dana hurried to her quarters, stripped off her flight suit and panties, and crawled into bed, where she lay for several minutes before she slipped her hand beneath the covers and between her legs. In an air force full of men, you'd think she wouldn't have to do this. But the only man she wanted, she wouldn't let herself have.

CHAPTER 13

By the next day, the entire mood of the base had changed. National Guardsmen roamed the halls with automatic rifles slung over their shoulders. The men moved carefully, either clumsy in the unfamiliar gravity or still recovering from the all-night binge in the Armstrong Lounge that Chase had heard about on the morning newsblips.

Men guarded the entrances to the housing and operations sectors. They watched the common areas, and presumably the commercial areas as well.

Warships, not trainers, occupied the air force hangar for the first time in history. Everyone knew the ships were armed; President Powers had said that much. They were there to protect the base, but their presence, like that of the National Guard, hung over Alpha like a threat of violence.

Chase propelled himself along the corridor railings all the way to the War Room, anxious to separate himself from the military presence in the halls. When the rest of his team arrived, he pulled up his list of unanswered questions. "Let's see what we have from yesterday. Stan, what do you know about the telnet threat?"

"It was made from right here at Alpha Base, from a public terminal in the Common, near the Armstrong Lounge, directly to Herrera's suite. They spoke to Agent Myers, one of the security team."

"Did you talk to Myers?"

"I reviewed his statement. The caller's voice was that of an adult male with a Chinese accent."

"That's it?"

Brower spread his hands in a gesture of helplessness. "It was a public terminal. What'd you expect? A recording?"

It would have been nice. But Brower was right. A deliberately anonymous caller would be hard to identify. "Video?"

"Turned off at the source."

Of course. To protect the privacy rights of the inhabitants, laws prohibited security scanners in the public areas of the base, and owners of private facilities could install them only if they posted signs to notify patrons of their presence. Whoever the perp was, he wasn't stupid.

It would've helped if Chase understood what kind of man would do this — if he knew the motive. But that would have to wait. What he needed now was some connection among the crimes.

"Mike, any more on the fire? Anyone see Forsythe that evening?"

"Negative. He must've been in his quarters from before dinner until late that night."

Suddenly Chase snapped his fingers and pointed to Brower. "There were security scanners in that bay." It was a NASA operations hangar with no public access.

Brower was already shaking his head.

"No?"

"That bay was empty for months before you moved in. The scanners were shut down. When you ordered a twenty–four-hour guard, there was no need to reactivate them."

So much for foresight. "Did you search his quarters?" Chase asked Mike.

"Chief Brower may have. Frank and I were busy talking to Forsythe's neighbors and anyone else who lives or works between his place and the hangar."

Chase shifted his gaze.

"Yeah, I took a look," Brower said.

"And?"

"Things were in disarray."

"Signs of a struggle, you think?"

"No." He pursed his lips. "It looked more like someone was looking for something."

"Any idea what?"

Brower shook his head.

Every lead seemed to dead-end. Armed ships occupied the air force hangar, soldiers patrolled the base, and Chase wasn't any closer to finding the criminals. Where the hell were the facts? "What about jumper flights to Montanari?"

"Several since the fire, about one every other day, counting both freight and passenger ships."

That was more than Chase had expected, but it made sense. Montanari was a sizable colony. The mine alone employed three thousand people, not to mention the businesses that served the miners and their families. "Did you get passenger lists for those shuttles?"

Brower slid a thinpad across the table.

Chase compared the lists with the ones he'd reviewed the previous night. "There's one match to the Stellarfare lists."

"Oh?" Brower said expectantly.

"It's one of the ticketing agents. She had access to the passenger information."

"But it was an Asian man who did the bombing. Isn't that who we're looking for on those flights?" Michelle asked.

"That's right," Chase said. "It's not likely the woman was involved, but it's worth finding out."

"I'll do that," Mike offered.

Chase nodded. "That brings us to the lists. I looked through them last night. There's no overlap between those who knew, or could have known, that Herrera was on the *Phoenix*, and those who had access to the ship after the decision was made."

"So we're back to square one," Frank muttered.

"Not quite. There're several Asian names on the list. From Stan's information on the telnet comm, that narrows the field a bit. It also tells us that one of a couple things is true. Either one of the lists is incomplete, or — "

" — Or we're looking for more than one person," Mike finished.

Chase pointed. "Exactly."

"We already knew that," Michelle said from the end of the table. "I mean, unless the Montanari bombing was totally unrelated, there must be more than one person involved. In fact, more than two. The bomber must have been at Montanari all along — "

"Wait a minute." Chase snatched up his thinpad. "The bomber. What was his name?"

"Zhou Zheming," Brower said.

Chase scanned the lists. The name wasn't there. "Never mind. You're right, Michelle. Please continue."

"Well, if the threat came from here, and the sabotage was done here, but the bomber was there, then there must be at least three people involved."

"Again, that's assuming the lists are complete," Brower pointed out. "The bomber could've traveled under an assumed name and somebody could've hacked into the passenger lists."

"Good point," Chase agreed.

Michelle sighed, as though deflating in her seat.

Chase shared her frustration as surely as he felt the press of time.

Frank, who hadn't spoken a constructive word since he'd come in, eyed Chase from across the table with a glare that seemed to smolder with suppressed rage.

"I'll find out more about this Zhou Zheming," Brower said. "Where he's lived. When he last traveled from Montanari. How long he's worked for Fusion Resource. That sort of thing."

"Good. Anything else?" Chase addressed everyone now.

"Yes," Michelle said. "Well, no, not really. We're doing some more tests on the chip."

"What kind of tests?"

"Metallurgy, mostly. It seemed odd to me that the saboteur would've used such a specialized technology for this application. The circuit could've been built from commercial parts available on the open market. If it was China, why risk a state secret for something like this? There must have been a reason."

"Let me know what you learn. In the meantime, I'll follow up on anyone in these lists who speaks with an Asian accent."

When the meeting broke up, Chase detained Brower until the others had left. "I hope you're not still upset that I took this away from you. I wouldn't have done it if I didn't think it was necessary."

"I know. I was pretty torqued at the time, but I'm okay now. It was your case to begin with. And you're picking up on some things I missed."

"You'd have gotten around to them eventually."

"Probably." Brower paused. "Still think it's not China?"

"The evidence does seem to be mounting, doesn't it?"

Brower's nod was almost imperceptible. "Time will tell, my friend. Time will tell." He patted Chase twice on the shoulder and left.

When Chase gathered his things and walked out a minute later, Frank was loitering in the hall. The young guard approached, his expression hostile. Then he seemed to change his mind and hurried away.

Chase shook his head and thought nothing more about it.

President Powers, her staff, their aides, and a delegation from the European Union filed into the Situation Room. The delegation, including the European secretary of state, their ambassador to the United States, and half a dozen representatives from the EU military and intelligence communities was present to discuss the unfolding crisis. On the American side, Tom O'Leary had added two intelligence men to his party.

President Powers began the meeting by replaying the recordings of the Chinese and Russian declarations.

As soon as the second clip finished, Dan Norton quoted President Li: "'Should the United States choose to attack China or Chinese-held assets on Earth, in space, or on any other world, we are prepared to protect those assets.'" Then he exclaimed, "What the hell is that supposed to mean?"

"It means that China has violated the Outer Space Treaty," said Wolfgang Das, one of the European intelligence men. "And it did so a decade ago,"

Several jaws gaped open and the room hung silent, but the European's features remained expressionless. Was he bluffing? Or guessing? He appeared genuine, but with his face shrouded in stubble and with a gray ponytail that reached his belt, he looked like a beatnik. Was he competent?

"Well then," quipped European secretary of state Andrew Yates with a strong English accent. "That brings us straight to the heart of the matter, doesn't it?" He pushed his glasses up on his nose and looked around the room, his boyish face smiling. "Oh, come now. What else could it mean? You didn't expect those rodents to abide by their sense of honor, did you?"

Powers' jaw tightened at the blanket remark, but she couldn't object to Yates' characterization where President Li himself was concerned. "Do you know the specific nature of the treaty violation?"

"As a matter of fact, we do. One of them, at any rate, and I had the foresight to get permission to disclose it before I left Brussels." He turned to Wolfgang. "Fill them in, if you please, Mr. Das."

The European stood and slid a data card into a slot in the table. He keyed the first image and the hologram emitter came to life. " This is *Mingyun-75*. Supposedly a Chinese communications satellite. It is, in fact, a weapon."

"*Supposedly* a communication satellite?" the president snapped at O'Leary.

"Not 'supposedly.'" O'Leary's red brows came together over his nose. "We routinely monitor its transmissions. It *is* a communication satellite."

Wolfgang advanced the display to a close-up view of part of the same satellite, a beam protruding from its main body with an array of solar panels attached, a feature found on nearly every satellite in Earth's orbit. "This center support for the solar collection arm is circular in cross-section. That's unusual for modern satellites. Even more telling is its construction material. The pipe is made of titanium, rather than the lightweight composites used for most modern space equipment."

He brought up the next image, a three-D design schematic of the same structure. "Note that all of the brackets have been welded to the outside of the pipe, leaving the interior smooth and unobstructed."

"A gun barrel?" the president asked.

"Not quite. More of a rocket launcher." Wolfgang pointed to a box-shaped structure near the bottom of the hologram. "See this here?" The image changed to a blow-up of the indicated component. "This is the magazine. It holds a hundred and eight projectiles, each mounted onto a cylinder of rocket propellant. A rocket is injected into the launcher, the satellite is oriented, and the rocket's released. Once it leaves the barrel, it jettisons the rocket stage and orbital mechanics direct the remaining projectile to the target."

My God. The president's fist clenched her cane with an intensity that squeezed the blood from her hands.

"How big are the projectiles?" Norton asked.

"You ever fly model rockets as a kid?"

Norton turned to face the man who'd spoken, another of the Europeans. "No, why?"

"Most model rockets are constructed from a cardboard cylinder about two centimeters in diameter with a plastic nose about five centimeters long. That's the size of what we're talking about here."

"So when the rocket stage drops away, all that's left is a five-by-two centimeter projectile?" O'Leary asked.

"If that big."

O'Leary took a few notes on his thinpad. "We'd never see that on radar. There'd be no way to see it coming."

My God, the president thought again. "How sure are you of your facts?"

"Of the facts I've stated, very sure. What we don't know is how many of these satellites they've deployed." Wolfgang nodded toward the hologram. "But we're sure of *Mingyun-75*. We've been monitoring some of their testing exercises." The wall panel lit with a list of satellites and dates. "They're using some of their old birds for target practice. This shows thirteen Chinese satellites shot down by *Mingyun-75*. A couple of these are recent launches, probably dummies deployed specifically for the purpose. Most of the rest had been up there for at least fifty years."

President Powers turned to O'Leary, still grappling for a point of stability. "Do we know anything about this *Mingyun-75*?"

O'Leary glanced around the room as though taking stock of those present, seeming to consider his response. "Not a peep." Then to Wolfgang, "You say they launched this thing ten years ago?"

"Nearly."

The president was no longer listening. Nothing. Not a peep. The US intelligence machine was supposed to be the finest in the world. This was huge, and nobody had known. It couldn't possibly be true. And yet she knew it was. In her gut, she knew.

She felt like she had when she was twelve, when she and her friends were playing in the surf off the South Carolina coast. She'd waded in a little too far and a particularly large wave washed over her, pulled her under.

China armed in Earth orbit and the United States ignorant. She couldn't breathe. A cold pressure squeezed in around her, holding her down while she was powerless to prevent it. She heard Norton slam the table through the muffled sound that filled her ears. They were arguing, Norton and O'Leary, but only Norton's voice penetrated the president's consciousness with the words *incompetent* and *consequences*.

Finally, like it had when she was twelve, the wave receded and she came up for air. She banged her cane on the hardwood floor to bring civility back to the meeting.

Norton, who'd stood during the exchange, resumed his seat. "We've got to know how many of those things are up there before we can take them out."

"Hold on, Dan," the president soothed. "Nobody said anything about attacking."

"I did." Norton's eyes blazed with vehemence from his artificially youthful face.

The president looked him in the eye to ensure that she had his complete attention. "We're talking about starting a war. I don't take that lightly." She didn't want Norton's explosive comments to spark a general call to that kind of action, especially from the Europeans.

"That weapon poses an imminent threat to the United States and its European allies." Norton was practically shouting. "Imagine that thing pointed at any target, at any time. Hell, combine it with satellite imaging, and they could probably pick you off just walking across the White House lawn."

"Not quite." Wolfgang was seated again, his presentation complete. "The projectiles are too small to survive atmospheric reentry. This weapon was designed for space-based targets only."

"Still …" Norton let the word hang.

Then one of O'Leary's men spoke. "We periodically track every satellite that China's ever put in orbit. If we make the assumption that all of these rocket launchers have recognizable components, then we can use that same satellite imaging technology and turn it outward, take a good look at each Chinese bird. Then at least we'll know how many they've got."

"How long will it take?" Powers asked.

"If we pull all of our imaging satellites off their current projects for the duration of the search — " the man shrugged. "I'd say twenty-four to forty-eight hours."

"You've got twenty-four," the president said. "Pull whatever resources you need. Dan, I want your people to work with those of Mr. Das and Mr. O'Leary. Do a feasibility study for taking out those weapons. All of them. Including a preliminary attack plan and timeline. I want a list of options by this time tomorrow."

"You'll have it."

"I'll inform President Hunt," Yates said, his face somber now.

"Please do," President Powers continued. "Now, let's talk about the Russians."

Chapter 14

Ever since President Powers had announced the launch of the warships, Chase had been free from the press. As far as the media was concerned, and probably the public as well, the case had been solved. President Powers herself had placed the blame. And as in the *North Star* case, reporters didn't particularly care whether the verdict was accurate as long as it was sensational. Powers' treaty violation was sensational enough to pull the spotlight off Chase.

It had done the same for Snider, allowing him to fade from the attention of the feds. The release of that burden had reduced the frequency and vehemence of Snider's demands for answers. Nevertheless, Chase still felt obligated to report his progress on a regular basis.

Chase was on his way to Snider's office for one such report when he passed Frank Lesperance in the hall. He nodded curtly as he approached the security guard, who glared back at him.

As he passed, Frank grabbed him by the arm.

If Chase hadn't caught himself on the railing, he'd have been pulled from his feet. Given the hostility of the guard's action, Chase expected him to follow it with a fist. He ripped his arm from the other's grasp and spun on him.

Frank's free hand was at his side, his fist clenched but not raised to strike. "Why did you come back?"

Chase's brow creased with the effort to stay calm. He tried not to return Frank's hate-filled glare. "I told you why. What's on your mind?" If Frank had a problem with his leading the investigation, Chase would need to ease the guard's mind or remove him from the team. He wanted to settle it here and now.

Frank leaned in so their faces were mere centimeters apart. "The case was going just fine until you showed up." He was just a kid, eighteen or nineteen years old, with fiery passion in his eyes and an obviously short fuse. His shoulders, broad as a battering ram, anchored thick, muscular arms.

"The case was going nowhere. You had no suspects and no leads."

Frank backed off, but his voice resonated with violence. "What do *you* know?"

"I've been around."

"We had lots of suspects."

Chase forced a chuckle. "Yeah, every Chinese national and Chinese American on the base."

"On the Moon. And yes, it was a long list, but we were working through it, eliminating each, one by one, until only the guilty were left." The edge came off his voice, but his face remained tense. "All you have are your lists, and there's no overlap."

That was true. There were still gaps in the data that needed to be filled, but it wouldn't take the months that Brower's approach would have, he hoped, and it left open the possibility of a non-Chinese perpetrator. Yet something about his own theory didn't add up either. It didn't explain the metallurgy or the connection the CIA had made to China. At least not yet. But now wasn't the time to admit it. "The lists aren't complete. We know that. But if you want out, just say the word."

Frank poked a thick finger at Chase's chest. "You can't throw me off the case. I've got friends, you know what I'm saying? And we'll see what's what."

Friends? Chase wondered. Authorities? Thugs? It took all of his self-restraint to keep from grabbing that finger and twisting it off. The boy's belligerence forced him into a mindset usually left in his past. "Careful, soldier. You're out of line."

That set the boy back. Frank hesitated before responding. "We're not in the military, and I don't report to you." Then he stormed off down the hall, looking every bit as furious as he'd been before.

Chase took a few breaths to shake off the disturbing confrontation. The threats didn't bother him, as such, but they did raise a number of troubling questions. What had prompted them? A fanatical loyalty to Brower fueled by youth and temper? Or was there more to it?

Instead of Snider's office, Chase went to Brower's. He reported the episode and asked if Frank had known about Herrera's transfer to the *Phoenix*. After all, Frank had compiled the list. It was a long shot, but sometimes you never knew.

Brower's eyes widened. "He might have. I pulled him off his duty station to run a ship manifest. The Secret Service had to know what was in the cargo before Herrera boarded."

"Did you tell him why?"

"It was an unusual request. He's a bright kid. I didn't have to tell him why."

"But you don't know that he knew," Chase said skeptically.

Brower shook his head.

"He left his own name off the list. Maybe he didn't know." If he did, that would explain his reaction to the investigation's sudden change of direction.

"We'll have to keep an eye on him," Brower said. "But we can't confront him. He's more likely to slip up if he doesn't know he's being watched."

"Agreed." Chase stroked his beard for a moment. "We'll have to redo his part of the investigation."

Brower spread his hands, palm up, in a gesture of resignation. "I'll go back through it myself. That keeps it between us."

"I think that's best."

With no training facilities on base except an exercise gym, Bill had resorted to cardiovascular and resistance training for two hours every morning for himself and his men. Along with calcium supplements, the exercise would keep their bodies in shape and stave off the long-term effects of lunar gravity, like the deterioration of muscle and bone. But without training simulators, a null-gravity cell, and actual flight time, the gym wasn't enough to keep their skills honed.

Once the CATS had been refueled and made ready for launch, all Bill could do was remind the crews that they were still on active alert. He ordered them to stay sober and confined them to the base.

Then, two days into their stay, Bill managed to separate Dana from the guys so he could enjoy some time alone with her, which he hadn't been able to do since their first night on the base. They went to the Tranquility Restaurant, which he favored for its reasonable prices — by lunar standards — quiet atmosphere, and the subtly masculine, romantic feel of the burgundy and brass decor.

Neither had mentioned what had happened in his quarters. It was safer not to. There never seemed to be any repercussions from his advances as long as he didn't press them.

"It's nice to have a bit of a break." Dana dug into her vegetable lasagna.

"From the training schedule, or from the guys?"

She laughed. "Both. How long do you think we'll be here?"

"Who knows? Weeks. Months. Hell, the CATS could be stationed here permanently for all we know. Though if they do that, they'll have to build a facility and bring up the other crews. Rotate us out on some sort of schedule."

"It'll feel like leave after a while," Dana said.

"It already does. It'll get boring, though. We've got a lot of time on our hands, and there's not much to do. I'm afraid the guys will start getting into trouble."

"Oh, they'll find something to do." She laughed again. "It's the girls they're with who're getting into trouble."

They fell silent for a time, comfortable in each other's company. Dana's eyes held a playful sparkle and he lost himself in them.

Finally, she raised the topic that had been on his mind since their arrival. "Does it bother you?"

"What?"

"That we've broken the treaty. That we might go to war."

"Doesn't it you?"

"Of course it bothers me. I'm not afraid of it, though. Not for myself. But I'm afraid of what it might cost us as a people. Does that make sense?"

He nodded, not sure that it did.

"You think they'll send us into combat?"

"Against what?" Bill swept a hand through the air to indicate the Moon around them. "There aren't any targets out here. They're all on Earth. No. We're here as a political statement by Powers. 'Mind your manners, you slant-eyed upstarts, or by golly, we'll jump up and down on your heads.'"

Dana frowned. "You don't think China will launch something? I think they're ready to. They wouldn't assume that there'll never be a conflict in space."

"No, they'll launch something. But we're here as a deterrent, to ensure that matters don't get out of hand."

She took another bite. "I hope you're right."

~(O)~

Stellarfare was a commuter starline that owned the bulk of the market for the so-called jumper flights on the Moon, at least for American passengers. They also ran at least one flight a month from Alpha Base to each of several major US spaceports and a small number of ships to Mars and the moons of Jupiter, when an orbital launch window was available. Lunar Alpha was their hub.

Chase stepped into the business-office reception area and crossed the plush red carpet in three arcing strides. Behind the desk sat a young blond girl who looked like she was still in high school. She must have been older, maybe twenty — Erin's age at the time of the divorce. Perfume clogged the air near the desk and made Chase's eyes water.

"Where can I find the staffing office?" he asked.

She looked bored. "Is Ms. Jackson expecting you?"

"No." He displayed his badge for her inspection. "I'm Ed Morgan, NASA Office of Accident Investigations. I need to speak with her about the *Phoenix*."

"Oh," she said. "I thought that was over."

"Is Ms. Jackson available?"

The girl shrugged, pressed a button on the intercom, and waited a few moments.

A voice came over the speaker. "Jackson."

"Ms. Jackson, there's a Mr. Morgan here to see you. Says he's from NASA, investigating the *Phoenix*."

"Send him in."

The girl smiled and pointed down the hallway. "Third door on the left. You can go right in."

"Thank you."

Sharon Jackson, the Stellarfare staffing manager — according to the plaque on her door — a middle-aged black woman, wore a sophisticated style of dress and pulled her hair into a loose bun at the back of her head in a manner too severe to be attractive. Her rich, expansive office was dressed with simulated wood paneling and a real fern that draped from the corner of her large mahogany desk.

The woman shook his hand firmly. "What can I do for you, Mr. Morgan?"

"I'm investigating the *Phoenix* incident." He again produced his credentials, which she scrutinized before motioning him to a chair opposite the desk.

"Most unfortunate," she said as she returned his badge. The way she said it, Chase wasn't sure whether she meant the incident or the fact that he was there to investigate it. "How can I help you?"

"I'm doing some follow-up on a few of your employees."

"Are they suspects?" Her brows cocked in a defiant manner.

"Ma'am, anyone who had access to the *Phoenix* on the day of the flight or access to any of the passenger information is considered a suspect until an alibi has been given and verified."

"What happened to, 'innocent until proven guilty?'"

"I didn't say they were guilty. I said they were suspects."

"That's a fine distinction, wouldn't you say, Mr. Morgan?"

"Not really." Chase sat up in his chair. "Look, Ms. Jackson, we know that the *Phoenix* suffered an act of deliberate sabotage — "

"By China, the news said."

"The media believes that, but I don't. Either way, we still need to identify the individuals involved. To do that, we must establish motive, means, and opportunity. So far, we know the means, and to some extent, who had opportunity or may have had opportunity. But I need more information on those who had access to the ship and passenger lists."

"How can I help you?" she asked again.

Chase held out a thinpad with a list of names displayed. "I'd like to review the personnel files for these people."

She made no move to take the thinpad or even look at the list. "Personnel records are considered proprietary information. I can't just let you into the files."

"Ma'am, company records are not privileged under the law. This is a criminal investigation. I could subpoena the documents, but that would delay the investigation unnecessarily. The longer it takes to catch the criminals, the less likely we are to do so."

"That's the second time you've referred to the criminal in plural. Is there more than one?"

"We believe there are."

"I'll tell you what, Mr. Morgan." She took the list. "It's part of my job to protect, to any extent possible, the personal information in the employee records. But I have no desire to delay your investigation. If there are criminals working at Stellarfare, we'll gain nothing by protecting them. I'll bring up the files and answer any questions you have. Will that be satisfactory?"

Chase nodded. He could always bring a subpoena later if he needed additional details or had any reason to doubt the information she gave him.

Ms. Jackson looked at the list for the first time. "All of these people are Asian. You said you didn't think the criminals were Chinese."

"I said I didn't think the Chinese government was involved. We know that at least one of the perpetrators is a male who speaks with an Asian accent."

"Oh? How do you know that?"

"Ma'am, I can't discuss the evidence without compromising the investigation."

The woman's expression soured, but she looked at the list again and began typing on her terminal. "What would you like to know?"

"For starters, their country of citizenship and the length of time they've been employed at Stellarfare."

⁂

"What do we know?" Victoria Powers surveyed her presidential council, twenty-four hours after their previous meeting.

One of O'Leary's CIA cronies stood to present. "We've visually inspected every satellite China's put into orbit in the past twenty years. We found three verified matches to the orbital weapon and seven possibles. These are the positive matches." He cycled through holograms showing three identical satellites and announced each by name. "The first two are in geo-synchronous orbit, at thirty-seven thousand kilometers above the equator. The third is in a polar orbit. The two at geo-sync are at opposite points in their rotation. Together they cover both hemispheres."

"How long have they been in orbit?" the president asked.

"The earliest launched nine years ago."

"Go on."

The presenter covered the next seven holograms more slowly, displaying four different satellite types. For each one, he named the satellite and pointed out the design similarities that marked it as a potential threat.

"Gut feel. Do you think these seven satellites are weapons?"

The presenter stared at the president. "Gut feel, ma'am?"

"Yes. Gut feel. Tell me what you think." She pointed to the hologram. "Is this satellite a weapon?"

"I don't know, ma'am. I don't think so."

"Is there any data to suggest that it is or isn't?" the president pressed.

"No, ma'am. None, other than the design elements I've pointed out."

"How many of these launched in the past ten years?"

"Two, ma'am. The last two." Both were of the same design.

"Were either of these satellites in a position to shoot any of the test targets we discussed yesterday?"

One of the military analysts responded. "Yes, Madam President. What we need to understand here is that any satellite can shoot down any target. One of these weapons can launch a projectile into an intercept orbit with a target that's out of its line of sight, no matter where it is, provided that it's programmed with the precise orbit parameters of the target."

"No matter where it is? Are you saying that an armed satellite around Earth can bring down a target orbiting the Moon?"

"I'm saying that a weapon here could theoretically shoot down a target orbiting a moon of Jupiter, or even Pluto for that matter, provided that the orbit of the target is well known and remains stable long enough for the projectile to arrive. Admittedly, in this example it would have to be an incredibly precise shot, but it's theoretically possible."

The president leaned back in her seat and let out a long, low whistle. She propped her cane against the table and sat, pensive, for several minutes, her fingertips forming a steeple before her mouth, tapping her lips. Missiles threatened the United States. The fact of it brought her mind back to the events of October, 1962. The Cuban missile crisis. The most significant event in the history of the worlds. Earth teetered on the brink of a nuclear catastrophe of imponderable magnitude, all because another country had dared to threaten the United States.

As China dared to threaten it now.

With the destructive powers of the world's nuclear arsenals at the time, and the political tensions that the situation created, there was far more at stake than at any other time in history, more even than during the great world wars of the previous century. And far more than there was now ... if it stopped here.

With the EU and Russia having each pledged their support to one side or the other in the growing conflict, the four major players had already come to the table. However this played out, it'd be a world conflict. And although nuclear weapons had fallen out of favor and had largely been dismantled, that was no guarantee against a clandestine stockpile among the nation's enemies. In this respect, Russia was of particular concern.

It had to stop here. It had to end now. Powers addressed her defense secretary. "Can we take them out?"

"Yes," Norton said without hesitation. "But with some risk."

"I don't see that we have any choice. They've got to come down."

"I agree," Norton stated.

"How do we do it?"

Norton prompted the advisor who'd spoken earlier to outline the tactical considerations. The man looked around the room at his audience. "What we're looking at here is a band of silent killers. These projectiles, once launched, travel at speeds close to a hundred-thousand kilometers an hour. They're too small to pick up on radar, except at very short range. If they miss the target, they'll fly by and the weapon can fire again. The target will never know it's under fire until it's actually hit. If the projectiles are explosive, then a single hit anywhere on a spacecraft will be enough to disable it, and probably knock it out of its orbit as well."

The president remained silent and attentive as the speaker continued. "Surprise is the key. Our warships are stationed at Lunar Alpha and it'll take them thirty-six to forty-eight hours to traverse the space between here and there. If China knows they're coming, the CATS will be shot up before they ever reach their targets."

"Can we fire our missiles early after launch? Will they find the satellites from that distance?" the president asked.

"Possibly, but I'd recommend against it. The missiles are designed to be launched at short range and guided by laser to their target, but we do have adequate thrust and mass information on the missiles to put them into an intercept orbit, if necessary. The problem is that the missiles can be seen on radar. In fact, they have a larger radar cross-section than the CATS. If the satellites can shoot down the warships, they can hit the missiles as well."

"What do you recommend?"

"The CATS were designed to be invisible, but they're not perfect. If the Chinese know what they're looking for and know where to look, they'll find them. But if they're watching for a sizable ship, the CATS' signal will be drowned in the noise."

Norton was quick to reassure the president. "Even if they are spotted, it's likely the Chinese will think they're looking at much smaller objects, jettisoned fuel tanks or some other space debris. The ships are most vulnerable to detection and identification during takeoff and landing, when their thrust rockets make them stand out optically. If they're spotted by an imaging satellite, they can be tracked by radar from there."

Concern etched the president's features. She was acutely aware that human crews would be at risk, and the chances didn't sound good.

The speaker continued. "Another thing we have going for us is that a long-range strike, by either side, requires the target to remain in a stable orbit. The CATS, because they'll launch from the low gravity of the Moon, will have a substantial fuel reserve during the mission. As such, they can change trajectory several times on their approach and return to reduce the probability of a successful hit. What we don't know is whether the satellites have a rapid-response tracking system that will allow them to strike an evasive target at short range."

"Madam President," Norton said, "I recommend that we take out the three known threats. We have to start with the basic assumptions that China's unaware of the stealth nature of our fleet, and that if they do see us coming, they'll give our boys the benefit of the doubt. After all, they may simply be coming home."

"We could even make a public announcement to promote that misconception," the advisor added, earning a glare from Secretary Norton.

"Madam President." Mariano's mustache flexed on his lip. "There is another option. We could ask China to bring them down under the threat of bilateral economic sanctions, which I'm sure the European Union will support."

Yates remained silent.

"I won't make an announcement of any kind until the strike is over," Powers declared. "And I won't warn Li Muyou. This mission relies on secrecy. He won't fire on our ships as long as he believes we don't know the true purpose of the Mingyun satellites. Diplomatic channels with China will remain closed until the satellites are gone. Dan — "

Mariano came to his feet. "We're supposed to follow protocol. Negotiat — "

"I don't give a damn about protocol — " Powers said.

"Ma'am — " Anne Portman began.

" — and I don't give a damn about the election. What I do care about are the CATS crews. They need secrecy to survive. I'll worry about protocol and public opinion after the attack. Dan, I want to take out the first three satellites presented and the last two. I'm willing to take my chances with the rest."

"Very well," Norton replied. "That'll leave us with four CATS and five targets. We'll hit the known weapons first. That may leave them defenseless while we go after the remaining two."

Now the president turned to the European delegation. "Do you have any concerns to voice at this time?"

State Secretary Yates spoke for the Union. "None. After our last meeting, I contacted President Hunt and notified him that you were pursuing the idea of striking the satellites. He was understandably concerned but reaffirmed his pledge of support. Our military is ready to mobilize in case of repercussions here on Earth."

"Very well." The president unconsciously tapped her wedding ring on the top of her cane. "We spoke last time about the potential for Russian interference. We know they've been shipping uranium to their Saturnine base for power generation for decades."

"That's true," O'Leary said. "We've verified the existence of fission reactors at those installations, but we don't know what they're doing with the plutonium byproduct. We suspect they're refining it for weapons, but we've never been able to locate their refinery."

"Is there any reason to believe that they threaten the current mission?"

"Not at the moment." Mariano was seated once more. "I spoke with the Russian ambassador yesterday and alluded to a treaty violation by China without giving any specifics. They're waiting to see if we can furnish proof."

"Very well, gentlemen, it's decided. Dan, finalize the tactical arrangements and draw up the orders."

CHAPTER 15

When Bill received the comm at two in the morning, he rolled out of bed, activated his link, and listened to the message. It said simply, "You have orders." He logged into his secure account and downloaded the encrypted transmission from Earth.

After reading the order, he forwarded it to each member of the four CATS crews and sent a second message to the hangar team. The transmissions would automatically relay a tone to the recipients' links to rouse them from their sleep. Bill's mind raced with the possibilities while his body went through the practiced motions. Years of training, drills, and exercises had brought him to this moment. They would launch in one hour.

In a quarter of that time, all of the crews assembled in a reserved briefing room near the CATS hangar. Bill could only repeat what they already knew; they'd read the same message he had. But he did make sure they understood that this was *not* a drill. They'd be firing live ammunition against hostile targets.

Despite their years of training and service, none of them had ever been in battle. A realization of the risk, to himself and to Dana, quickened Bill's pulse. He could read a rare tightness in Dana's expression. Apprehension or excitement shone in the eyes of his men. They all felt it.

He handed each captain a data card with the orbital parameters for his assigned target. Then they hustled to their ships.

Dana caught up to Bill just before he reached the hangar door. She touched his arm to delay him. "Be careful, Bill."

"You too. And don't worry about me. You just worry about your target."

He was touched by her gesture and hadn't meant to be abrupt, but their best chance of success would come when each person focused solely on his or her task. Personal distractions could be deadly.

"Yes, sir." Hurt filled Dana's eyes as she started to turn.

He took her in a long, firm embrace. "I love you," he whispered before releasing her to her duty. He hadn't meant to tell her that way, but the words were genuine and he couldn't risk losing her without her knowing.

Without replying she hurried to her crew.

Bill caught up with his own men and the three helped each other into their combat gear.

The ground crew was leaving the hangar by the time Bill climbed into the hatch. He pulled himself into the cockpit, closed the door, and verified that the seal integrity light shone green. Then he found his seat, snapped the flight harness into place, and requested hangar depressurization.

When all four crews announced readiness, the air handler evacuated the hangar. It took twenty-two minutes to depressurize the bay to match the lunar atmosphere and another four for the CATS to taxi into position on the launch pad. Three minutes later, a full five minutes after their ordered launch time, all four CATS were ready for liftoff.

Bill gave the order and the ships blasted into space, starting a return trajectory to Earth orbit and the attack that would initiate the first armed space combat that humankind had ever known.

Later that morning, before he'd gotten himself out of bed, Chase received a telnet communication. "Good morning, Michelle." He rubbed his eyes to clear away the sleep.

Michelle was already dressed and appeared as though she'd been up for some time. She looked worried. "Sorry to wake you, Mr. Morgan, but I wanted to catch you before you went out."

"What's up?" Her use of the formal appellation concerned him.

"Can I come by? I want to talk to you about the chip."

"Sounds important."

"I think so. I mean, it might be — " She paused for breath. "Yes, it's important."

"Okay, give me thirty minutes."

"Thanks."

"Michelle." He caught her before she keyed off the link. "Have you had breakfast?"

"No."

"I'll make something when you get here."

◆

When Michelle arrived, she was unsure of what she was going to say. The conclusion she'd drawn was far-fetched, to say the least, almost to the point of absurdity. She'd present her opinions, of course, but the data she'd use to support them was fairly technical and she wasn't sure how much Chase would really understand. There was also no way to know if she'd missed anything in her analysis. So she'd tell the story, just as clearly as she could, and let him decide if she was out of her mind.

She entered, carrying a thinpad full of data, and was greeted by the scent of fresh pancakes. She smiled in spite of herself and her stomach growled. Lunar pancakes were her favorite. They rose light and airy in the low gravity. There was nothing like them on Earth or even Mars.

Chase served the cakes with juice before sitting down to join her. Suddenly, she was in no hurry to broach the topic she'd come here to discuss. She knew her findings were important, through she wasn't sure how. But they could wait until after breakfast.

Throughout the meal, they discussed the investigation and the relative lack of recent progress. They'd held meetings daily since Chase rejoined the team, but the last few had been sparse in the new-information department. Then she asked Chase about his plans for retirement. They talked about his daughters until they finished breakfast and he'd cleared the dishes.

He returned to the table with two cups of coffee. "What have you got?"

She didn't know where to begin. "Well, you know we've been doing some additional tests on the chip."

He nodded.

"We've been trying to determine the purpose of the alloy. And the bottom line is, there isn't one."

"What do you mean?" he said after a moment's pause.

"I mean that someone went through the trouble and expense of developing a new metal composition for nanochip manufacturing, an alloy that nobody's ever used or experimented with before — for this purpose or any other that I can find in the literature." Her hands gestured her exasperation as she spoke. "Then they supposedly classified the process, kept it top-secret, and made sure that nobody else in the worlds has it. Am I right so far?"

"Yes. Go on."

"Well, they must've had a reason. Nobody would design a technology, develop it to the point of manufacturability — which generally takes years to do — and then classify it, unless it was better for some application than anything already available."

"Makes sense."

She found his quiet attention encouraging. "So the guys in the lab and I have been asking ourselves the questions, 'In what way is this alloy better than those used in the commercial sector?' and, 'To what application would that improvement best be employed?'"

"And what did you find?" He took a sip from his mug.

"I'll show you." She turned her thinpad so Chase could see the display right-side up. "We started with the obvious, electrical characterization. The resistivity of the alloy is slightly higher than that of the standard. For reasons of internal heating and power consumption, low resistively is categorically better than high. Then, because the chip was used for a space application, where temperatures can vary by several hundred degrees from sunlight to shade, we did a temperature response analysis. The response is virtually the same as that of the standard, though the melting point of the new alloy is two degrees lower."

Michelle displayed a variety of results for a wide range of physical tests, including material hardness, reliability, corrosion resistance, and others. She stopped to explain the significance of the various aspects of the graphical data and answered any questions that Chase asked. All showed the confidential alloy's performance to be the same as, or inferior to, the more commonly-used metal.

Chase seemed to be remarkably perceptive. His questions demonstrated a clear grasp of the technical considerations and a sharp mind for absorbing the subtleties of the data. When Michelle commented on this, Chase said he was used to investigating accidents, not crimes.

"Accidents are generally caused by a complex sequence of procedural, judgmental, and technical errors. You can't investigate an accident without a technical understanding of the hardware," he said.

Next, she went into an analysis of the engineering issues associated with the manufacture of a computer chip, how materials were integrated into a manufacturing process. "The material must be easy to deposit onto the chip, and it must be easy to etch off." She and the lab techs had speculated on the former and tested the latter. "Copper has always been a challenge to manufacturers, but the trace elements of nickel and palladium don't significantly improve its manufacturing characteristics." Her arguments in regard to other integration questions were more speculative, and she admitted as much, but she believed them to be well-founded, based on the available literature.

Finally, she went into cost.

"It's unlikely that a government would classify a technology on the basis of cost," Chase said.

"Even so, the alloy would be both harder and more expensive to produce than pure copper. You'd have to purify not only the copper, but the other elements as well. Then you'd have to combine the constituents in a controlled manner to achieve the desired percentages in the final alloy and ensure that they were uniformly distributed. All that adds cost."

"What about radiation hardness? Electronics in space are constantly exposed to solar radiation. They last longer if they're radiation-hardened."

"We thought of that." She searched the files for a specific chart before continuing. "The new alloy broke down more readily in a radiation environment than the commercial standard."

"Maybe that's the point," Chase said. "Maybe they hoped it would break down after it'd served its purpose and prevent us from determining its function."

Michelle shook her head. "They'd want to make sure it worked when it should. Besides, the location in which we found it is clue enough to its purpose. Anyway, the difference in radiation performance was minor, on the order of ten to twenty percent, depending on the type of radiation."

Chase leaned forward and placed his elbows on the table. "What do you think it means?"

"I think it means that the purpose of the alloy was to make the chip unique. Recognizable."

"Why?"

"I don't know. I thought that's what you were here for." She smiled to show that she wasn't admonishing him, only saying that she didn't have an answer.

Chase sat back in his chair, one hand on his beard. He took a long draw from his mug. "That would explain something else that's been bothering me."

"What?"

"Why the saboteur didn't include an explosive charge with the device. If it were me, I'd have blown up the chip after it'd served its purpose. It would've made it a lot harder to prove sabotage, or at least harder to locate the device and trace it back to the Chinese." His eyes shot open. "Jesus Christ!" he exclaimed, as though responding to some inner voice. "You've got to be kidding me." He put his hand on his forehead, closed his eyes, and shook his head.

Michelle was beside herself with impatience but didn't speak.

Chase looked up. "That would put it all together."

"What?" she asked, finally unable to contain herself.

"Damn it!" Chase slapped the table with his open palm. "That's it. They wanted us to prove sabotage. They wanted us to trace it back to the Chinese. They're trying to start a war."

"Who? How?"

"I don't know who, but we've got to find out. Somebody developed that technology and reported it to an American spy working in China, and that spy dutifully passed it on to the CIA. Then they used it to assassinate Herrera and followed it up with additional attacks."

"Wait a minute. Why would anybody do that?"

"I don't know."

"Maybe it was China after all."

"No. They'd just strike first. They wouldn't have gone through all this." He waved his hand at the data on the table. "The perpetrators must have known that simply claiming Chinese responsibility wouldn't be enough to spark a conflict. It's too uncertain. They wanted us to come to that conclusion on our own, with their so-called proof."

Michelle was speechless. Chase's speculations were even wilder than her own. But she had to admit that it made a weird sort of sense. So far, it was the only explanation that fit all the facts: the diplomatic target, the new chip technology, Chinese denial of the *Phoenix* attack, the fire's occurring immediately after the device was found, the bombing, the predictable US military response, everything.

"We must find out who's behind it," Chase said, "before the US does something that we can't take back."

"Well then, I've got some more bad news for you. The air force ships are gone."

His head snapped up. "Where?"

"Nobody knows, but it's all over the station. They left during the night last night."

"Sounds like we're running out of time. I'll contact O'Leary and see if I can find out where the report of this chip technology came from."

"What can I do?"

"Pray."

Chapter 16

The CATS orbited the Moon once, flying in formation. Bill had no way of knowing if the Chinese were tracking their flight, but it was safest to assume they were. So he ordered each ship to deploy a radar decoy, a small metallic shape designed to return a radar reflection about twice as strong as that of the CATS. The signal observed on any tracking radar would jump when one was deployed, but the radar operator would probably attribute it to a change in the orientation of the ship being tracked.

They came around the Moon and Bill assigned a different trajectory to each ship. As they broke orbit, one at a time, any radar operator would probably choose to continue tracking the larger signal of the decoy dummies. The other advantage of this approach was that if someone spotted them on radar later, they'd each be drifting in a slightly different direction, thereby giving the appearance of debris. Four objects in formation would be much more likely to attract unwanted attention.

On the other hand, this would take longer and would require a mid-flight course correction. But the ships carried sufficient fuel, and time was less important than the element of surprise.

Once the maneuver was completed, with each of the CATS proceeding on their prescribed course, Bill ordered radio silence and settled in for the trip back to Earth.

~(O)~

Despite the urgency of the situation, the air force ships off to God knows where to do God knows what, Chase had to wait for the CIA office to open before he could contact O'Leary. So at two that afternoon, nine A.M. Eastern Time, he keyed O'Leary's connection.

It took several minutes to get through the protocols before the agent's face appeared. "What can I do for you, Mr. Morgan?"

"I spoke with you several days ago regarding the sabotage of the *Phoenix*."

"Yes, I remember." He seemed distracted. "That caused quite a stir in the hornet's nest down here."

"I know. It's been all over the news."

"Oh, you don't know the half of it."

"I can imagine. Look, Mr. O'Leary, the reason I called is because I need more information on the source of that chip technology."

The agent glanced at his watch. "There's not much I can tell you. What is it you want, specifically?"

"I need to know who reported it to the CIA, or at least how your agent found out about it. It's key to my investigation."

O'Leary's expression hardened. "Please understand. I can't reveal the identity of our field agents or their sources. Not for any reason."

"Tom — can I call you Tom?" Sometimes it helped to deal with people on a more personal level.

O'Leary made a gesture that seemed to say, "Who cares?"

"Tom, this single piece of information may be enough to lead me directly to the perpetrators."

"I'm sorry. You'll have to find some other evidence to take you there. If we compromised our informants' identities every time some investigation came up, we wouldn't have any sources left."

Chase sighed. "Can you tell me how long ago it was reported?"

"Sure. Let me look it up. ... Let's see ... July of last year."

"Where is the agent now? Still in China?"

"That's classified."

It was like pounding his skull against the bulkhead, and it gave him just as bad a headache. But he had to try. This wasn't about Randy any more. It was bigger, much bigger. It was bigger even than Secretary Herrera. "Look, Tom, I'll level with you on this because I need your help. I'm certain that the Chinese government is not involved."

"I'm sorry. Did you say *not* involved?"

"That's right."

"What makes you say that?"

"Circumstantial evidence mostly." Chase shrugged. "Call it a hunch."

"Can you prove it?"

"Not yet, not without this information. I'm afraid that this whole thing's going to explode into a war that nobody can stop. In fact, I'm convinced that's the whole point of the attacks. But if we can prove that China's innocent, we might be able to prevent it."

O'Leary was shaking his head.

"Okay, how about this?" Chase said. "I don't know if you have the president's ear, but I'll bet you know someone who does. I need time to work this out. Can you get this knowledge to whomever it takes to slow things down until I find out who's behind it?"

"What knowledge?" Exasperation crept into O'Leary's tone, but he kept his words civil. "All you have are speculations. You bring me proof and I'll see what I can do. Besides ..." He trailed off.

"The orders have already been given," Chase finished for him.

O'Leary paused. "I'll tell you what. I'll contact the agent and see if there's anything he can tell me without compromising his informants. Then I'll get back to you."

"Make it quick. There's a lot at stake here."

"You have a gift for understatement. Have a nice day, Mr. Morgan."

"Temperature's low on the starboard tank, Captain," Abrams said as he prepared to make the midflight course correction.

Bill leaned forward in his seat. "Hold the burn and run a diagnostic."

"Coil current and input power are both normal," the pilot reported a few minutes later. "And the thermostat seems to be working."

Sometimes the thermocouples could be temperamental. Fortunately, the temperature readout was still within the thruster's safe-firing range, so it was easy enough to test.

But the diagnostic had taken several minutes to complete and had put them out of position for their originally-planned trajectory. "Update the burn parameters and fire both engines." If the temperature really was low, they'd see a few milliseconds' delay in the ignition of that thruster relative to the port side.

Abrams punched the new numbers into the console and thumbed the ignition. Both engines fired on time.

Bill shrugged. "Must be a bad TC."

"In that case," Townsend said, "it looks like we just had our glitch for this mission."

Bill grunted. "We should be so lucky."

~

A day and a half after speaking to O'Leary, Chase sat at his kitchen table eating breakfast and watching the newsblips for the latest developments in the military arena. Something was about to happen. And when it did, the media would know.

The door buzzed.

"Come in," Chase hollered, loudly enough for anyone in the corridor to hear.

Penny got up, walked halfway to the door, and stopped.

A moment later, the buzzer sounded again.

"Come in," Chase yelled, a bit more loudly this time. But still no one entered. Maybe the door was locked. He rose to answer it himself.

Just then, it slid open and two Asian men stepped in. One of them, a full head shorter than the other, had a hand buried in a pocket of his gray jumpsuit, which displayed no patches, embroidery, or color scheme to designate a job or company affiliation. Neither said a word.

Penny growled.

The men just glared at Chase with eyes that held a grim threat of violence.

In that moment, Chase knew he was in trouble. As a ruse, he glanced toward his open bedroom door, then poised himself for whatever happened next.

The short man looked at his buddy, then jerked his head in the direction of the bedroom. The taller man walked behind him to cover the other room.

Still growling, Penny backed out of his way.

Chase reached under the table and watched the hidden hand closely. When it began to move, so did he. The man leveled a Lancaster pistol at Chase's chest. The weapon, allowed beyond Earth solely for security purposes, was issued only to security personnel. And the plain jumpsuits told him that these two weren't on the force.

Chase flipped the table up between himself and the gun. When the assailant pulled the trigger, the aluminite table top scattered the microwave pulse, which was designed to overload the neural synapses to create a conscious but catatonic state in the victim for up to twenty minutes.

The attackers were young and fit, a contrast to Chase's fifty–eight–year-old frame. And they were armed. The gunman thumbed the recharge button, generating a long, high-pitched whine from the weapon.

But Chase had learned much during his years in the military and was far from defenseless. He heaved the table at the gunman and knocked the weapon to the floor.

While the attacker scrambled after it, the other man returned from the bedroom with a knife in his hand.

Penny charged him and locked her teeth around his ankle. With a curse, he shook her loose and kicked her in the head. She yelped and tumbled into a stack of moving crates. As soon as she found her feet, she retreated into the bedroom.

Chase's mind barely registered the second man's return, focused as he was on the first and the pistol lying between them.

Before Chase could retrieve it, the knifeman launched himself in the low gravity, sailing across the room and over the upset table to collide, elbow-first, into Chase's chest. His knife hand came up, but without leverage there was no force behind the strike.

Chase grabbed the man's wrist to keep the knife at bay, then kicked at the attacker's feet, and both men tumbled softly to the ground. Still laboring to breathe, Chase came out on the short end of the exchange, with the attacker on his knees, straddling his prone body. But Chase had retained his grip on the assailant's wrist.

A man's weight is nothing on the Moon. Chase pressed his free hand against the attacker's chest and shoved him up and away.

When Chase started to rise, the short man slammed him backwards into a stack of moving boxes along the kitchen wall. The man's knee plowed into Chase's stomach, just below the rib cage, and doubled him over.

The gun still lay among the upset table and chairs.

Chase took another blow from the man's knee. He cocked his arm back and swung, but the man ducked, leaving Chase overextended and off-balance. Then he hooked an arm over Chase's neck and clamped it in a vise-tight grip.

A blurred fist hammered into Chase's eye. A second blow pounded his cheekbone and caught the edge of his nose. Blow after blow, the punishment continued. Bright lights flashed in Chase's vision with each impact. His stomach soured and his head swam in a whirling nebula. Blood splattered the countertop, the boxes, the floor, and the clothes of himself and the enemy, but Chase could no longer grasp its significance. A long tendril of red mucus dangled from his nose.

His mind swooning, Chase kneed the man in the rump, lifting him from the floor and stealing a bit of his leverage. The blows stopped and the grip on his neck loosened, though only slightly. Chase staggered, blind and barely conscious, but the movement pushed the enemy farther off balance.

Acting on instinct alone, Chase jabbed his fist into the attacker's kidney. The man grunted and the grip loosened further. Chase ripped the arm from his throat and pulled his head free. He shoved the intruder away with all his remaining strength to land among the table and chairs amid the clattering of splintered pieces.

Chase wiped the blood from his eyes but saw only a blur as the taller man closed, leading with an arcing sweep of the blade. Chase reeled backward. The knife slashed through his shirt and left a slit as wide as his hand in the fabric across his belly. He barely perceived the hot sting of the wound and the warm flow of blood past the throbbing in his skull.

Chase's muscles ached and his strength waned. His right eye was swollen completely shut and the left wouldn't seem to focus.

The knife came in again, nothing more than a vague movement in Chase's vision. He sidestepped, trapped the man's arm against his body, reached up with his other hand, and grasped something — hair, maybe. He swept the assailant's feet from beneath him and slammed the back of the man's head with a sickening thud against the corner of the aluminite countertop.

The man slid to the floor.

Chase struggled to locate the other intruder, the smaller and more dangerous of the two. The whole apartment seemed to be swirling.

Chase heard a sound to the left and spun his head. For a moment, his vision went black and the pain in his skull soared. One hand sought the support of the countertop while the other went to the rip in his belly. Both came away sticky with blood. He heard the sound again. Oh, God.

Then his vision began to return. The assailant stepped cautiously forward with a long, white object gripped in his hand like a bludgeon, probably a chair leg.

Chase reached across the counter for a butcher knife and flung it. He didn't expect to cause any harm. But the act forced the man to stop and reassess. Chase grabbed a chair leg of his own.

He stepped away from the corner into which he'd been forced and nearly fell on the blood-slick floor. He and his opponent circled, each holding a healthy respect for the other. Although Chase was still blind in his right eye, the vision in his left improved and he managed to catch his breath. Blood continued to stream from the wound on his belly, but he didn't dare look down to assess its severity.

As soon as his sight cleared enough for him to compete with reasonable confidence, Chase lunged at the man's face with the butt of his club. The man swept the thrust aside and came at Chase with a swift backhand. Chase back-stepped and landed a solid hit across the attacker's ribs, and a *whoosh* rushed from the man's lungs.

But the intruder pressed on. He advanced with an overhead chop.

Chase blocked, his stick held with one end in each hand. Then he kicked the attacker in the stomach, throwing the man backwards and himself off balance.

The attacker recovered first and rushed back in. With his club held in both hands like a baseball bat, he swung like a madman, left, right, high, low, overhand, and backhand. Chase blocked or dodged the worst of them, turning his whole head to see those coming in from his right. Forced now into a defensive posture, Chase stepped back as the other came on.

When the fury of the blows lessened, Chase struck out. The man ducked, but too slowly. The blow clipped his forehead and sent him staggering back. Chase pressed the opening with another backhand. This one the man blocked in time, though he appeared to be swooning and disoriented.

Chase kicked and the intruder made a two-handed block across Chase's shin. The blow stung fiercely but left the man's head exposed.

Holding his club in two hands, Chase swung sideways, smashed the man across the temple, and dropped him like a sack of potatoes at one-g.

Chase watched him for a moment, then stepped away.

He lifted his shirt, now soaked with blood, and inspected the wound. The cut was long but appeared shallow. Weak from loss of blood, he grabbed a towel from the bathroom and pressed it against the wound to slow the bleeding.

Because the kitchen terminal was smashed, he went to the bedroom to contact security and medical services. When he returned, the gunman was just disappearing through the doorway into the corridor beyond. Chase lacked the strength to pursue.

Instead, he went to the other man, still motionless on the kitchen floor, and rolled him over. The back of his head was gone. Pooled blood coagulated around scattered bits of bone and brain. The metallic scent of it assaulted his nose.

Chase staggered into the cardboard boxes behind him and slumped to the floor. This wasn't some faceless enemy destroyed by a distant air strike. Chase had murdered this man with his bare hands. His laboring lungs drank the foul air until he felt as though he could stand. Then he returned to the comm and keyed the security chief directly.

"Jesus Christ. You look terrible," Brower said. "What happened to you?"

"I was attacked. In my own apartment. Security and medical are on their way, but I figure you'll want to see this for yourself."

He killed the link and eased himself onto the bed. Penny hopped up next to him and began to lick his bruised face.

"Easy, girl." He smiled and drew her gently against his side. Still pressing the towel against his wound with his other hand, he waited for the medtechs to arrive. By his count, this was attack number four. *It's getting decidedly dangerous to live on the Moon,* he thought just before he lost consciousness.

Chapter 17

The *Snow Leopard* coasted to within missile range of the Chinese satellite *Mingyun-81*. "Slow down, Miller," Dana urged. "Match her orbit."

The ship rotated to face the thrusters forward, and the weight of her body pressed into the seat as they fired to slow the craft. Then the ship came around to view the satellite once more.

According to the mission schedule, they were first to reach their target. They'd wait there while the clock counted down to give the others time to get into position as well. Dana kept a close eye on the satellite. The barrel of the weapon pointed into space as it coasted along its path, seemingly oblivious to their presence.

"Ready the missiles," Dana ordered at one-minute-to-strike.

Allistair opened the missile bay door beneath the port wing. "That'll make us easier to see."

Dana nodded. Anything that interrupted the smooth lines of the radar-absorbing hull increased their radar cross-section.

"Ten seconds. Nine. Eight. Seven. Six. Five."

Allistair flipped on the targeting laser and waited for the tone.

"Four. Three. Two."

Beeeeeeeeeeeep. "Target lock acquired, sir."

"Fire the missile, Lieutenant."

With a loud snap and a sudden jolt, the missile catapulted through the open bay door. A second after it cleared the ship, its rocket fired, propelling it toward the satellite. It took a minute for the missile to traverse the gap to the target. When it hit, *Mingyun-81* exploded into a shower of debris.

"Evasive action, Lieutenant Miller," Dana requested calmly.

She keyed the link and announced over the encrypted comm channel, "Target two destroyed. *Snow Leopard* returning to base."

"Target one destroyed. *Cougar* returning to base," Gabaldon reported moments later.

The *Snow Leopard* cleared the expanding debris field that used to be *Mingyun-81*. "Give me a burn calculation for the Moon," Dana ordered, "and thrust when ready."

"Aye, Captain," Miller replied.

"Target four destroyed, proceeding to target five." It was Captain Etre on the *Jaguar*. He'd been given the more difficult task of taking down two satellites.

What had happened to Bill? Why hadn't he reported? Dana considered breaking radio silence to request his status, but that was forbidden. The only authorized transmission was the one she'd already made.

The *Snow Leopard* rolled into position and the thrusters fired, a long push this time. "Release the other decoy." A muffled thump, then the decoy drifted away.

Several minutes passed. Still no word came. Dana's chest tightened with each passing second. It was nothing, she told herself. Bill was always late. She should have expected it. But she was sweating in her pressure suit.

More minutes passed. *Come on, Bill.* The mission was timed to bring down the first four targets in the first two minutes of the attack. The last would come down two-and-a-half hours later, after the *Jaguar* shifted orbit. Yet no report came from the *Puma*.

⁂

Bill checked the mission clock as the *Puma* executed the final burn to bring it onto an intercept course with *Mingyun-75*. *Damn!* "Abrams, we're behind schedule. Did you update the burn for the target's new position?"

"Yes, sir, but we'll still enter striking distance eight minutes late."

"Thank you, Lieutenant. Carry on."

When the report came through from Dana and the others, Bill could see the satellite in the long-range imager and watched it carefully for any response. He was now six minutes out, but at 25,000 kilometers per hour, that put the target a long ways off.

Thirty seconds later, *Mingyun-75* began a slow roll in space.

"Stand by, gentlemen." It could be just a routine maneuver.

Light flared as three rockets streaked from the barrel of the satellite. It was pointed away, but the rockets' trajectory could bring them to intercept the *Puma*'s path nonetheless. It was just as likely, though, that the rockets sought another CATS or somebody's decoy. If so, the projectiles would take some time to reach their targets.

"Release the decoy. Evasive maneuvers," he ordered.

Mingyun turned again. Three rockets launched on another vector.

Puma's thrusters pushed them out of orbit, leaving the radar dummy behind. Two minutes later, *Mingyun* rocket rounds shredded the *Puma*'s decoy.

The satellite rolled and fired again.

"Evasive again, Lieutenant." The maneuver would cost them several minutes, but it was a necessary precaution. He had no more decoys to launch.

Mingyun-75 went still.

The evasive course brought them into missile range seventeen minutes late. "Fire when ready," Bill told his weapons officer. Eight seconds later, two missiles sped toward the target.

The satellites rotated again, this time coming to bear directly on their approach.

"Get us out of here, Cory," Bill ordered unnecessarily. The ship was already rotating for their next burn, and the *Puma*'s missiles impacted before *Mingyun-75* could fire again. "Target three destroyed. Projectiles were launched. Repeat, *Mingyun-75* did launch projectiles on several trajectories. All units alter course. Acknowledge. Over." Each ship acknowledged the course change and Abrams turned the *Puma* toward Alpha Base.

A little over two hours later, Etre's voice came over the comm. "*Jaguar* to *Puma*. Target five destroyed. Major, we have sufficient fuel to return to lunar base, but not with a comfortable margin. Request permission to land on Earth. Over."

"Permission granted, *Jaguar*. Good work, guys."

A heavy sigh escaped Bill's lips as he closed the comm channel, expelling all his pent-up tension in that breath. But there would be repercussions from what they'd just done. It seemed simple enough: launch a few missiles, destroy some equipment, and fly away. But that equipment belonged to a nation of proud people and substantial military means.

Chase lay in a room at the base infirmary. Scanners monitored his vital signs from a console cantilevered over the bed. Status lights told him that the sensors were operating, but he couldn't see their readouts, which were positioned on the wall behind his head.

The knife wound in his gut had required more dermaplast to close than he cared to consider, but it wasn't life-threatening. He'd received synthetic plasma to replace lost blood and accepted some non-narcotic pain medication. But he refused the strong stuff. He needed his head clear to think things through.

Frank Lesperance came immediately to mind, of course. But Chase had no proof that the guard was in any way involved, recent threats not withstanding. He had only circumstantial evidence. Brower, he knew, would follow up on the possibility.

Before long, Michelle came by to visit. He smiled, then winced at the pain of it, when she passed the guard that Brower had stationed at the door.

She blanched when she saw his face. "How are you, Ed?"

"I've been better, but I'll live."

She sat down by the bed and examined his face. "Looks painful."

"You have no idea." He managed a weak laugh, then winced again.

Michelle laid a cold-pack from the nightstand over his swollen eye and cheek, pushing his hand away when he tried to protest. "Anything broken?"

"Luckily, no."

They made small talk for a time, and then a look of doubt came over her features. "What does it mean that they came after you like this?"

"It means we're getting close. It means they're scared."

She stared into her lap for a moment before meeting his eyes again. "It also means they have someone close to the case. Doesn't it? I mean, how else would they know if we're getting close? You haven't held a press conference in days."

"I called Tom O'Leary and asked him about his sources on that chip technology. I don't think he knew who was involved on the Chinese side, but he was going to do some checking and get back to me. He might have stirred something up."

Just then Brower walked in, bracing against the door jamb to correct the angle of his stride as he crossed the threshold. "Hey buddy, how you doing?"

"As well as can be expected."

"Good. They've pretty well got your place cleaned up by now."

"You get any prints from the gun?"

"Didn't have to. I just followed the trail of blood. Found the perp dead in his apartment. You messed him up pretty good. We found this with him." He tossed Chase a blood-smeared thinpad. "That yours?"

Chase set aside the cold-pack and examined the number on the back of the pad. "I've been using it for the case."

"The guy must have taken it when he left. It's been wiped clean."

Chase shrugged. "Everything's backed up on the mainframe."

"Who were they?" Michelle asked quietly.

"The one in his quarters was Lu Chin, a Stellarfare maintenance tech. We haven't ID'd the other one yet."

News played silently on the terminal. The picture changed from a human-interest piece to a head-and-shoulders shot of Victoria Powers. "Hold on." Chase turned up the sound. "I need to hear this."

"My fellow Americans," the president began, "late last night, United States forces attacked and destroyed several armed Chinese military satellites."

"Military satellites," Brower echoed, his eyes fixed on the screen.

"These satellites were in direct violation of international treaty," the president continued. "They represented a clear and present danger to the security and welfare of the United States, its citizens, and its assets in Earth orbit and elsewhere."

Chase felt the need to move, to launch himself back into the case despite his injuries, but he was too late. The war had begun. His clock had run out. He listened for some sign that a point-of-no-return hadn't yet been reached.

"The engagement was a swift and effective demonstration of America's willingness and ability to defend our interests and those of our allies. The targets of the attack were unmanned and there were no human casualties on either side."

That, at least, was good.

"Our intelligence organizations will continue to monitor the skies of this and other worlds for additional threats. In the meantime, our forces remain on alert. Let us hope and pray that further need to employ them will not arise. God bless America."

Reporters shouted questions as the president vacated the podium and left the press room.

Chase clicked off the sound. "Well, there it is."

Neither of his visitors offered comment.

"How long will you be in here?" Brower asked after a period of silence.

"They want to keep me overnight for observation. If there're no complications by morning, I'll be released then."

"Well, rest easy. I'd say we got the perps. I'll keep a guard by the door, though, just in case." With a glance at the silent newsblip, Brower left the room.

Michelle stayed behind. "Do you think he's right? Do you think we got them?"

"No." The conviction with which he said it surprised even him. "Not all of them, at any rate. The maintenance guy, Chin, he couldn't have been working alone. Unless the fellow with him had access to the passenger lists, there's a third person we still need to identify. Besides, if our conspiracy theory is correct, there's a whole organization to reveal. One with the resources to develop a technology, put it into production, and use it. We've got to uncover that operation and hope it's not too late to stop the war." Or to salvage his relationship with Erin.

"No," he said again after a pause. "I'd say we're far from done."

~(O)~

That evening, the Chinese president made a public statement denouncing America's latest "act of war" and issued an ultimatum. "US and European citizens must vacate all Chinese facilities on the Moon within twenty-four hours. Any remaining after that time will be considered prisoners of war and will be detained, as such, until the end of American hostilities."

CHAPTER 18

When Chase left the infirmary the next morning, the base was alive with activity. People milled in the corridors, carrying armloads of belongings and trying to determine where they were supposed to go. Evacuees flooded in from every Chinese base and outpost on the Moon. The first refugees of the war. There'd probably be many, many more to come.

They served as a reminder that Chase had already run out of time, that the war had begun. Every moment that passed made it harder to stop. They reminded him also of why he'd once again separated himself from his family in a time of need for the sake of his job.

According to the newsblips, everyone in residence at Lunar Alpha had been asked to host a refugee family for an indefinite period of time. Hotel rooms and empty apartments were given away for free to those lucky enough to secure them. Two separate hangars were cleared to house the rest.

Snider had secured every available transport. Government, NASA, and commercial and privately owned ships, including the military troop transports, were collecting as many American citizens as possible from Chinese outposts before the deadline. Arrangements were being made to import additional supplies to support the added population and to relocate as many people as possible to Earth. According to rumor, similar measures were also being executed at Lunar Bravo, Montanari, and Capricorn.

Chase stopped by his quarters. The place had indeed been cleaned up. The body was gone, along with the broken pieces of chairs and other furnishings, the shattered telnet terminal, and the weapons used in the brawl. The floor, cabinets, and countertop had been scrubbed clean of blood, and the table set upright. Everything else had been left where it was: the stacks of moving boxes, still stained with splatters of blood; the dishes in the sink from yesterday morning; the seal-pak mug on the end table, everything.

Chase went into the bedroom and activated the terminal to download his personal and investigation files back into the thinpad. But the case files were gone. Someone had deleted them from the mainframe, someone with access to his personal account, someone with extraordinary hacking skills or someone in telnet administration or security.

Someone like Frank Lesperance.

But even as he cursed the delay, Chase realized that all he really needed were the lists. And those he could recreate.

At the moment, however, there were other, more pressing matters to attend. He activated the telnet and contacted the CIA.

"The agent involved," O'Leary said, "refused to disclose any information regarding his Chinese connections."

Chase made a final plea for the name of the agent so that he might contact him directly, but O'Leary said it was "out of the question."

Chase went to the bathroom, carefully wiped the blood off the frame and keyboard of his thinpad with a damp cloth, and threw the rag into reclaim. He swallowed two pain capsules to help silence his pounding skull and examined his face in the mirror. The entire right side had turned purple with bruises and his eye was still swollen shut. He put on his sunglasses to conceal the worst of the damage. What remained was disguised somewhat by the darkness of his ebony skin.

He spent the morning recreating his deleted lists. Those with access to the ship consisted primarily of the five Stellarfare employees whose names appeared in the maintenance log. Those he remembered. He remembered also that Lu Chin wasn't among them.

The list of people with knowledge of Herrera's flight change proved more cumbersome. The *Phoenix* passengers and crew he knew. The Secret Service contingent he got from Brower, whose name he added along with that of Jack Snider and Frank Lesperance. The rest required a trip back to the Stellarfare staffing office.

Then he went to see Augustus Watson, the maintenance supervisor on duty the day of the accident. He made his way by leaping strides through the maintenance hangar to get to the office. The bay held four ships, including the hangar queen — cannibalized for parts in order to keep the rest of the fleet operating. Chase grinned. Until his first NASA case, he'd thought that only the air force kept hangar queens.

As he walked past the tool chests, fueling hoses, power umbilicals, hoists, and racks of spare parts, he estimated about thirty men working in the hangar. If that many were there when the *Phoenix* was inspected, considerably more people had access to the ship than those whose names appeared in the log.

Chase skirted the edge of the hangar to reach the office marked MAINTENANCE SUPERVISOR. No accompanying name adorned the plaque. Four cluttered desks, a large roll-around tool box, several metal cabinets, and stack upon stack of boxes filled the room. But of people, it was empty.

In the hangar, a man separated himself from the throng and approached. His large mass of curly black hair and thick beard had grown too long to look tidy. His heavy build hindered him not at all in the lunar gravity. The cleanliness of his coveralls, in Stellarfare teal and white, set him apart from his staff, and a patch above his left chest pocket read simply, GUS.

"Can I help you, inspector?" the big man asked.

Chase held out his hand. "I'm Ed Morgan. I'm here to — "

"I know why you're here. I seen you on the news. Come in, please." He offered Chase a seal-pak mug of coffee and cleared off a seat. "Now, how can I help you?"

"I have some questions about the maintenance staff who performed the last safety inspection of the *Phoenix*."

"Just a minute. Some of the fellas are here now." Watson got up, took a single leap to the door, and closed it. "Fire away."

"Can you tell me which members of your staff speak with an Asian accent?"

Watson blinked. "The security chief was down here a week or two ago asking questions. But he didn't ask nothing like that."

"Well, the investigation's come a long way since then. So the questions are getting more specific."

"That's good, I guess." Watson scratched at the mass of unkempt hair dangling from his chin. "Now, let's see. I guess the fair way to do this is to bring up a staff list and consider each one, see if I can recollect how he talks. Know what I mean?"

Chase didn't reply.

Watson mumbled to himself as he worked his way through the list and occasionally spoke a name out loud, which Chase typed into his thinpad. "That should just about do it," the supervisor said finally. "How many is that?"

"Four."

"Four it is, then."

"Can you tell me how long each one's worked here?"

"Sure." Watson took the list. "Lu Chin has been here for about ten months, maybe a year. Huong Tran, a year and a half or so. The others, longer. I'll have to look up their records to be exact."

"That's close enough. Do you have an image of Lu Chin on record?"

"Sure. His badge photo's part of the file." Watson punched some keys, then turned the screen for Chase to see.

A brief wave of fear washed over Chase when he saw the image, that of the shorter man who'd attacked him. He took a moment to calm himself. "Was he here the day the *Phoenix* was inspected?"

"Let's see." Watson turned the screen around and tapped some more. "No. He was off that day."

"Perhaps, but was he here?"

"He was off the clock, but he may have come in. Most of these guys hang out together, ya know. It's not uncommon for them to stop by on their day off to chat with a buddy. I usually don't say nothing, so long as the visits are kept short. It's a small price to pay to keep up morale. Ya know what I mean?"

Chase asked for a copy of the *Phoenix* log and to speak privately with each man listed there.

"They're all working today," Watson said. "I've got everybody in on overtime to support the evacuation. You can use my office for your interviews if you like, but I'd rather you wait until tomorrow, after the evac deadline."

Chase shook his head, starting it throbbing again. "I'm afraid this can't wait."

Watson gave him a long stare.

"There's a war on," Chase said. "The information's vital."

At that, Watson stood. "Anyone in particular you want to see first?"

Chase selected Tyrone King, a technician that was listed as having attended the inspection for its entire duration.

Watson nodded and left the room.

He returned, accompanied by a burly man with a dark complexion, black hair, and a thin mustache. Tyrone wiped grease from his hands with a rag as he entered, then tucked the rag into the pocket of his stained coveralls. "Mr. Morgan." He extended a not-quite-clean hand. "I understand you want to talk to me?"

Chase shook the man's hand firmly. "Yes, Mr. King. Please sit down." They both took a seat on the same side of Watson's desk. Then Chase thanked Watson and waited for him to leave the room.

When the door slid shut, Tyrone glanced at it with the frightened look of an animal that's stepped into a snare.

"There's nothing to worry about, Mr. King," Chase assured him. "You're not a suspect. I just have a few routine questions for you."

"Isn't that what you guys always say?"

Chase managed a half-smile through the damaged muscles of his face. "I suppose it is, but this time it's true. I have a copy of the *Phoenix* maintenance log from the day of the accident. I'd like you to read through it for me." Chase handed him the thinpad. "Take your time and read it carefully. Think back to the events of that day. I'm going to ask you if the record's complete."

"All right." Tyrone spent several minutes reviewing the few screens of data that the record contained. Occasionally, he looked at the ceiling as though trying to recall some detail. Then he handed it back. "I think the propellant tank seals were actually inspected after the injector flow calibration."

"You seem to have a good memory of the events."

Tyrone shrugged. "It wasn't that long ago."

"The names listed in the log for that day are Mortensen, Torres, Shaffer, Hudson, and yourself. Is that everybody who worked on the *Phoenix*, or were others present?"

"It's company policy for everyone involved in a maintenance procedure to electronically sign the log."

Chase leaned forward in his seat. "That's not what I asked."

"Let me see." Tyrone stared at the ceiling some more. "I think Gus came by once or twice, but I never saw him working on the ship."

"Gus Watson?"

"Yeah." Tyrone lowered his voice. "Is that what this is about? You suspect Gus?"

"I can't comment on that." Chase set the record on Watson's desk. "Do you know a man named Lu Chin?"

"Sure, he works third shift."

"Was he here during the *Phoenix* inspection?"

Tyrone's eyes popped open. "Yes! Now that you mention it, he was. He talked to Tony, Tony Shaffer. I think he worked on the electronics. Didn't he sign the log?"

"No. There's no record of his presence here at all that day."

The interview continued for another half-hour. Chase went through the maintenance record in detail, trying to spark any additional points that Tyrone might have forgotten. He repeated the process with each tech in the log and again with Watson. Two other men, including Shaffer, confirmed Chin's presence. Shaffer had even left Chin working alone on the electronics panel for several minutes, long enough to have spliced the device into the control circuit, a procedure that Shaffer estimated would take no more than two minutes "if it was a simple plug-and-play installation."

Chase left Stellarfare confident that he'd determined the man, motive, means, and opportunity in the *Phoenix* murders. But it wasn't enough. He had to prove conspiracy to have any chance of stopping the war. There had to be a support structure behind Lu Chin, and Chase was determined to find it.

European president Peter Hunt entered the chamber with his vice president and best friend, Clinton Everhart. The meeting, a top-secret council to discuss war strategy, wasn't held in the Executive Mansion, where most presidential conferences took place. Instead, he conducted this business in the basement of an Intelligence Agency safe house, which had been certified secure from technical surveillance by Scott Lamm, the director of the agency himself, who also attended the meeting.

The room's plush gold carpeting and rich wood paneling were lost in shadow. The lights had been dimmed to illuminate little more than a narrow spot on the table's dark, cherry-wood surface before each chair. Arthur van Arsdel of the European Space Agency and Antonio Asabtino, director of the Defense Agency, were already present. No one else knew the president's whereabouts except the pair of bodyguards that had escorted Hunt and the vice president to the meeting. Coffee, tea, and pastries sat on a smaller table in the corner.

The men would be left alone for the duration, no matter how long the discussion might last.

Everhart took his seat, and the president, still standing, began without introductions. "As you know, the European Union has shared its knowledge of Chinese military satellites with the United States. In response to this information, and in response to recent provocative behavior by the People's Republic, the United States launched a squadron of military attack spacecraft and destroyed the illegal orbiters."

Everhart and van Arsdel shifted in their seats.

"In doing so," President Hunt continued, "the United States has put itself into a posture that could open the door to interplanetary conflict. The European Union has pledged its support to the US in that conflict. To do otherwise would send a message to China that it can take advantage of democratic attitudes toward peaceful prosperity."

Because the president needed the support of these men, he built his case carefully. "In return, the United States has shared their suspicions of a Russian space-weapons program. We have suspected for some time that they've been preparing for interplanetary conflict. It would be foolish of any nation with space technology to neglect such a program. What we lacked before — evidence that their program included a treaty violation — the US has now provided."

Now Lamm looked decidedly uncomfortable. Good. If he felt his agency had slipped up, he'd look for ways to recompense.

Hunt leaned over the table, bringing himself under the spotlight. "Because of the Russian plutonium, the Chinese armed satellites, and the US space fighters, the Union finds itself behind in the deployment of forces for the space-based conflict that is rapidly approaching." He fixed upon the eyes of each man in turn. "Now is the time to correct that deficiency."

His audience had been silent and attentive. The Space Agency director was the first to comment. "You're proposing that we launch our own armed satellites?"

"That's correct, Mr. van Arsdel. And what's more, I propose that we do so immediately."

"'Immediately' is a relative term when it comes to launching satellites into orbit," van Arsdel said.

"Especially if you don't want the worlds to know they're there," Lamm added.

"Of course, gentlemen." President Hunt waved away the comment. "I simply use the term to emphasize urgency. What I propose is to replace the payload, as discretely as possible, on the next several scheduled launches with Centurion satellites."

"That's still going to raise some eyebrows." Van Arsdel's voice betrayed alarm at the consequence of discovery. "There're some important payloads scheduled for those launches."

"Mr. President, may I speak freely?" Vice President Everhart said quietly.

"Of course, Clint." And then to the assembly, the president added, "Gentlemen, this is a monumental decision that will have far-reaching and long-term consequences. It must be considered carefully and debated candidly. We must all speak freely if we're to have a worthwhile discussion with a positive outcome." He turned his attention back to Everhart.

"Very well." Everhart leaned forward. "From what we know, the American-Chinese conflict has consisted only of an American attack on a few unmanned satellites — satellites that were illegal by international law. I'd hardly call that a full-scale interplanetary war."

"Don't forget the attacks on the Moon," Asabtino said.

"Attacks for which China denies involvement." A hint of exasperation tinted Everhart's voice. He took a slow breath before continuing. "The Chinese have lost their satellites, and with them the strength of their military position. It's entirely possible that they'll apologize for the treaty violation, Russia will deny the existence of nuclear weapons — which nobody can prove they have — the Americans will bring their warships home, and the whole political crisis will dissolve."

"I'm afraid I agree with the president," Asabtino said. "If the war continues, we'll need the Centurions in orbit. That's what they're for. If the crisis subsides ..." He shrugged.

"We'll be asked to destroy them," Everhart said, "or at least to return them to Earth."

"No, we won't." Hunt's statement brought all eyes back to him. "Because nobody's going to know they're there."

"You're going to keep this from the Americans?" Everhart blurted. "They requested our approval before they violated the treaty."

"But violate it they did." Hunt raised his voice. "And so did every other country that signed it."

Then he sat down and continued in a more even tone. "Clint, please understand. The Union has an opportunity here that we must exploit. In the event that the conflict continues, these satellites will be a tremendous asset to us as well as to our allies. If it doesn't, the other countries will either disarm their forces in space, or they won't." He spoke to his friend now, the rest of the assembly momentarily forgotten. "If they don't, we'll need our own weapons to maintain the balance necessary to encourage peace. If they do disarm, and if they're aware of the Centurions, they'll request that we do the same. And we will."

That assurance did much to ease the apprehension in Everhart's eyes.

"If they're not aware, the Union will retain a dominant military position after the conflict." President Hunt turned now to the others. "And that, gentlemen, is my ultimate objective."

Everhart was silent at last. He looked only at his pen.

The meeting continued long into the night while they worked out the details of the deployment plan.

The first satellite would launch within the month. Others would follow.

CHAPTER 19

Before Chase went to the meeting that afternoon, he stopped by the lab. He had to warn Michelle of what he planned to do and ask her not to challenge him on his decision. The arguments he was going to make weren't that strong, and he wasn't fully prepared to defend his position, so he didn't want a heated debate.

At the meeting, he announced his findings regarding Lu Chin's presence during the *Phoenix* inspection. "I have recorded statements from three witnesses who saw him there and one who says that Chin was left alone, working in the electronics cabinet, for more than enough time to have installed the device." He played the relevant portions of the recordings he'd made on his thinpad at the time of the interviews. "That gives us means and opportunity."

"What about motive?"

"The man's dead, Mike. We may never know what drove him. What's important is that he left behind falsified maintenance records to hide his activities while three eyewitnesses put him at the scene and working on the *Phoenix*. He also attacked me in my apartment to prevent our discovering the truth. There's no question that the man's guilty.

"What's more, I'd say that we now know how Forsythe came to be in the hangar on the night of the fire. He was probably attacked in his quarters with a pulse gun, as I was in mine, knocked out or killed, and then moved to the hangar. Stan, you said that you searched his quarters. Did you find his thinpad?"

Brower shook his head.

"That's what Mr. Chin and his friend were looking for. It would've contained any investigation notes he might have taken."

"Very clever," Brower muttered.

"How did Chin know Herrera would be on the *Phoenix*?" Mike asked.

"He might not have," Chase lied. "Not definitely, anyway. There was an awful lot of activity on that ship all of the sudden. Chin may have made the threat on Herrera's life to force a change of flights and then watched to see where the activity was." This is where Chase's argument fell apart. He'd pressed this line of reasoning with the Stellarfare maintenance techs. All had been told that the *Phoenix* had been selected by the NASA Safety Board for a random inspection. There was no fanfare around the event, and random safety inspections were required by all commercial starlines. None of the men working that day had perceived it to be at all exceptional.

Chase hadn't yet mentioned his conspiracy theory. That made his arguments now much more convincing than they might have been otherwise.

Mike seemed satisfied.

"Therefore — " Chase took another difficult breath — "I propose that we close the investigation. Over the next few days, I'll wrap up any loose ends and write the preliminary report, which we must all review and sign before we submit it to Snider. Comments?" He glanced at Michelle, who remained quiet. He took the others' silence for approval and adjourned the meeting.

Afterward, he returned to his apartment. What he'd just done had been a calculated move to buy himself time. He knew there were more people out there with a malicious hand in the unfolding events, and Michelle had warned him that they might include someone close to the investigation. Chase considered that to be a distinct possibility. It could be one of the investigation team, one of the lab techs, or a friend or colleague who received formal or informal updates. Hell, it could even be Snider, for that matter. The only person that he was sure he could trust was Michelle. She was the one who'd brought the conspiracy to his attention. And that's the one thing the perpetrator would never do.

It was just as likely, however, that the attack in his apartment had been prompted by O'Leary's inquiries. Chase had no way of knowing at this point. Either way, disbanding the team on the pretense of completion seemed the best way to ensure his own safety while he continued to investigate alone.

Tying up loose ends for the report was a sufficient facade for him to pursue the one lead he had left.

~(O)~

The thrusters fired and the *Snow Leopard* eased into orbit. Dana waited for Lunar Alpha to clear the horizon before deploying her reflector plates and switching her comm to the control frequency. "Alpha tower, *Snow Leopard* requesting approach. Priority one. Repeat, priority one. Over."

"Alpha tower to *Snow Leopard*, please stand by. Over."

Dana was incensed. "Tower, this is *Snow Leopard*. Are you listening? I said this is priority one. Acknowledge!"

The controller remained calm, her voice steady. "Acknowledged, *Snow Leopard*. Priority one. We didn't know you were coming. The landing pad is full. We're clearing a site for you now."

Alpha was large enough to accommodate twenty-five ships the size of the *Snow Leopard*. Dana had never known there to be more than half that number on the pad at any one time. But it was a civilian base. They weren't privy to the details, or even the existence, of the CATS mission. "*Snow Leopard* to tower, what is your situation? Over."

"I'm sorry, *Snow Leopard*. Evacuation activities are clogging our facilities. All routine flights have been canceled."

"Alpha Base is being evacuated? Confirm."

"Negative. Americans are being evacuated from Chinese lunar facilities *to* Alpha. I'm sending orbit parameters now, *Snow Leopard*. Recommend that you circle once. We should have room for you on your next approach. Alternatively, I can send a vector for a landing beyond the base — we can spare a transport to pick you up from there. But if you want a spot on the blacktop, you'll have to wait. I'm afraid that's the best we can do."

Dana considered her options. They'd be on the ground sooner if she accepted the immediate approach. But it'd probably take a day or more to move the *Snow Leopard* from there to the hangar, which would expose the ship to observation by enemy satellites. On the other hand, she saw no immediate risk in waiting for base personnel to clear a landing site. "Thank you, tower. We'll take the trip and see you on the next pass. Be advised, you'll need to clear three sites."

"Copy, *Snow Leopard*. We'll make room for you. Tower out."

The *Cougar* must have been mere minutes behind. As soon as Dana concluded her conversation, Captain Gabaldon called in. "*Cougar* to Alpha, we've been advised of your situation and request a priority-one approach vector."

"Tower to *Cougar*, we're sending orbit parameters. We'll bring you in on your next approach."

"Copy, tower. *Cougar* out."

Lunar Alpha came back over the horizon three-and-a-half hours later. Lieutenant Miller received an approach vector and rotated the ship in preparation for their de-orbit burn. The seat pressed into Dana's back as the ship slowed and the lunar gravity began to pull them toward the surface.

The servos hummed as Miller reoriented the thruster nozzles for landing. "Did you see that?"

"What?" Dana asked.

"There!" Miller pointed. A flash of light passed the windshield, followed by another.

"Orbiting debris," Allistair said.

"No," Dana corrected.

⁂

"Approach vector received," the pilot of the *Cougar* said over his shoulder. Gabaldon opened the comm to relay receipt to the control tower.

Suddenly, the weapons console exploded. Pieces flew past the gunner toward a hole the size of a man's fist that had appeared in the ship's hull. "What the fuck was that?" Gabaldon yelled. "Marcus, you all right?" Air rushed out the breach. Their pressure suits sustained them.

"Delaney! Thrust, now!" Gabaldon shouted over the whistle as the last of their air escaped into space.

A second missile smashed through the durapane and caught Delaney square in the chest. The exploding shell turned his torso to paste within the shreds of his pressure suit. The flow of air from his O_2 tank sprayed a fine red mist across the cracked remains of the windshield.

"Shit!" Gabaldon keyed the mike and spoke on the traffic-control channel, partly because he was already on it, and partly because he knew the other CATS were monitoring it. "All units, evasive maneuvers! We're under fire — "

A third missile struck the port fuel tank and that side of the ship disappeared in a ball of flame and debris. In Gabaldon's last moments, he drifted away from his shattered ship, still harnessed to his seat. Shards of durapane, plastic, and steel protruded through the pressure suit into his broken body.

⁂

"Evasive descent, Lieutenant." Without knowing where the shots were coming from, Dana had no way to return fire. She could only hope the enemy wasn't close enough to correct, real-time, for rapid changes in trajectory.

"Aye, sir," Miller said. "That'll bring us off our assigned approach."

"Can't be helped. You'll have to compensate manually." A difficult task. He'd have to land the ship, traveling over three thousand kilometers per hour, on a thirty–meter-square patch of ground on a surface revolving at four hundred kilometers per hour.

The *Snow Leopard*, oriented horizontally with the main thrusters pointed at the surface, obstructed Miller's view of the ground below, so he used a vid-scan image of the landscape to guide the ship down.

Gabaldon's transmission came over the comm, and a brief flash lit the distant sky.

"Get this thing on the ground," Dana said.

The base appeared below them and Miller matched their speed to the revolution of the Moon. But they were coming in too fast. The area cleared for landing looked to be the size of a data card. And it was supposed to be large enough to land three ships.

Miller fired the thrusters on full burn, trying to slow their descent. The fuel gauge plummeted toward empty. They were close enough now to make out the people below. Some just stared at the approaching ship. The wise ones ran for cover. Dana looked back and forth among the fuel gauge, their velocity, and the landing pad. It was going to be close.

~(O)~

Bill Ryan was beyond the horizon and missed Gabaldon's final message. So he braked into a standard orbit, deployed his reflectors, and waited for the base to come into line for clear communications.

An explosion rocked the ship and spun it out of control, off its trajectory, and toward the surface.

"Abrams, stabilize. Townsend, what happened?" Bill began a mental inventory of the possibilities and options. Malfunction or attack. Those were the possibilities – most likely the former, but he wouldn't make that assumption. Cabin pressure was holding steady, but options were limited. The *Puma* had only two missiles left, and no decoy buoys.

"Sir," Townsend said, "it looks like we lost O_2 tank four. The gauge is reading empty and half my electronics are out."

"I've got flashing lights all over the place," Abrams added. Buzzers and alarms sounded from every station.

"I need status reports, system by system. Disengage reflectors. And drop a missile, zero thrust. It'll act as a radar decoy." The ship tumbled toward the surface. The giant scar of the helium mine passed before the window and disappeared from view, replaced by the stars. "Abrams, can you stabilize?"

"Yes," he shouted over the noise, "if I do nothing else."

Bill keyed the comm. He should be able to raise Alpha by now. "*Puma* to Lunar Alpha. Mayday. Mayday. We are requesting an emergency landing. Acknowledge. Over."

The channel hissed static in reply.

"Negative on the missile release," Townsend said. "Weapons remote is down."

The tumbling motion of the ship began to slow. Bill tried the comm again. "*Puma* to Alpha control, do you read? Over."

Static.

Abrams began to wrestle the ship into obedience as Bill tried two more times to reach the base.

Still static.

"Communications down. Navigation down," Townsend reported.

Bill didn't think consciously. He'd seen every conceivable scenario in the simulator, over and over again. Today felt no different. His mind was on autopilot. Status, options, action, status again — all automatic.

The *Puma* settled into a stable flight orientation.

"Excellent," Bill said. "Now give me altitude. Townsend, get back and release both warheads manually. I don't want the munitions on board if we hit the ground."

Cabin pressure remained steady.

The navigation control terminal was live, but the flashing status light signaled an unknown state. Bill started a vid-scan of the surface below. The computer would capture a series of images, compare the scans with a database of lunar surface features, and calculate their current orbit. The entire process was supposed to take about three seconds.

The screen came back with a system error.

Bill didn't bother to look up the failure code. Instead, he reached for the lunar atlas in the pocket beside his seat, grateful that regulations required ships to carry such paper documents along with procedures manuals so they'd have some resources in the event of a total electrical failure. He hoped to determine their location from the landmarks below.

Once he pinpointed their position, he gave it to the pilot, who took the maps and began calculating their speed and direction based on the rate at which the features passed by. Knowing the ship's mass, Abrams could then perform a fuel consumption calculation.

Status. Options. Action.

Townsend returned from the crawlspace. "Munitions separated, sir."

Abrams completed his calculations and turned to face the commander.

"What've you got?" Bill asked.

"The good news is we're still in line for Alpha Base."

"And the bad?"

"We have two choices. I can keep us off the ground until we reach the base, but with no fuel left to slow us down when we get there, or we can slow down now and land in the middle of nowhere, between here and the base."

"With no chance of rescue before our air runs out."

"Pretty much," Abrams conceded.

So much for options. "How fast are we going?"

"About forty-five hundred kilometers an hour."

~(O)~

The *Snow Leopard* slammed down within the space provided on the blacktop. The port side gave a little more than it should've, but they were down.

"Oh, I bet that broke something," Allistair groaned.

Dana wasted no time in heading for the hatch. Bill was still out there somewhere. "Everybody's suit sealed?" She barely waited for an answer before she popped the door seal and rushed outside.

By the time she reached the bottom of the ladder, a truck waited to take them to the compound. Together, they hopped on the back and grabbed the handrail. When she signaled thumbs-up, the driver kicked the truck into gear and they sped across the landing pad.

Dana had never seen such activity at the base before. Shuttle busses unloaded refugees from passenger and freight ships alike. They rolled up to each ship, latched the docking collar, pressurized the tube, and hustled everybody off just as quickly as the operation could be managed. Fueling trucks, maintenance rigs, and tugs shuffled back and forth in a chaotic dance from one end of the platform to the other. Crewmen and other workers bounded across their path. It was amazing that nobody had been clobbered in the confusion.

They passed the air force tug on its way to the *Snow Leopard*. Dana smiled and shook her head. A path large enough to accommodate the CATS had somehow been cleared. The stealth machine would be under cover within the hour.

The truck drove straight into the hangar and across to the airlock. Dana and her crew climbed down, cycled the door, and stepped in. Air hissed into the small compartment and the fabric of their suits draped onto them as the pressure equalized. When the lock on the inner door popped and the status light shone green, she stepped into the dressing chamber beyond, where they shed their EVA gear and hung it on the racks provided.

The three propelled themselves, hand-over-hand, along the railing that edged the crowded halls of the station. At one point, Dana knocked down a young mother laden with belongings and a small boy, who trailed behind and complained of hunger. Dana mumbled an apology and hurried on her way. When she reached the traffic-control tower, a guard tried to stop her at the door, but she forced her way past into the control room.

The place was packed. Controllers occupied eight of the ten stations and each monitor seemed to display a different image. The hologram showed the Moon in the center of a swarm of different-colored dots, each accompanied by a call number or other ID designator. Most of the terminals had at least one person watching over the controller's shoulder while several others, whose function she couldn't guess, milled among the aisles. All were civilians.

If this had been a military base, the CATS would've been on the ground and under cover by now. But it wasn't. By the Outer Space Treaty, it couldn't be.

Director Snider, standing behind a terminal to Dana's left, turned when the guards protested her entrance. "Come in, Captain," he said politely before addressing the guard. "It's all right. They can stay."

He glanced back at Dana. "These ships of yours are causing an awful lot of confusion. We've got blips flashing on and off the screens all over the place. And we're holding all the incoming evacuation traffic while we sort it out. Maybe you can tell us what's going on up there."

"China's got a satellite taking pot shots at us. That's what's happening." Dana followed Snider to a terminal operated by a young black man.

The controller looked up as they approached. "We can't see your ships on the scope. You said there're three of you?"

When Dana thought of Gabaldon's message and the flash in the sky, she clenched her fist and vowed to keep the tears from welling in her eyes. She'd never been in combat before, had never lost a friend to enemy fire, and she struggled to keep her voice calm. "There were."

"Pad's clear for the other priority-one, sir," a female controller announced from across the room.

Dana took a few steps so she could see the video image of the landing pad on the woman's terminal. A tug pushed the *Snow Leopard* toward the hangar. A picture-in-picture box showed a graphic of the entire field with occupied sites shaded in red. Four adjacent slots flashed green, probably for the air force landings. She turned her attention back to the nearer display.

"I'd like to replay some of the images we saw earlier," Snider said.

"You said there was another priority-one?" Dana asked.

"That's right. The *Cougar*."

Her heart became a rock in her stomach. "Have you heard from the *Puma*?"

Snider looked inquiringly at the young man in front of the terminal.

"No, sir."

Dana bit her lip. It had been at least four hours since her first comm. Bill shouldn't be that far behind. The very real possibility of disaster threatened to overwhelm her. She couldn't stand not knowing. But the tower hadn't heard from him, so she asked about Gabaldon. "What do you know about the *Cougar*?"

"We got this." The controller played back Gabaldon's last, frantic message. "Nothing since."

Dana's mind tried to take it all in, to digest it.

"I'd like to play back some images for you," Snider said again.

Dana gave a tired nod, still distracted by unfamiliar thoughts and emotions.

"Go ahead, Robinson," Snider prompted.

The controller typed a series of keystrokes and the display went dark except for a single blip with no ID code. "I'll superimpose the audio."

Gabaldon's message played again. Then the blip grew larger and split into separate, diverging markers. The image changed to a two-D representation of the main hologram. Robinson pointed to a cluster of white markers toward the left-hand side of the screen. "That's those markers now."

"The *Cougar*." Dana's voice caught in her throat. "We saw the explosion. Anything else?"

"Just this." The display changed again. The lunar surface showed as a band of gray at the bottom of the picture. A blip appeared in the center of the screen, diverged into two dots, both moving toward the surface. About halfway to the gray band, they vanished. "That's where they went below our radar horizon," Robinson said. "But it's pretty clear that those objects hit the surface."

"You think that's your other ship?" Snider asked.

Robinson reset the display. "Whatever they were, they were pretty small."

"Or large, with a low radar cross-section," Allistair said from behind Dana. "What was the time difference between the two images?"

"Twenty-eight minutes. This one just before you got here."

"And where were they located?" Dana asked.

The display changed to match the hologram again. Robinson pointed out two locations on the chart. "Here. And here."

"Too far apart to have come from the same ship," Allistair observed.

Dana's mind was slow to accept the implications, but there was no other explanation. "Yes, I think that was our other ship. But suppose it wasn't." She had to hope. "How long can you maintain a holding pattern for them?"

Snider checked his watch. "We passed the evacuation deadline a little over an hour ago. Anybody up there now is incoming with whoever they could get." He shrugged. "I can hold them up there for as long as we need to. Besides, it'll give us a chance to catch up and clear some of the landing pad. We mixed things up pretty good, making room for you guys."

"Well, we appreciate it. Can you keep the space clear for the next six hours? That'll give them time to orbit at least once if they're out there. We might hear from them by then."

"If there's a chance they're still alive," Snider said, "then they deserve every effort we can make to help them. In the meantime, Robinson, try to raise the *Puma* on the comm."

Dana moved to the window and looked down at the bustle of activity on the launch pad. The *Snow Leopard* looked small and fragile from up here as it disappeared into the hangar. Her gaze drifted out over the horizon to the stars and she started to cry.

Johnny Miller put a reassuring hand on her shoulder, gave her a cup of coffee, and said nothing. He didn't tell her that they could be wrong. He didn't promise that Bill was all right.

Dana held the cup dumbly before her. "I never told him that I loved him."

Chapter 20

Not enough fuel to keep the *Puma* aloft until they reached Lunar Alpha and to slow the ship once it arrived, Abrams had said. Well, fuel consumption in either case depended heavily on the ship's mass. Bill looked at Townsend. "Feel like going for a walk?"

"Sure."

"Good." He held up a power wrench in his gloved hand. "Grab your tools. We need to lighten the load."

They each checked the state of their pressure suit and harness. Then Bill triggered the exploding bolts on the cockpit door and the cabin pressure blew the plate away. In the next three seconds, everything that wasn't tied down was sucked into space. "Abrams, jettison any consumables we don't need. Transfer the fuel into one tank, if it's not already. And if we don't need more than one O_2 can, ditch the rest. Then go through the cabin and throw anything that's not essential out that hole." He pointed. "Got it?"

The pilot nodded. "Hold on, I'll do a nice long burn to give us some altitude. Then I can let it coast for a while."

That done, Abrams eased the ship into a nose-forward attitude.

Bill and Townsend each donned a belt with a retractable life line attached at each hip, hooked a line to the handrail beside the door, and made their way outside. The design characteristics that gave the *Puma* its stealth body-shape didn't allow protruding handholds or railings, but a few recessed hooks could be accessed by manually sliding the cover panels.

Bill made his way back along the top of the wing. A fuel tank and two oxygen bottles separated from the tail end of the ship and drifted away. Bill reached the back of the wing and examined the damage. "My God," he whispered into his helmet microphone. There was no doubt now. They'd been hit by an enemy shell.

Dana came unbidden to his mind. She should be on the ground by now, but approach protocol would have required her to deploy her reflector plates to make herself visible to Lunar Alpha radar.

And to the enemy.

"Holy shit!" Townsend said when he saw the damage from his side. "Thank God for redundant systems."

"Amen to that. Come on, we don't have much time."

The *Puma*'s wingspan was well over twice its length. As such, the wings constituted a large percentage of the vehicle's mass. Fortunately, the ship's design allowed removal of the wings for separate storage in hangars too small to accommodate a fully assembled CATS. Each attached to the body by four staunch bolts.

Bill clipped a second life line to a hook at the back of the ship, then took up the slack and set the tension with the retracting spools. He touched the end of his power wrench to the head of the first bolt and set the torsion lock. The bolt was stuck fast.

Townsend removed two bolts from his side and went on to the third.

When Bill stripped the bolt head, he gave up on the stubborn pin. He loosened the tension in his cables and moved forward to the next one in line. Within minutes, Townsend dropped the port wing and it drifted away.

All the while, discarded instrument consoles, tool chests, and other equipment flew past from the cockpit.

Then Abram's voice came over the comm. "Hang on, guys, I've got to burn." The ship's thrusters rotated to the nozzle-down position and the rockets fired. Bill slammed against the fuselage when the ship jumped in altitude.

"That's going to hurt in the morning," Townsend said. All the loose debris that had been coasting with them disappeared below.

Returning to the task at hand, Bill removed the next-to-last bolt from the starboard wing, fit a drill bit to his power wrench, and made his way back to the stubborn rear bolt. He worked it for several minutes while Townsend removed and discarded the communications gear.

Then it was time for another burn. Bill grabbed a handhold and braced himself for the maneuver. But when the ship shot up, it smashed him against the hull again. The drill flew from his hand and struck his helmet like a sledge. But the wing sheered the damaged bolt and broke free.

The thrust stopped and Bill reoriented himself. His mind and body froze as he stared at a single chip that had been knocked from his faceplate.

"Hey, Major. You okay?" Townsend asked over the comm.

That simple question got Bill breathing again. He *was* okay, at least for the moment. He was alive, at any rate. His suit-integrity light shone green and no cracks spread from the chip.

He forced his eyes from the blemish and made his way back to the cockpit.

By now, the crew compartment was almost completely bare. The control panels, terminals and wiring for the weapons, navigation, and communication systems had been ripped out and discarded, along with the spare passenger seat, the machine guns, ammunition crates, and any personal belongings. "That's everything," Abrams said. They no longer knew the mass of the ship, so a new set of fuel calculations was impossible. "Let's hope it's enough."

⁂

Three-and-a-half hours into Dana's vigil, she was sitting in a seat near the window of the control room beside a cold cup of coffee and staring at the stars beyond the pane. Ground crews had managed to clear a substantial portion of the landing field. Any ships that could be moved had been, although about half of the spaces remained occupied. Snider had ordered all maintenance crews and other ground personnel to clear the field and take a break. They'd be needed soon enough when Snider began landing the dozens of ships still waiting in orbit.

Her mind numb and her eyes bleary from unshed tears, Dana didn't notice the new star that appeared in the sky until its brightness grew unmistakable. "Oh my God," she breathed, rising to her feet. The ship was coming in way too fast, ass-end first, fifty meters off the ground, with thrusters firing full throttle. It approached the landing field like a bullet. Its dark exterior told her that it was a stealth ship, or what was left of one. Otherwise, it was unrecognizable.

Suddenly the thrusters cut out, flared again, sputtered, and then died. They'd run out of fuel.

The ship touched ground about half a kilometer to the far side of the landing pad. It skidded in the dust, slowed rapidly, and left a long, shallow trench in its wake until it hit the edge of the blacktop. Then it bounded upward and tumbled end-over-end across the pad like a football bouncing into the end zone, wiping out a half-dozen parked ships in the process. Dana's breath caught when the *Puma* took a bounce toward the tower. But the ship tumbled to the side and came down with a crunch onto a section of the habitat wall. A shudder reverberated through the tower when it hit the base.

~(O)~

When Chase was lying in his hospital bed discussing Lu Chin's gun with Brower, he remembered something that had fallen through the cracks in the investigation. So the morning after his release, he made his way to the forensics lab to follow up.

Unlike the materials lab, the forensics lab consisted mainly of scanning microscopes and data terminals, each connected to a vast database of substances and biometric information that could be compared to a forensic sample. Only one tech was present, a kid in his twenties with a crew cut and glasses so thick that the image of his eyes filled the frames. The kid clicked off the terminal he was using and jumped to his feet when Chase walked in. His lab coat hung from him like draperies, as though he couldn't find one small enough to fit his gaunt frame. Bags and wrappers from the nearest food-vend, some of them probably weeks old, cluttered every working surface. And the equipment appeared to be in a state of borderline repair. Lunar Alpha just didn't have enough work to support the lab. Chase was lucky he'd caught anyone there at all.

"Do you have the fingerprint scans we collected from the *Phoenix*?" Chased asked.

"Sure." The tech was one of two who'd helped with the initial reconstruction.

"Where are they now?"

"On file."

"You identify them?"

"No." The tech frowned. "Once we got pulled from the case we were never asked to pursue the matter."

Chase wasn't surprised. He, one Soaring engineer, and the techs were the only ones aware that the prints had been taken. And Chase had had too much on his mind to recall them. "Well, I'm pursuing it now." He handed the tech a data card. "This contains two lists of names" — the same lists he'd been working with. "Compare the prints from the *Phoenix* with those on file for each person in the lists."

"Piece of cake." The tech wiped his hands on the front of his lab coat before taking the card. "I should have something by this afternoon."

"Excellent. In the meantime, don't tell anyone, on or off the investigation team, what you're working on." He gave the tech a stern look.

"You're the boss."

Dana paced back and forth across the carpeted waiting area outside the base trauma center, where the survivors of the *Puma* had been taken. The elongated strides of lunar-g failed to satisfy her sense of urgency. They were too slow, just like the doctors and the hospital staff, and she couldn't fit enough of them between one bulkhead and the other.

Cory Abrams, the pilot and the man most responsible for getting the *Puma* back to Alpha Base, had been dead on arrival. Duane Townsend sustained minor injuries and was listed in satisfactory condition. Dana and her crew had visited him briefly, but he had little memory of the events that had taken place.

Bill was an unknown, alive when he was recovered from the wreckage but now in critical condition. He'd been rushed into surgery with numerous shattered bones and massive internal bleeding. By now, he'd been in the operating room for nine hours and all the hospital staff could say was, "It's too early to tell."

Miraculously, there were no other casualties, either on the landing field or in the base proper. The hangar breached by the collision had been vacated when Snider ordered the ground crews to rest up for the next wave.

While Dana waited, her crewmates sat in a pair of plastic chairs nearby and newsblips played on the monitor in one corner of the room. The big story on the American network, of course, was the brutal attack by China on the American space fighters. The attack had come from an armed satellite in orbit around the Moon, the reporter speculated, but nobody knew which Chinese satellite, or whether there was more than one.

Finally, Bill's doctor emerged from the surgical wing wearing a white smock that looked like it had never been worn before. He was an angel or an apparition, his face devoid of any emotion that might reveal the state of his patient. Dana might have imagined him. Nonetheless, she rushed forward.

"His condition has stabilized," the surgeon said when she came to a stop before him.

Dana breathed a sigh. Her hands clenched the front of her flight suit in an effort to contain her relief.

"But the damage is substantial," the doctor continued before Dana could find her voice. "The patient's resting. He may regain consciousness in a few hours, or he may never regain consciousness at all."

He'll make it, Dana told herself over a wave of panic. *Bill's a fighter. He has to make it.* "May I see him?"

The surgeon glanced at the men seated behind her. "Only one visitor, for now. And only for ten minutes."

"You go ahead, Dana," Miller offered. "You're closer to him than we are."

Allistair nodded his agreement.

"Thanks, guys." She followed the doctor to Bill's room and tried not to imagine what he'd look like.

Her breath caught when she saw him. Tubes and wires ran everywhere, from his arm, mouth, nose, chest, and several from beneath a blanket that had been pulled down to his waist. Each connected him to equipment in his headboard.

Meaningless numbers and graphics lit the display. She heard the hollow pump and hiss of a respirator and a series of beeps with the rhythm of a steady heart, but she'd cautioned herself against false hope for too many hours to draw encouragement from the disembodied sounds.

Bill himself looked small and fragile, his face clean and undamaged, his hair disheveled. Bandages wrapped his ribs as if they'd been broken. Splints bound his left arm and both legs. And a dermaplast closure crossed his abdomen from below his navel up under the bandages on his chest. They hadn't put a gown on him. Why would they? He wouldn't be up and about for some time and they'd need to clean and tend his injuries.

"I'll be done here in a minute," the nurse said.

Dana stopped in the doorway to wait.

When the nurse completed her exam, she pulled the blanket up to Bill's neck and keyed several commands into the computer that sustained him. "You may see him now."

Dana crossed to the bed and laid a hand, and then a kiss, gently on his forehead. She didn't know how she was supposed to act or what she was supposed to say, but it was apparent that the nurse wouldn't leave them alone. So she tried to forget the woman's presence, lowered herself to Bill's bedside, and ran her fingers through his hair. Her other hand found his beneath the covers and held it.

She sat in silence and stared at his relaxed features for fifteen minutes before the nurse put a hand on her shoulder. "It's time."

Dana stood and leaned over the bed. "You come back to me, Bill Ryan." She kissed his lips, wiped the tears from her eyes, and walked quietly from the room.

Chase stopped by the forensics lab again that afternoon, hoping that the prints would lead him to Lu Chin's accomplice. He needed this case to be over. He'd been away from Erin too long already.

The tech had cleaned up some of the trash and changed his lab coat. "We scanned two sets of prints from the device and several from inside the cabinet. Based on the breakdown of fats left in the prints by human sweat, the ones on the board were about two weeks old at the time the scans were taken. The others varied from two weeks to indeterminate."

"Let's focus on the device itself. Did you find a match for those?"

"One of them. Lu Chin."

Chase nodded. "And the other?"

"No match."

"No match to anyone on the lists?"

"No match, period. When I didn't find a match on the lists, I expanded the search to all Lunar Alpha residents. Still no go, so I submitted the request to the International Space Consortium database. Anyone who's ever left Earth should have prints in that database."

"And?"

The tech grunted. "Nothing. Zippo."

"Then the other person who touched the device is still on Earth," Chase concluded.

"Unlikely. The prints were the same age as those of Lu Chin's, though Chin's were on top."

"Hmmm." That was important, but Chase wasn't sure what to do with it. "What about the prints in the cabinet?"

"Anthony Shaffer and Andrew Torres."

Chase recognized the names from the *Phoenix* maintenance logs. But without their fingerprints on the device, there was nothing to suggest they'd done anything more than legitimate maintenance work. "Nobody from the other list showed up at all?"

The tech shook his head.

"Then I'm back at square one. Thanks for your help." Chase stood and made his way to the door.

"Sir," the tech called after him. "I did notice one thing I thought was rather strange. One of the names didn't have any prints in the local files."

Chase waited.

"Well, like I said, I thought it was strange, so I checked the international database, and they weren't there either."

"You're saying that somebody managed to catch a shuttle from Earth without getting his fingerprints taken."

"Yes, sir. Either that or they've been removed from the records since."

Chase frowned. "Frank Lesperance?"

"No." A long pause. And then, "Stanley Brower."

CHAPTER 21

Somebody had left prints on the sabotage chip, somebody on the Moon whose prints couldn't be matched to the database. And Brower's prints weren't in the database. Coincidence? Perhaps. It all depended on why Brower's prints were missing. The records may simply have been lost, but it was suspicious enough to warrant follow-up.

Chase arrived in the NASA records and data management office a few minutes later. It was the only part of the base besides the fusion power generator that was located below the Moon's surface. He flashed his credentials to the receptionist and then to the records custodian. "I need to see any and all records for Stanley H. Brower, starting with his employment application and date of hire."

The custodian, a frumpy redhead who wore her jumpsuit like a pair of sweats, sat down at a data terminal and typed a few commands. Beyond her lay the network vault, the core of the base's computing system. When a picture of the security chief appeared on the screen in front of the custodian, she scrolled down to the first few text lines of the file. "He started work eight months ago."

That seemed right. Brower had been on Alpha for only a little while. A year or less, he would've guessed. "What about his application?"

"What do you want to know?"

"Hmmmmm." He was fishing, not sure what he'd catch. "How about prior work experience? Previous employers, that sort of thing."

She scrolled down. "That's odd."

"What?"

"It just says, 'Government service' and some dates. Nothing specific."

"What are the dates?"

"June, twenty years ago, to present. That was in August of last year, according to the application date."

"Twenty years," Chase noted. "He'd have been retiring from service at that time. The question is, what kind of service and what government agency?"

"Let's try — " She tapped some more. "Huh."

"What?"

"His application includes a link to a resume, but there's no file attached."

"Deleted?"

"Must have been."

"Well, well, Mr. Brower," he said out loud. One lost record was one thing. But two, in independent databases, managed by separate organizations ... that was too much to be coincidence. Furthermore, Brower was involved in the case and had access to Security's weapons stores. He could've easily arranged the attack in Chase's apartment. "Thank you," he told the custodian. "You've been very helpful. If I need anything else, I'll holler."

Chase went straight to Snider's office.

"He's gone for the day," the admin said. "He was pretty wiped after the vigil he pulled in the tower during the evacs."

Chase thanked the girl and headed for Snider's apartment, sickened by his own thoughts. He respected Stan. And though the events of the past few weeks had leeched any semblance of friendship out of their association, Chase wouldn't have thought him capable of these crimes. Yet Brower's guilt would put a number of disturbing pieces together. He was the link to the other list, he knew of Herrera's flight plans, and he could have worked with Lu Chin to sabotage the *Phoenix*. But where did Brower get the chip? Who developed it? Who manufactured it? And Why was Brower involved at all?

The questions stayed in his mind as he buzzed Snider's apartment.

"Come in, Morgan." Snider stepped aside. "I'm surprised to see you here. Can I get you something to drink?"

"Is there someplace we can talk?"

"Sure." He led Chase into his study and closed the door. "What's up?"

"You already know that it was Lu Chin who sabotaged the *Phoenix*. I confirmed that today with fingerprints pulled from the chip. And I now know who provided it to Chin and told him which ship to plant it on."

"Who?"

"Your security chief."

"Brower?" He looked shocked. "Do you have proof?"

"Yes. His fingerprints were also on the chip — the only other prints found there." Chase was hedging a little here. He didn't actually know that they were Brower's prints, but by a process of elimination, they must be. Anyway, he'd verify his guess after he had the man in custody.

"Could they have gotten there after the incident, during the investigation phase?" Snider asked.

"Chin's prints were on top of Brower's." He gave Snider time to absorb the news before continuing. "I have to arrest him, but it's an awkward situation. The guards I need to make the arrest all work for him."

"And he works for me."

"That's why I'm here."

Snider paused. "I'll tell you what. As of right now, Brower is on administrative leave. That means Deputy Chief Cordova reports directly to me. I'll issue a directive to take Brower into custody, but only for questioning. Take Cordova and two of the National Guard troops with you. They've been ordered to work with us on any security issue, but they report to Cottington, so they won't have any personal ties or reporting issues to complicate the arrest. Cordova's presence and my administrative-leave order will give you the authority."

"Thank you, sir."

"But, Morgan, if you don't have sufficient grounds for the DA to press charges within twenty-four hours, I'll release him on his own recognizance and confine him to the base. You hear me?"

Just then, Mrs. Snider poked her head into the study. "Excuse me for interrupting, Jack. You have an urgent comm."

Snider keyed the terminal on his desk.

It was Cordova, looking much distressed. "Sorry to bother you, Director, but I thought you'd want to be notified right away."

"About what?"

"About Chief Brower, sir." He spoke quickly. "I got a report that he and others have seized the ERT staging area. They're armed, sir, and shots have been fired. I'm organizing a response now."

"Are you sure Brower's with them?"

"If the reports are right, he's leading them."

~(O)~

Chase and Snider arrived at the staging bay a few minutes later.

Cordova, already there with a team of security guards and military troops, was looking through a window into the hangar.

"What's the situation?" Chase asked.

"It looks like they've cleared out and taken one of the transports with them."

That made sense. They were the fastest vehicles available over rough terrain; they had incredible range and emergency rations; they were always stocked, fueled and ready to go; and they were simple enough that anybody could drive one. Brower could get to any one of a half-dozen bases from there.

Chase looked through the portal in the airlock door. The bay was small, as hangars go, with a variety of crates and boxes stacked on the near side. At the far end sat the other ERT transport, identical to the one Brower had stolen. Stretchers and other first-aid and medical gear lined one wall. Beyond the transport lay the ERT administration office, accessible only from the hangar. The bay was unoccupied.

"This wasn't an impromptu escape plan." Chase turned from the window. "They had this worked out ahead of time. What doesn't make sense is that they left the second transport behind. It's the only thing that can catch them, so why leave it for us?"

"Maybe it's been disabled," Cordova said.

"Or booby-trapped," added one of the soldiers.

Snider looked at Chase. "It's your show. How do you want to proceed?"

"We can't let him get wherever he's going. We need that truck." He turned to the senior National Guardsman, Lieutenant Cottington, and poked a thumb over his shoulder at the transport. "Are any of your men qualified to inspect that thing for booby traps?"

"Sure," Cottington said. "They all are."

Chase turned to Cordova. "How many men are with him?"

Cordova shook his head. "We just got here."

"Hostages?"

"I assume so. He either killed the witnesses, took them with him, or locked them in the office."

Chase took a long look into the bay. He was still missing something. It still didn't add up. There was some connection, some thread of evidence, channel of communication, or chain of events that he knew nothing about, except that it existed and that it eluded him at every turn. "Okay." He pressed a panel on the wall and both airlock doors slid open. "Let's go find out."

"Perhaps you should let us go first, sir." Cottington selected two of his men. "Someone may still be in there." Together, the men proceeded through the airlock and checked the walls just inside the door for a hidden ambush. Then they stepped into the bay and moved cautiously past the supply crates. Two soldiers followed the first.

Chase and Cordova moved in behind. Their footsteps echoed over the hum of the air handler, giving the bay a hollow, vacant sound. The sick scent of hemoglobin hung in the air. Just past the crates, the body of a medtech sprawled facedown in a pool of her own blood.

Shots rang out and the first two soldiers went down. The two behind, along with Chase and Cordova, dove for the cover of the supply crates. One of the victims tried to crawl to cover. The other lay on his back, motionless, with three holes in his chest.

Adrenaline and rage percolated in Chase's blood.

"Cover me," the soldier nearest Cordova yelled.

The woman beside Chase clicked her rifle into automatic and sent a spray of ammunition across the bay. Chase had seen muzzle flashes between the tread gears of the transport. The woman aimed her rifle there, raked back and forth along the length of the tread, and forced the snipers into cover of their own.

The man near Cordova pulled his wounded buddy, who'd been shot in the shoulder and side, behind the barricade. "Live rounds."

"No shit," cracked the wounded man. He choked on the words, then coughed blood into his hand.

"What are you using?" Cordova asked one of the soldiers.

"Rubber. Nonlethal, except in the head, and they won't shatter the habitat windows. But they'll incapacitate a man with a single shot if he's not wearing body armor."

"Let's back off," Chase said. "We have no idea what we're up against."

The woman sent another volley of covering fire over the barricade and they retreated to the safety of the corridor.

Once the wounded man was out, medtechs rushed him to the base infirmary.

"Now we know why the other transport is still here. Can you lock the bay doors?" Chase asked Cordova.

"Already have. They require a security access code, which we've changed so they can't use Brower's." He waved a hand at the hangar. "Those guys aren't going anywhere."

"The security scanners working in there?" Chase asked.

"Let's find out." Cordova keyed the central control room on his portable link. "They're still on," he said a few minutes later. "I've asked the controller to pan each scanner in sequence and feed the vid-file here." He tapped the display on his thinpad.

"How many scanners?"

"Two in the hangar, one in the office."

They gathered around to watch each scanner make its sweep. The first, mounted along the same wall as the door, revealed nothing more than what they'd seen already. The second, located in the opposite corner, showed the far side of the transport and the closed office door. There was no one in sight.

The third scanner showed an armed Asian standing guard over four hostages in the office. "We'll need to neutralize him before we proceed," Chase said.

"Is there any other way into that room?" Snider asked no one in particular.

"Sure," Cordova said. "Through the air handler. There should be a vent somewhere in the ceiling."

They spent the next thirty minutes developing an assault strategy and getting a soldier into position over the office. The one chosen for the task was the smallest one present, identified by her uniform as Private Sena, the woman who'd accompanied them into the hangar.

Meanwhile, Brower was getting farther and farther away.

Chase's comm link crackled, then emitted three clicks as someone tapped on an activated microphone, the prearranged signal from Sena. Two soldiers, privates Vargas and Goodman, readied themselves by the airlock door. From the scanner images, Chase knew that the terrorists beneath the transport hadn't moved from their concealment.

A single shot sounded. "Office is clear," Sena transmitted.

On cue, Vargas and Goodman opened the door and tossed a pair of smoke grenades into the bay. Within seconds, visibility shrank to a few meters. The two privates sank to their bellies and crawled through a continuous ring of gunfire into the smoke.

ও(O)ঔ

As the shots died away into silence, Private Vargas made his way along the stack of crates to the right-hand side of the door. The shadowy bulk of the transport loomed in the smoke ahead. He aimed under the vehicle and sent a volley of rounds into the enemy position.

The sound of cursing and screaming came to him from one of the snipers along with that of someone scrambling out from under the far end of the transport.

ও(O)ঔ

Private Goodman moved down the left side of the bay, along the external door, until he made out the vague shadow of the transport. There he stopped and waited. The gunfire and swearing started. Then a shape moved in the smoke, took on a human outline, and separated from the transport.

Goodman fired three shots.

The shape fell with a thud and a rifle clattered across the floor.

"Clear!" Vargas called from across the bay. Cautiously, Goodman moved to apprehend the fallen man. But before he could react, the terrorist fired several shots from a pistol, not at him, but at the window in the main hangar door.

A long whistle sounded as air escaped through the bullet holes and an isolation door slammed closed at the airlock. The smoke stirred violently in its race to escape with the air. By the third shot, a crack split the length of the durapane. Suddenly, the window was gone, shattered and carried away by the pressure in the hangar. Goodman and the enemy gunmen careened into space, followed by Vargas and the two dead bodies.

Chase watched in horror as the men vanished into the void. "The office?" he hissed at Cordova, his jaw set, his fists clenched.

"The hostages are safe. Sena's evacuating them through the air shaft."

"And the terrorist guard?"

"He's dead," Cottington said. "Shot in the head."

Chase approached Snider. "Stan's lead isn't getting any smaller. Request permission to take the transport and go after him."

Snider considered the request before raising his voice and calling for everyone to gather around. "Listen up! Morgan's made a request to pursue the offenders. After what just happened, I'll send only volunteers to go with him. Who's willing?"

Everyone present raised a hand.

"Very well. Cordova, take two of your people and two National Guardsmen and go with him. Arm yourselves. Obviously Brower and his friends are extremely dangerous." Then he turned to Cottington. "You may select which two of your men will go, but I need you here to manage the rest of the military forces. Your volunteers will report to Cordova. I just promoted him to security chief."

"Thank you, sir," the new chief said.

"And you," Snider pointed at Cordova, "will report to Morgan until you get back. He's ex-military and it's his operation." Cordova gave a perfunctory nod and Snider turned to Chase. "Suit up and get on the road. I'll see if I can commandeer an intelligence satellite to track Brower. He could be going anywhere."

Mike Penick and Frank Lesperance were the first two chosen for the pursuit. They had more invested in the case than anyone else on the security force did and therefore deserved a seat on the transport. With them were Private Gloria Sena and another soldier, Clark Mathers. Chase and Cordova brought their number to six.

Chase had reservations about Frank, of course, but with the confirmation of Brower's guilt, Frank became less suspect. If he was guilty, forcing him to stay behind would tip him off to Chase's suspicions. And while bringing him along had its risks, it would allow Chase to keep an eye on him and give Frank a chance to prove his guilt or innocence through his actions. Chase accepted the selection.

It took them forty-five minutes to gather the supplies they needed, cycle through the airlock, and certify the transport safe to board and use.

"Ask Michelle to take care of my dog for me?" Chase asked Snider just before he stepped onto the transport.

Because of Brower's unpredictability, Chase ordered everyone to don full EVA gear for the duration of the pursuit.

He and his team spent the next twenty minutes patrolling the edge of the landing field before they were sure they'd found the correct tracks to follow. By that time, they'd decided to rotate drivers so they could travel twenty-four hours a day, if necessary, to catch the fugitives.

Several hours into the pursuit, they learned that they wouldn't have the use of an imaging satellite to track the fugitives. "They're all tied up searching for the satellite that brought down the air force ships," Snider said. "And we just lost Brower's transponder signal. He must've shut it down."

CHAPTER 22

On the long stretches of open terrain or when he topped a rise, Brower saw a cloud of dust in the distance behind him. The transport was equipped with a magnification imaging scope to assist in rescue searches, so Brower stopped and turned his to view the trailing vehicle. Either the men he'd left behind had lost their nerve and fled Lunar Alpha, or they were dead and Chase was pursuing. Probably the latter.

He hailed the pursuing transport and asked for Chase by name.

"Hello, Stan," Chase said. "We know where you're headed. Why don't you give yourself up and save us both a lot of time and effort?"

"Not on your life. I just needed to know who was back there."

Chase's was the voice of reason. "You're in more trouble than you can handle, Stan. Come on back. I'll advocate for a light sentence."

"I'm afraid even a light sentence is more than I'm willing to endure at this point. From where I'm sitting, my chances look pretty good."

Chase replied, but Brower switched off the receiver. He'd confirmed his pursuer's identity, and that was all he needed.

He spent most of the next two days racing across the lunar desert with a pair of his Chinese colleagues, rotating drivers to prevent the need for rest stops.

At first he'd struggled. Vertigo and space sickness hit him as soon as they'd cleared the hangar and gave him the sense of riding the open ocean in a tin can. His only saving grace was the feel of the Moon's surface beneath the transport. It gave him a solid foundation on which to anchor his sanity.

For hours, he sat behind the driver and stared out the window at the ground. Every time he looked away, vertigo consumed him once more. And outside, the void called to him. Her siren song promised eternity, if only he'd let her in. But eventually his senses came to trust the walls around him and he was able to take his turn behind the wheel.

Finally they reached the rugged transition between the dust-covered landscape and the lava-like basalt formations. This transition, which signaled their proximity to the geological survey camp, slowed their progress to a crawl.

When he saw that Chase had reached the same area, Brower was only a few kilometers ahead, but that few kilometers represented hours of navigating the hazards of the landscape.

At last he came around a long basalt ridge to view the structures of the camp. The habitation dome was maybe a hundred meters in diameter with the semicylindrical protrusion of the equipment garage on one side, the only obvious entrance to the structure. From afar, it looked like a giant igloo on a vast stretch of dirty ice.

Outside the huge door of the igloo was a stretch of graded basalt that served as a parking lot and maneuvering area for the drilling and coring machines required for geological studies. But the vehicles generally parked there were now gone, probably moved inside the garage. Two rectangular outbuildings — shacks, really — stood nearby.

As Brower approached the outpost proper, he hailed the residents in their own language. His fluent Chinese carried only a slight American accent.

One of the outpost occupants acknowledged his hail and welcomed him to their home. "We don't get many visitors," the man said.

Brower brought the truck to a stop near an airlock beside the main equipment entrance. For several minutes, he just sat behind the wheel, listened to his own labored breathing, and contemplated what he must do next.

"Let's go," one of his men said finally.

Brower pried his butt from the seat, talked himself to the airlock, and cycled out. He took one step from the transport and his world came apart around him, whirling off kilter and spinning out of control. He found himself floating away into space.

No, not floating away, he realized when his face hit the ground. All he could see then was dirt, with the empty void of space concealed behind the bubble of his helmet. "Oh, thank God." He took several deep breaths to clear his mind and steady his nerves. He'd never been EVA before. It made him suddenly small and insignificant. Helpless.

No. He refused to be helpless. One of his colleagues tried to help him up, but Brower pushed the man away and collapsed again. He would do this for himself. He refused to be helpless.

Brower pushed himself to his knees and crawled a few meters. The spinning stopped and he managed to swallow his stomach. Carefully, he came to his feet, then stood stock-still, eyes closed, until the spinning subsided again. By the time he reached the building, it'd taken him ten minutes to traverse as many meters. His men had already gone inside.

He turned around to face the transport. Then, with the purpose of a madman, he marched to it and back with careful steps that always kept one foot on the ground despite the lunar gravity, convincing himself that he could repeat the task without losing his senses again, if necessary.

Finally, he stepped into the outpost airlock.

Once inside, he stripped off his environmental suit, surrounded by a clamor of activity. Men hauled equipment and crates everywhere, it seemed. Several, standing nearby in pressure suits of their own, waited for the airlock to clear so they could cycle out. Two pallets of sandbags sat on big-wheeled hand carts. Next to them lay a 33mm machine gun and two crates of ammunition.

Chase must have warned the "geologists" of Brower's arrival. The men of the China Dominion had put their stronghold on alert, and there wasn't a real scientist among them.

⁂

Brower and his colleagues stood in the outpost command center, relieved of their weapons and well guarded, before General Chang Lei, the head of the movement. They waited while the Dominion leader directed the distribution of his defense forces, his attention split between a diagram of the base layout splayed on the conference table and the displays from security scanners that covered every passage on the base.

When Chang was satisfied that his men were doing everything possible to prepare for Chase's arrival, he faced Brower with a cold stare. The wrinkles at the corners of his eyes might have been etchings in stone. "I should kill you where you stand," he said in his native tongue.

Brower forced a laugh and replied in the same language. "You should pay me what you owe me and thank me for my service."

"You are in no position to make demands."

Brower understood the general, who led through fear — military to the core. If he'd intended to kill them, he'd have done so already, but the Dominion leader could show no weakness. Brower shrugged. "It was not a demand. Just a suggestion."

Chang considered the white man's words. "You brought the Americans to our doorstep — and in doing so, will expose our operation. You call this a service?"

"It will expose only that the base is military in nature. You can lead the Americans to believe you're Chinese military. They needn't discover the truth."

"If you hadn't come here, they need not have discovered anything at all."

Brower knew long before he'd arrived that this conversation was inevitable, and he had been planning his arguments ever since he'd made the decision to flee the American port. "My contract was to report your computer-chip technology to American intelligence, and then put myself in a position to assist in planting the device on a high-profile target. That contract has been fulfilled. Successfully, I might add."

"We got a comm from Lunar Alpha to go rescue the crew of that ship you selected. We nearly had to finish the job for you."

"Nevertheless, Secretary Herrera is dead. You wanted a war. And you got one."

"The war was to be brought to America and to the People's Republic. Not to the China Dominion." Chang leaned into the table. His voice was deadly calm, but fury raged in his eyes. He looked over his shoulder at the exterior security monitors. The images, taken by hidden vid-scanners mounted on the coring towers outside, showed Chase's transport picking its way over the treacherous approach to the compound. Chang stabbed a finger at the display. "And yet, it approaches."

"An unfortunate development, I admit, but an unavoidable one. You see, Morgan is clever and resourceful. Somehow, he's put the pieces together and deduced the objective of your China Dominion. Once that happened, he was in a position to put an early end to our efforts. And that would serve neither of us."

"So you bring him here?"

"Yes. I bring him here. He can't have more than eight men on that transport. Less than a third of your numbers. And he's separated from support. Let's put an end to that pain in the ass before he can gather the proof he needs to stop your precious war."

General Chang ground his teeth. He looked from the exterior display to those showing his own men inside the outpost. "Very well." He turned to the guards and gestured to Brower and the others. "Arm them."

Then he keyed the link in his ear and spoke to the men stationed outside. "You may welcome our guests at your convenience."

❧

When Chase rounded the bend to reveal the geology complex, the first thing he noticed, other than the buildings themselves, was Brower's transport, recognizable by its tractorlike treads, passenger space sufficient for multiple rows of seating, and large aft compartment. "They're here, all right. Request permission to enter the compound."

Cordova keyed the link and made the request in English. Fortunately, one of the geologists spoke a bit of the language and the two managed to laboriously communicate.

Three drilling sites loomed nearby. A team of scientists worked on a small rise to Chase's right, though he couldn't discern what manner of work engaged them.

The transport came into the open and turned broadside to the geology team. Seconds later, all hell broke loose. Holes perforated the right side of the transport and a whirlwind of air rushed out. Sparks flew, equipment shattered, men screamed, and bullets ricocheted throughout the compartment. The security guards and soldiers dove for the relative safety of the floorboard, where lockers of medical equipment, survival stores, and maintenance tools provided some measure of protection. Without time to think, Chase hunched down in the seat and swerved away from the source of the onslaught.

A frantic call came over the comm. "I'm hit! Oh, Jesus, I'm hit!"

As they sped away, bullets tore holes in the rear doors and perforated the durapane windshield. Almost immediately they found themselves in vacuum, sustained by their pressure suits.

Ahead, a lava shelf dropped an unknown distance to a plateau below. It was their only chance, so Chase aimed the truck for it. Depending on the height of the drop, it would give them salvation or death, but one way or the other, it'd get them out of the shooting gallery.

They sailed out over the edge and found themselves suddenly weightless in the cabin. The rain of bullets ceased and the cries of the wounded fell silent. The transport nosed over, then crunched into the mattress of lunar dust. Chase hurtled forward into the instrument console. Then the truck stabilized, upright and barreling at full speed across the sand.

He steered along the base of the escarpment to take advantage of the natural cover it provided. The shock of the event had passed and his mind raced to make sense of it. The ambush had been well prepared and well supplied. That meant the base was not scientific, but military. Chase had found his conspirators. He picked up the comm, synch'd it to his helmet link, and tuned to the emergency channel.

If the enemy pursued, Chase and his team might never make it back to Lunar Alpha to report their findings. So as the truck rattled and bumped over the terrain, he transmitted everything he knew of the Chinese base, but without response. The jostling made it difficult to retain his seat and only static came back to him over the channel.

Finally, having said all that he needed to say, he addressed the men in the back. "Everybody okay?"

Mike shook his head. "Frank's dead."

"I'm sorry."

Clark and Gloria looked alert, but neither spoke.

Then a pair of four-wheeled, all-terrain cycles flew over the ridge behind them, carrying men in pressure suits, armed with automatic rifles. The machines had the air of grizzled beasts, predators on the trail of frightened prey. The distance they covered in their graceful flight was tale enough of the power and speed they possessed. And the complete, eerie silence produced by the intervening void only added to their hunter's image. They landed many meters from the lip of the ridge and disappeared in a cloud of fine gray dust. When they emerged, they wheeled directly for Chase's transport.

"Here they come," he warned.

Clark pulled himself to his feet. "Oh, this ain't good. We don't have live rounds. I don't think they'll even feel rubber bullets through a pressure suit."

"And a single hit anywhere on ours will be fatal," Gloria added.

"What else have you two got?" Cordova asked the soldiers.

"A knife, a flash-bang, and a smoke grenade," Gloria replied. The jostling made it difficult for her to speak. "Because of treaty concerns and the risks of using live rounds in space habitats, that's all we were allowed to bring from Earth."

Chase was barely listening. The ATVs were almost on them, one approaching on either side. Unfortunately, they were out of each other's line of fire, with one leading the other by several seconds.

The first came alongside and leveled his weapon at the transport, which wasn't meant to be a fighting vehicle. Its sides, constructed from thin sheets of composite, offered little protection from even small-arms fire. And the treads, which allowed the truck to traverse nearly any landscape, weren't designed for quick maneuvers. Too tight a corner at this speed could overturn the truck.

"Hit the deck!" Chase called.

The muzzle of the rifle flared and bullets streamed through the cabin. Chase slammed on the brakes and sent the lead ATV out in front. Then he pulled the wheel to the right to cut off the other cycle, causing it to swerve and slow down. That bought them time, but only seconds. The transport was no match for the agility and firepower of even one of the hunters.

Gloria hooked an arm around the nearest seat and kicked open one of the rear doors. Then she lay on her back, her rifle aimed between her feet, and waited for a clear shot at the man behind. The door flopped open and shut as Chase swerved to prevent the rider from coming alongside.

The ground, though fairly level, offered many dangerous rock outcroppings and loose boulders. Chase dodged the ones he could and bounded over the rest. Each time the ATV came into sight behind them, Gloria fired a burst. But she either missed the target or her rounds had no effect — Chase couldn't tell which. The opportunities were fleeting and the difficult terrain demanded his attention.

Meanwhile, the other bike raced ahead. The rider pulled to one side and took aim at the transport.

Chase and Cordova dove under the dash. Durapane shards joined a stream of ammunition into the cabin. Chase kept one hand on the wheel and the other on the throttle, but he was blind to their path until the gunfire stopped.

When he looked up, a lava boulder the size of the transport loomed in their path. He spun the wheel, arresting the tread on the left-hand side. The transport pivoted but continued its forward momentum in the meager traction. Immediately, it began to tip as it slid sideways into the obstacle.

Six bodies and every scrap of loose gear in the truck smashed against the wall as the impact crushed the side of the transport and they all came to rest.

As the survivors threw off the blanket of equipment and sorted themselves out, one of the riders came to a stop with a clear line of fire through the open rear doors. Chase pulled himself into the driver's seat and tried the ignition.

The transport was dead.

Several rounds swept the compartment before Mike returned fire. When he did, the rider rolled off his bike and took cover behind it. Clark and Gloria joined the offensive. Cordova moved behind Chase and fired out the driver's window, forcing the second rider to take cover as well.

Chase turned up the O_2 bleed and tried the starter again. The motor roared once and died. More O_2. He cranked up the fuel intake as well. The transport came to life and he pulled away.

A distinct, rhythmic wobble originated from the damaged right tread. Chase could only hope it would last. He steered the truck around a bend in the basalt formations and brought it out of sight of the ATVs at last.

But the hunters resumed the chase.

The trio in the back of the transport began throwing out the loose equipment and medical supplies that had become dangerous projectiles inside the careening vehicle. They threw tool boxes, first-aid kits, and medical scanners. Even a stretcher that had been shaken from its mounting was hurled out. Each item hung for an unnaturally long time in the air and provided an additional obstacle to the riders behind, forcing them to watch the ground for hazards and the air for makeshift missiles, some of which had sufficient mass to potentially topple them from their bikes.

Mike grabbed a crow bar and dislodged one of the rear doors, which was hanging by a single hinge. It landed on its corner and tumbled toward the lead rider. The man swerved as the flying panel passed over his head, clearing him by a finger's breadth. Then Mike threw the crow bar out behind it.

Still the riders came on, both along the hobbled right side. Clark fired a long burst of rounds into the second rider, who tumbled from his bike with a spasm. "That's one."

Chase stood on the brake and sent the lead rider once again out ahead. As soon as the transport stopped, Gloria ran for the vacated cycle.

"Go get him," Chase said, referring to the fallen man.

Mike jumped out into a boulder-strewn valley between two basalt cliffs, each standing from three to five meters in height. Clark followed close behind.

Chase and Cordova took up arms and laid a barrage of fire through the shattered front window at the rider ahead, who seemed to question the wisdom of continuing the attack alone.

Then Gloria climbed onto the vacated bike and tore off in the direction of the remaining rider, spinning up a cloud of dust and gravel as she went. Seemingly oblivious to the riskiness of her actions, she sped ahead with her rifle held before her like a lance.

Mike and Clark approached the fallen man cautiously. He hadn't stirred, but with his gun lying beside him, they took no chances that the man might still be alive and conscious.

Sure enough, before they'd covered half the distance, the rider moved. He reached for his weapon and forced Mike and Clark to scramble for the cover of the nearby rocks. The enemy struggled to rise, but his leg collapsed beneath him. So he scrambled on his belly to secure cover of his own. Once he did, he fired barrages of bullets wherever he saw movement to keep the two men at bay.

Mike, pinned down behind a solitary clump of cover, hooked his arm over the top of a boulder and sent a spray of ammunition at the injured rider.

Clark began to work his way, rock by rock, around behind the enemy, but a stretch of open ground thwarted his efforts. After scanning the area for alternatives, he belly-crawled as well as he could in his bulky gear toward the lava wall behind him.

When he reached the escarpment, he worked his way along its base until he found a gap that would shelter him while he climbed to the top. From there he might find a clear line of fire.

Then the pit of Chase's stomach hardened. Dust clouded the horizon. At first, he thought it was residue, suspended in the low gravity by the passage of the ATVs. But then Brower's ERT transport came into view.

Chase grabbed the imaging scope. He could see through the front window of the newcomer that it was laden with men. And one rode on top, viewing Chase through the sight of a high-caliber rifle. The riders weren't hunters after all. They were merely dogs, sent to force the hunted up a tree and prevent it from fleeing before the hunters could arrive.

Chase set the scope aside. His lame vehicle was capable of only half the speed it had done before the collision. The dogs, it seemed, had succeeded.

CHAPTER 23

Private Gloria Sena approached the rider carefully, ready to swerve if he brought his gun to bear.

He watched her for several long seconds, as through he considered challenging her. But at the last possible moment, he fled down the canyon. Almost immediately, a curve in the escarpment took him out of sight.

When Gloria came around the bend, the rider was gone, so she followed his tracks to a rough section of wall where the slope wasn't quite as steep as the rest. She slowed to a crawl and allowed the front wheels to find purchase on the rough lava bank.

The bike could climb it — her opponent's had — yet she hesitated. At three times her height, the wall concealed the plateau above and provided a great place for an ambush.

That couldn't be helped. So she slung her rifle over her shoulder, grabbed the handlebars with both hands, and eased down on the throttle. The front wheels climbed the near-vertical face until the rear wheels connected and found purchase as well. Then she gunned it.

The bike surged up the bank in a single bound and leapt high into the air at the summit. It landed on its rear wheels, well onto the plateau. Gloria leaned into the handlebars until the front wheels came down as well.

The escaping outlaw fled before her. He hadn't gone far, but the plateau was a continuous, rugged formation. It took both hands and all of Gloria's considerable strength to steady the front wheels and maintain her direction as the bike clawed its way over the terrain.

The man dropped off the far side of the plateau, and from there sped through a broad valley, its sandy floor spotted with lava hazards. Gloria raced after him. Minutes passed as the two ripped through the slalom course of their raceway. The gap closed, but only slightly.

Gloria checked her oxygen gauge, then threw caution away and urged the bike to greater speeds. Her only thought was to stop the man, though she didn't know how.

As she drew closer, the terrorist raised his pistol and fired sporadically behind him. But he could divert no attention to aim on the treacherous course, and Gloria by necessity darted back and forth to avoid the hazards. The effort slowed the terrorist's progress, and the gap narrowed.

When the pistol clicked on an empty chamber, he threw it away and took up his automatic rifle, which was cumbersome but required less accuracy.

Gloria took broad arcs around the obstacles, moving first to the man's right, then to his left, forcing him to shift the rifle from side to side.

When she came up beside him, almost twenty meters distant, along a parallel path, he took too long to spot her. He turned back just in time to see his bike slam into a boulder. It stopped dead and wrapped what it could of itself around the obstruction. The rest of the bike shattered, decorating the landscape with debris.

The rider flew over the obstacle in a graceful arc and somersaulted for some distance before he came down, face-first, on a protruding rock. Durapane shards from his faceplate sparkled in a halo of twinkling light. The man lay still. The fabric of his suit collapsed over his body as his life-sustaining oxygen escaped into space.

Clark reached the top of the escarpment and worked his way along its edge. The enemy crouched behind his cover with his legs exposed, but it was doubtful that a rubber bullet to the leg would do more than reveal Clark's own position. So he bided his time and waited for a better opening.

Mike was also hidden by a barricade and had achieved a stalemate with the enemy. The fallen rider had no place to go, but Mike couldn't approach for a capture.

"We have company," Chase said over the speaker.

Clark crept back for a short distance to better conceal himself from the approaching transport and particularly from the gunner perched on top. When it arrived, it came to a stop just past the fallen rider. The rear doors flew open and the men inside laid down a thick blanket of covering fire on Mike's position. Flakes and chunks of lava engulfed him in a cloud of rock and dust. He tucked himself into fetal position and mumbled incoherently into his helmet. Nothing Clark could do would help him.

When the rider broke from cover and ran toward the truck in a series of awkward, limping bounds, Clark had a clear shot at him. But all he could hope to do was knock the man down and cause half the gunners to turn their fury on him.

Chase and Cordova had already pulled out, trying to put as much distance between themselves and the newcomers as possible. Good. The wounded transport was their only chance of survival. But it was a futile effort. It was too slow.

Maybe, just maybe, Clark could help them.

The rider climbed aboard.

Then Clark was up and running along the top of the escarpment. The enemy gunman, anchored to the roof by nylon cables that ran from his hips to hooks on each side of the transport, seemed oblivious to his approach.

Clark took several leaping strides forward. On the third step, he stumbled and twisted his ankle on the uneven ground. His rifle tumbled from his grasp, but he didn't fall. Gritting his teeth against the pain, he kept running. The transport sprang into motion, so Clark corrected his angle to lead the vehicle and launched himself through the ten meters of intervening space.

He crashed down against the side of the transport just as the men inside slammed the rear doors closed. He wrapped his left hand around one of the rider's cables as he hit, then dangled there, catching his breath while the truck gained speed in its pursuit of Chase.

Suddenly, a gun barrel appeared above him. With his free hand, Clark grabbed the combat knife from his belt and cut the safety restraint that he shared with the enemy. The gunman toppled away.

As Clark cut the cord, his end slackened. His bulky gloves prevented a firm grip, but a deft flick of his wrist wrapped the loose end once around his hand before the slack came out of it. He dangled by one arm with his feet dragging on the ground and his body bouncing off the side of the truck. He had to replace the blade in its sheath, a delicate task with his legs flailing and the blade sharp enough to pierce the fabric of his pressure suit. But after several tries, he stowed the blade. When he hooked his hand over the top of the transport to pull himself up, the gunner was nowhere in sight.

But a hand appeared at the far edge. Then an elbow. Clark struggled to gain the rooftop first. By the time his waist cleared the side, the other man's chest had risen into view. So Clark swung his legs around and kicked out with what meager leverage he could achieve. The gunner fell back over the edge.

The rock escarpment fell away on either side and the valley opened up.

When the enemy's hand reappeared, Clark released his lifeline and slid on his belly across the rooftop with his arms and legs spread for stability. He slipped the knife again from its sheath and plunged the blade through the back of the gunner's hand, which disappeared once more.

Clark replaced the blade and peered over the edge. The man dangled there, flopping like a fish on a lure, his eyes and mouth open in a scream that Clark couldn't hear. Only the gunner's hand had been injured, but that didn't matter. The pressure suit was punctured. He'd die in seconds.

Suddenly, the truck swerved and Clark began to slide. He grabbed the side of the transport with one hand and a protruding flood lamp with the other. Ahead, the terrain was flat and clear. The truck swerved the other way and back. It kept up for several cycles, back and forth. Then a breaking and accelerating motion added to the challenge. Eventually, the driver gave up and returned to a fixated pursuit of Chase.

Clark made his way to the side. "Tough break," he said to the body as he cut the remaining restraint.

~(O)~

Chase shook his head, not in despair, but in amazement at how circumstances had changed so quickly.

He'd sacrificed everything, most of all his family. Erin sat at home, listening to Sarah portray him as a stranger or deserter — perhaps even a traitor or monster. He never for a moment forgot Erin's pain or her need for him. But those thoughts weren't in the forefront now, having been crowded out by the more urgent needs of the larger political events. He had no idea how much time he had left, but he knew it was running out.

Chase picked up the comm and keyed the link. He had to reach Lunar Alpha. He had to explain the plot hatched by this militant gang, had to convince someone to hunt down Brower and seek the proof that he'd hoped to acquire, had to make somebody stop the absurd war that neither the US nor China wanted. He had to get through.

He tried the emergency channel, calling repeatedly without response, making his plea into the pervading static in hopes that someone would hear.

He'd left Mike and Clark behind. The fact gnawed at the back of his mind, but he didn't second-guess his decision to do so. The two were at least as safe there as they'd be in the transport. And waiting for them would have cost all their lives. Beyond that, Chase had no time to think about it.

He navigated a minefield of bumps and boulders, favoring the right tread whenever the landscape offered a choice.

Michelle was the only other person aware of the terrorists' plot. She had the chip and all the technical data, but none of that meant squat. It had allowed Chase to deduce the foul motives of the perpetrators, but it proved nothing. Maybe she could convince someone to take up his cause. But she was green. She didn't know the right people. She didn't know her way around or through the bureaucracy and politics of NASA to get things done. Her pleas would fall on deaf ears.

Their pursuer was closer now, almost within gunshot. Cordova grabbed a rifle and moved to the back, but his bullets wouldn't even break the enemy's windshield.

The canyon walls dropped away and they broke into open ground.

Undeterred by the continuing static, Chase tuned to the traffic control frequency and repeated his appeal.

As the enemy truck drew closer, Chase put down the link. Earlier, he'd thought the man on top was armed, but he saw now that he wasn't. Nor did the man have a lifeline. Perhaps he intended to jump from one transport to the other. If he did, a single hand grenade could be the end of both Cordova and himself.

The transport pulled up alongside and swerved toward Chase, who veered away. Then it moved out in front and the back doors flew open. Inside, a dozen men in pressure suits aimed automatic rifles.

Chase swore as he and Cordova threw themselves under the dash.

Bullets, sparks, shards of durapane, and broken bits of transport swept the passenger compartment. A rain of debris pelted his helmet with the sound of hail on a skylight. The remains of the windshield vanished and the roof began to collapse, its supports sawed clean through by the gunfire. Only the bulk of the motor protected the men from the deluge.

∞(O)∞

The ride stabilized enough for Clark to look around. Sparks flew from Chase's transport into the void and smoke poured from the engine compartment. The riddled truck began to slow, and with it, the enemy's transport.

Clark pulled the pin from his flash-bang and dropped it into the passenger compartment with the gunmen. The device exploded silently but with a bright flare. The shooting stopped and the transport swerved. Clark tumbled toward the roof's edge and grabbed the light bar. The truck careened onward at an angle to its previous heading, weaving drunkenly as it went.

Clark looked for a place to jump off and seek safety, but the transport moved much too fast for a safe landing, and the terrain, though rough, offered no features large enough to hide a man for any length of time. So he stayed put and hung on.

Then the transport slowed and made a wide turn back the way it had come.

A line of holes appeared in the rooftop beside him. He grabbed the remnants of a nylon strap, threw his legs over the side, and hung there as the roof exploded with the shells of a dozen machine guns.

Chase's transport crawled away ahead.

Beyond it, a flare lit the sky. A ship flew straight at Clark. And a moment later, a missile.

Chapter 24

Dana spent most of the day after Bill's surgery sitting at his bedside. The doctors and nurses came and went, but she didn't talk to them, afraid her voice would fail her if she did. Instead, she watched their faces and tried to read Bill's progress in their expressions.

She'd lost her friends and her innocence, taken by an enemy upon whom she'd fired the first shot. So she buried her head in her hands to block out everything from her sight but the man she was helpless to aid.

"Visiting hours are over, miss," a nurse said from the doorway.

"I'd like to stay with him." She saw the answer in the nurse's eyes and added, "He has no family here."

"I'm sorry. Hospital policy — "

To hell with policy. "I'd like to speak with the doctor."

"He doesn't have the authority to waive our visitation policy any more than I do."

Fury boiled beneath the surface and threatened to dissolve Dana's weakening façade of composure.

"I'll call security if I must." The nurse's tone remained soft and reassuring. "But the disruption would be bad for the patient. Our policies are for his benefit. If a part of him is aware of your presence, that part needs rest."

Something inside Dana understood the woman's logic, but that something was buried beneath layers of grief and anger. Nonetheless, this was a battle she couldn't win. If the nurse called security, Dana might not be allowed to return tomorrow. So she stormed from the room before her temper broke free from the vestiges of her restraint.

But she didn't go home. The nurse had triggered her anger, but she wasn't the source of it. So Dana did the only constructive thing that she could. She directed it, focused it, gave it a target. She turned it toward its source, the Mingyun satellite.

She went to the intelligence office, where the search for the orbital weapon was taking place. To the eye, there wasn't much to it: a communication uplink, a radar display, and a single operator with a couple of telnet terminals.

"I'm sorry," the radar operator told her. "We've lost it."

"What do you mean, you've lost it?" She slammed her fist into the bulkhead and the vibration rattled equipment clear across the room. "How do you lose a satellite?"

"Relax, Captain — "

She wheeled on the man, screaming now. "Don't tell me to relax!" Then she checked herself. This operator was no military subordinate. He was an agent of the CIA.

Breathing heavily, Dana brought herself back into control.

Only then did the radar man continue. "We know which satellite is the weapon, but we weren't tracking it at the time of the attack. Shortly afterwards, China shifted its orbit. It's out there somewhere, and there's a lot of sky to search, but sooner or later we'll find it. When we do, we won't take our eyes off it until it's gone."

Dana's fists clenched and unclenched in spasmodic cycles. Though her anger had a focus, it lacked an outlet until the satellite was found.

So she stayed in Satellite Operations until nearly two A.M. and when she got home, she tossed in her bed and checked the clock every few minutes until morning.

The next day, Bill's condition was unchanged and the day was a repeat of the last — until late that night. As she paced the length of the satellite control room, Chase's distress comm came into the security office across the hall.

"Alpha, this is Chase Morgan." He yelled into the radio, as if conversing in a noisy barroom. "We've followed Brower to the geology outpost. It is *not* a science base, it's a damned military installation. We're under fire and need help. Are you reading me, Alpha?"

Dana migrated across the hall. A rattle and thump came through from the transmitting end, some static, and then the voice resumed. "... under fire ... vacuum integrity compromised ... man down."

Dana pulled Cottington into the hall. "Where is that base? Do you know?"

"About thirty-three degrees east, seventeen north."

She keyed the link in her ear and spoke to the hangar crew. "This is Captain McCaughey. Is my landing strut fixed yet?"

"Yes, sir," the man replied. "*Snow Leopard*'s ready to fly."

"Good. Clear the hangar — we're conducting an emergency launch."

Chase Morgan was lucky. Cottington commanded the National Guardsmen, but he had no authority over the air force ships. Here, the CATS were autonomous. Only Bill — tears welled again in her eyes and she swept them away with the back of her hand. Only she herself could command them. If she'd been able to sleep, she'd never have heard the distress call.

She fired a priority comm to Miller and Allistair to tell them of her plans.

"Do we have the authority for that?" Allistair asked.

"We have orders to neutralize any foreign attack on US citizens, installations, or assets," she snapped. "We not only have the authority, it's our duty to respond."

Cottington stood nearby. "What about that satellite? It's still out there somewhere."

"They caught us with our reflector plates down. That won't happen again."

Dana scrambled toward her ship, propelling herself through the dead halls by the stability of the railings and the strength of her arms. She stopped only to don her pressure suit, a practiced maneuver that took fewer than four minutes. By the time she was done, Miller and Allistair joined her. The three climbed into the cockpit and sealed the door, and Dana called for an explosive decompression of the hangar. Seconds later, the bay doors opened and air whistled through the widening crack. The heavy equipment and tools remained undisturbed by the gale while lighter objects littered the tarmac. Immediately, the crew began the ignition sequence, skipping the customary preflight safety checks. There simply wasn't time.

As soon as the gap was wide enough for the ship and Miller had visually cleared the space before them, he punched the throttle and the *Snow Leopard* shot from the bay like a rocket round from a Mingyun satellite. Dana hadn't cleared their launch with traffic control, an oversight that would earn her and Miller a formal reprimand in their personnel records, but they'd avoid serious repercussions if the mission was ultimately successful.

Miller hugged the terrain, flying an evasive course well below the horizon of any enemy radar, and in twelve minutes they buzzed the enemy compound. Three men in a machine-gun nest near the main building looked up as the ship passed, but they never had time to bring their weapon to bear.

"There." Dana pointed. Dust clouds directed them to the combatants. "Mr. Morgan, this is the *Snow Leopard*. We're at your disposal. Please advise. Over."

"*Snow Leopard*, this is Colonel Morgan." *Colonel?* "If you can, take out the rear transport. Over." Even at that short distance, his words barely penetrated the cloud of static. His communications antennae had been sheered off. Nevertheless, Dana recognized his voice. "You heard the man," she said to Allistair.

"Yes, sir." He lit the enemy truck with the targeting laser and let a missile fly.

A man clinging to the side of the target propelled himself away from the vehicle and escaped the explosion that engulfed and destroyed the transport and its occupants. He hit the ground and tumbled for some distance, limbs flopping in an unnatural fashion.

Satisfied that the man was dead, Dana didn't bother to pursue him with *Snow Leopard*'s guns.

"Thank you, *Snow Leopard*," Chase said.

"My pleasure, Colonel. Are you planning to enter the compound?"

"We have to. This bucket won't make it back to Alpha. And we can't just sit here and wait for help. They'll come after us."

"I'd offer you a ride, but we haven't got the room. Shall I go open the door for you?"

"Anything you can do, *Snow Leopard*."

With that, Miller steered toward the enemy base.

"Good luck, Colonel," Dana said as Chase's transport vanished from sight. When she reached the compound, she approached the machine gun emplacement from the back side at an extremely low altitude. "Let's try out the guns."

Allistair opened the ports as Miller brought the ship over the last rise. All three enemies scanned the sky. One spotted the ship and pointed.

As the others turned, a hail of bullets rained down on the foxhole. The maneuvering thrusters kept the nose pointed toward the pit as the ship coasted past.

The men convulsed with the impact of the gunfire. When the bombardment ceased, nothing moved in the hole.

At Dana's order, Miller brought the ship to a hover just outside the igloo's main equipment door. Then Allistair released a missile that disappeared through the structure's shell. It released a conflagration inside that blew off the door and caused a portion of the roof to collapse.

The action released much of Dana's pent-up tension. She flexed her hand twice, only now beginning to feel the pain from her outburst in the satellite center the night before. "Well done, boys. Let's go home."

She had but one missile left with which to oppose the Mingyun satellite.

Chase's transport limped only a kilometer or two back toward the point where Mike and the soldiers had disembarked. Then it gave up and died. He exchanged glances with Cordova. "That's all she's got."

"More than I would have expected." Cordova checked the oxygen supply. "Several tanks are ruptured. There's just enough for a day, maybe a little less."

"Noted." Chase's mind was on the others. They were out there somewhere. And, dead or alive, they were his responsibility.

"What do you think?" Cordova said, as though guessing his thoughts. "Do we go find them?"

"We have to. They might be injured."

"Hold on." Cordova pointed.

Chase squinted into the sunlight. An ATV sped toward them. The two grabbed their rifles, but as it approached, Chase recognized Gloria's small stature in the bike's driver seat. A larger man rode on the seat behind her.

When they arrived, Mike Penick climbed off and bounded to the transport. "Did you see that, Louie?"

"What?"

"The ship. She was beautiful, wasn't she?"

"That was the *Snow Leopard*," Chase said. "We have her to thank for our immediate survival."

"The *Snow Leopard*? That's the one that chick flies. I met her the other night. Charming woman."

"Put it in your pants, Penick," Gloria said, then turned to Chase. "Where's Clark?"

"He got out with you."

"The crazy bastard jumped onto the other transport." Mike snapped a fresh magazine into his rifle. "Took on the shooter. Didn't you see him?"

Chase's gaze sought the enemy truck, though it was out of sight now. "Yeah, I saw him." He squeezed his eyes shut. "He was still there when the truck was hit. I didn't know it was him." Chase couldn't look at the others. His voice was barely a whisper. "I didn't know."

"What do we do now?" Mike asked, eyeing the shattered transport.

Chase spun on him, bitterness thick in his tone. "We go in after that son-of-a-bitch Brower."

"That's absurd," Mike declared.

"It's our only option. We've little air, no transportation, and we're sitting ducks out here."

"The captain of the *Snow Leopard* said she'd open the door for us," Cordova added.

Gloria fired up the bike. "Then let's get moving before they close it."

Chapter 25

Chase clung to Mike as their ATV neared the enemy stronghold. They approached the compound from behind one of the outbuildings, where they were least likely to be observed, and found Gloria waiting where Mike had left her.

She sat in a small crater with a 33mm machine gun lying across her lap. "Present from the *Snow Leopard.*" She held it up for inspection. "It's the one that shot us all to hell when we got here. Everyone in the nest is dead."

Chase climbed off the bike. "What else did you see?"

"There's a hole in the hangar door big enough to drive a transport through. The bay's pretty well shot."

"And inside the building?"

She shrugged.

Mike turned the bike around and went back for Cordova.

Chase peered into the portal of the outbuilding, which was filled with spare parts and machining tools. Designed for EVA use, the building lacked an airlock. He'd find no oxygen there or in the other shed, more than likely. That left the igloo.

The level ground between the maintenance shack and the igloo was clear of obstructions and several windows dotted the facing side of the main building. There was no help for it. They'd have to make a run for it and get lucky.

So after Mike arrived with Cordova and Chase had double-checked the windows and the rest of the compound grounds, the four of them made a dash for the igloo, bounding up and down in a ragged line like so many horses on a merry-go-round.

They reached the building without incident and crouched below the window ledge, then crawled around the perimeter toward the breach in the equipment garage. Gloria led the way, clutching the huge machine gun before her. When she reached the opening, she motioned for the others to wait while she took a second look inside. Two people in the bay, she signaled.

Chase peered through a shattered windowpane. The vehicles inside ranged in size from ATVs to a cargo truck to drilling and coring rigs. Those near the center had been hardest hit. Mangled pieces of frame and body from overturned equipment cluttered the bay and smaller debris littered the floor. The men inside appeared to be assessing the damage.

When the workers finally came together, Gloria brought the machine gun to her hip and pulled the trigger. Designed to be anchored, the weapon recoiled. The force of the shots threw her back. Without comment, she righted herself and crept back to the opening.

Both men lay in the middle of the floor. Neither moved. Chase waved for the others to follow him inside.

"They're dead," Gloria said after checking the bodies.

The interior wall, opposite the door, had survived the explosion intact and maintained the environmental integrity of the dome interior.

"Listen up." Chase stopped the group. "We have two options. If any of these rigs are working and we can find enough O_2, we might be able to make it home and get some help. But if we do, that'll give Brower and his friends several days to run in the meantime. On the other hand, we could go inside. We don't know their number or the layout of the base. But we do know they're well equipped and willing to kill."

Gloria spoke first. "I say we go in and wax the bastards."

"Let's do it." Mike's voice was full of bravado that his eyes couldn't match.

Cordova was already nodding.

Chase looked into the faces of his three young and fit companions. It had been twenty years since he'd been in the military. He was their age back then. Older. Naturally, he'd tried to stay fit.

NASA's astronaut program was pretty rigorous, but he'd washed out of that four years ago. "Failed the stress test," the doctors had said. "Can't hack the physical rigors of the job." It was bullshit, of course. But there were too many pilots in the program for NASA to keep one that had failed his stress test.

Two Asian men looked back from inside the habitat. Both sported body armor and weapons. Neither wore an environmental suit, so they couldn't compromise their habitat by shooting into the bay.

Was it bullshit? Chase wondered. If it wasn't, he'd probably have a heart attack. Or he'd fall behind, or get shot. *Let's find out,* he thought with a grim sense of defiance.

"We can't kill the terrorists," Chase told his team. "Not all of them, at any rate." He outlined what he knew of the terrorists' plot. "But we need proof. We need somebody who'll testify so that we can convince both President Li and President Powers that these people are the source of the violence."

"Will they care, at this point?" Gloria asked.

"I hope so. Neither country started this war, and neither wants it. But they'll both need an excuse to back down without admitting defeat or giving concessions to the other. Proof of the source of the attacks will give them that. And proof of war as a motive will apply additional pressure to cease hostilities. Neither president will want the outlaws to succeed in their objectives."

"How do we get inside?" Mike asked.

"Easy," Gloria said quickly. "I climb into that drilling rig over there and drive it through the bulkhead."

"I have a better idea. Let's use the front door." Chase made his way through the wreckage to the airlock.

The men on the other side of the durapane followed.

Chase punched the controls for the outer door and waited for the chamber to pump down to vacuum. When it did, the door opened and he stepped inside.

Gloria went in with him.

The Asian men smiled and laughed with one another. They raised their weapons and waited for the airlock cycle to complete.

But Chase pressed the control for the inner door while the outer door stood open. A warning light came on and a Chinese message illuminated the display. He opened the safety override panel and reached for the lever inside.

One of the militants tapped his buddy's arm with the back of his hand

and spoke a few short words. Chase couldn't hear the men, but their expressions said that they grasped his intent. The two men fled down the hall.

When Chase pulled the lever, the inner door seal separated and a stream of air rushed past. A sensor detected the pressure change inside and slammed isolation doors shut at either end of the hall. Both terrorists had made it through before the doors came down, leaving the corridor evacuated of both persons and atmosphere.

Gloria tossed the unwieldy 33mm back into the bay and the four companions moved inside. Then Chase sealed the airlock and air handlers began pumping oxygen back into the space. There was an isolation door on the wall to his left, near the end of the hall. To the right, the passageway ended in a door that faced them.

Cordova voiced the thought in Chase's mind. "When those doors reopen, we're sitting ducks."

"Maybe not." Gloria reached into a pocket and pulled out a fist-sized object.

"What's that?" Mike asked.

"Camouflage."

Mike's brow knitted.

"It's a smoke grenade." Chase recognized it from his own military days. "And a good idea."

Gloria pulled the pin and the passage began to fill with thick, white smoke.

Meanwhile, Chase motioned for Mike and Cordova to cover the door on their left.

As they moved to do so, Cordova used his hands to form a box around his face, indicating the head as the target. The bullets would be lethal there, but Cordova was right. On a man in body armor, a hit anywhere else would just be wasted.

Chase dropped to his belly against one wall and aimed high, as Cordova had advised.

The doors slid open, smoke stirred, and gunfire swept the hallway, drowning out the sound of Chase's heart. He squeezed the trigger and swept the gun from side to side until his hand ached.

When the shooting stopped and the smoke dissipated into the air-handling system, four terrorists lay dead beyond the doorways.

Any others had retreated farther into the complex.

Hundreds of dents puckered the enviro-dome from enemy bullets, but the structure took the damage without breach. The militants must have anticipated the possibility of discovery and assault when they built the complex.

None of Chase's team had been hit.

Three of the bodies lay at the other end of the hall, but one sprawled in front of Chase. There was no way to know if he had killed the man or if Gloria had. He tried to tell himself that it didn't matter; in combat, one did what one must to survive. But the issue ran deeper than that. These men had been bent on murder. You might say they deserved what they got. But what of their families? If they had children somewhere, their kids didn't deserve to be fatherless any more than Erin's did.

Chase kicked the man's gun down the corridor, shunning the lethal rounds it carried. "Take them alive if you can."

He chose the hallway to the right, which ran along an exterior wall with numerous windows, where the enemy would be more reluctant to fire live ammunition. The curve of the building took them past two adjoining corridors. Down the third, a fleet figure ducked behind a bulkhead. Chase motioned Mike and Gloria to retrieve the man while he and Cordova stood guard at the intersection.

A moment later, two militants appeared at a corner farther down the hall. Chase and Cordova took cover in the adjoining corridor. Cordova shot a volley of rubber shells that knocked one of the terrorists down and forced the other to duck behind corner. Without bothering to rise, the downed man scrambled to safety.

"Cover me," Chase told Cordova after trading a few ineffective rounds with the pair. He took a few running strides, then dove into a headfirst slide down the corridor with his gun extended before him.

As soon as Chase hit the floor, Cordova launched a stream of covering fire over the investigator. One of the terrorists stuck his head around the corner to squeeze off a shot but dropped instantly, leaving a stain of blood on the bulkhead behind him.

Chase fired a short volley down the militants' corridor as he slid past, but he needn't have bothered. One man lay dead. The other was nowhere in sight.

Chase came to a stop just past the intersection, got up, and walked back to it, intent on holding the position until the others caught up. They were driving the enemy deeper into their lair and he refused to give up ground already taken.

While he waited, terrorists began to gather at an intersection down the adjoining corridor, which led farther into the building. Chase shot the last few rounds in his rifle to make the men cautious, then swapped magazines. Blood pooled at his feet from the body lying in the intersection. The man's gun was gone, apparently taken by the terrorist who'd retreated.

Cordova pointed down the hall beyond Chase. The investigator turned, expecting company, but all he saw was a short stretch of empty corridor and a closed door, which he'd have to watch.

He nodded his understanding.

The security chief shook his head and pointed again, more emphatically this time.

Chase fired a few blind shots toward the gathering terrorists.

Then Cordova indicated "up" with his thumb and pointed again to the dead-end corridor.

This time Chase spotted the security scanner near the ceiling at the end of the hall. He shattered it with rubber shells, then sent another volley toward the enemy. "What's keeping them?" he asked over the comm.

Cordova shrugged and looked off in the direction that the others had gone. "They're coming."

"One dead and no exits," Gloria said as they rejoined the chief. "That section's secure." The three moved up to join Chase. "How many?" she asked.

"At least four."

Gloria glanced uneasily at the window behind her and the void beyond. Then she snapped the seals on her helmet and moved it to her waist. "Cover me."

Chase, the only one on the far side of the adjoining passage, poked his gun barrel around the corner and pulled the trigger. While the deluge poured down the hall, Gloria peered around the corner, much less exposed then she'd have been if she'd retained her bulky fishbowl helmet. She drew back and Chase ceased firing.

"They're down about ten meters," she said through the microphone in her collar ring. "At least one on either side. Poised to aim below the windows."

Chase took a moment to check the closed door at his end of the hall, which led to a custodian supply closet. A dead end.

Chase's heart raced from the physical exertions and excitement of battle. Storming the corridor was likely to get someone killed — a distinct possibility in any case — but he wasn't into pressing his luck. He was about to signal a retreat to one of the corridors they'd passed when a hand grenade skipped down the hall. Before it came to rest, he kicked it down the passage from which they'd come and all four companions hit the deck.

When the grenade exploded, it blew the nearest window into space. Air rushed from the corridor until an isolation door slammed down between them and the breach, sealing off their retreat.

Gloria unfastened her pressure suit enough to retrieve a pistol from a shoulder harness and stuff it into an outside pocket. She refastened her suit and, with a nervous glance at the pressure door, put her helmet back on.

They no longer had a choice. They had to run the gauntlet.

CHAPTER 26

Dana was back at Bill's bedside shortly after returning to the base. She hadn't slept for more than four hours total since he'd been hospitalized and was coming down off the adrenaline rush of their race to save Chase. Her head ached from lack of food, but she was too exhausted to care.

She sat by the bed with one hand beneath Bill's covers, grasping his limp fingers. Her other hand toyed with a few locks of his unkempt hair. Dana mumbled a story from her childhood. It was one he'd heard before, but she told it again now to keep herself awake and because it seemed better to talk to him than to sit in silence. Maybe somehow it let him know she was there.

Ever so slightly, his hand moved in hers. It was just a twitch. She thought she'd imagined it. When it happened again, she sat up, squeezed his hand gently in return, and stared at his face. "Bill? Bill, it's Dana."

He moved his hand again and his head rolled from side to side.

"Bill, come back to me." She must have said it at least a hundred times in the past few days, but this was the first time he might actually hear. "Come back, Bill. I miss you."

He opened his eyes and squinted against the glare of the light. "Dana?" His voice was barely a whisper.

"I'm here, Bill. Oh, thank God." She leaned over him so he could see her face and blocked as much of the light from his eyes as she could. "Bill, I love you."

His mouth stretched into a weak grin. "Dana."

She smiled back and kissed his forehead, then reached for the nurses' call button on the headboard instrument panel. Dana eased herself onto the side of the bed, where he could look at her, careful to avoid the IV tube and urinary catheter. Over the past two days, the nurses had removed the rest of the tubes and wires. Bill was breathing on his own and vital-sign monitoring had been transferred to remote sensors over the bed. She brought his hand to her lips, kissed it, and wept.

When the nurse arrived, Dana moved away to give her room to work.

The woman reviewed the monitor screens, checked his IV, and verified his vital signs. In hushed tones, she asked him a few questions that Dana couldn't quite make out. As she left, she gave Dana a reassuring smile.

The sun warmed the room through the durapane window, suddenly now bright and cheerful as if it had just risen. Dana returned to Bill's side and kissed him again, this time on the mouth. "I thought I'd lost you."

He smiled weakly. "You can't get rid of me that easily."

She took his hand. "How do you feel?"

"Tired."

"That's all right. Just sleep. I'll be right here." She lay her head on the bed by his shoulder and both fell instantly asleep.

⁂

The corridor that stretched between Chase and the waiting enemy was only a few strides long, so he checked his magazine, gathered his courage, and broke into a rush toward death, his gun blazing. With the barrage of shells that he and his friends sent before them, the enemy didn't dare look into the passage. But one man fired blindly at the onrushers. A spray of blood shot from Cordova's leg and he went down in the hall.

Chase saw him fall, but there was nothing he could do. If they stopped to help, they'd all be fodder for the gunman. So he and the others went on.

When he reached the enemy position, a single terrorist threw his weapon down and thrust his hands into the air. A live prisoner, at last. But four of the man's buddies retreated down the hall behind him, one of whom saw his comrade trying to surrender and put a bullet through the back of the man's skull. The prisoner crumpled into a heap on the floor and the rest fled through a doorway to their left.

Mike recovered the dead man's rifle and checked the magazine. "Empty." He threw it down the hall in disgust.

Chase went back and helped Cordova to his feet. "How are you?"

The chief could stand, but he favored his left leg as he walked. "Hurts like a mother."

Gloria held the intersection, watching all four directions at once, while the two men caught up. When they did, she crouched to inspect Cordova's damaged leg. "I can't see the wound, but there's an exit hole in your suit, so the round's not still in your leg." Her voice sounded comforting. "The bones are whole or you wouldn't be walking at all. We'll need to stop soon to arrest the bleeding, though. And you'll need a new EVA."

"You a medic?" Chase asked.

"Not really, but combat first aid is part of our field training."

Mike looked sullenly at the dead man. "We won't take anyone alive."

"We must," Chase insisted.

"Well, then you'd better tell them that."

Advancing cautiously, they reached the door through which the men had fled. Gloria put her back to the wall beside it.

Mike stepped beyond and did the same on the far side. Then he pressed the panel next to the door. It slid open and bullets rained out.

When the gunfire stopped, Gloria eased her head back from the wall so she could see a sliver of the room. "It's a dining area." She nodded to Mike, who provided covering fire while she took a better look. "Six tables, several overturned for cover. About five men. Three exterior windows along the far wall. One other exit."

"A kitchen," Mike guessed.

Chase nodded. "And a dead end, or they would've taken the way out."

No one suggested a course of action, so Gloria drew her pistol from the pocket of her suit. With a wicked smirk, she hooked her arm around the edge of the door frame and fired into the windows. The isolation door between the dining hall and the corridor slammed down, trapping the men inside as their air escaped into space.

"Where the hell'd you get that?" Mike demanded.

Gloria shrugged. "It's mine. Why? You want to arrest me for it?"

"No. I want to know where it was outside. It would've come in handy then."

"Inside my pressure suit. I couldn't get at it."

"Come on." Chase led them down the hall.

The team made two turns, shot out a security scanner, and searched several more rooms before meeting the enemy again. When they did, the resistance was less intense. They seemed to have whittled the militant forces to a few remaining men. But they'd seen no sign of Brower.

"Could he have been in the dining hall?" Chase wondered aloud.

"I didn't see him," Gloria said.

Two terrorists moved before them as they wound their way through the labyrinthine passages. The men were without body armor and Chase's hopes of a live prisoner soared. "Aim for the chest," he said. Rubber bullets wouldn't be fatal there.

The defenders stopped at each intersection to fire a few odd rounds, which slowed Chase and his party, but the men never stayed in one place for long. Twice the terrorists fired through a window to bring down isolation doors and seal off part of the complex.

"They're running out of ammo," Mike concluded.

"They're herding us." It didn't bode well, but there was nothing Chase could do about it. He had to take the open passages wherever the enemy left them.

Cordova stumbled frequently, but Chase didn't dare stop to tend the wound. He had nothing to dress it with in any case. So he tried to speed their progress by leaving some of the rooms unsearched, a practice to which Gloria objected.

Halfway down the next corridor, one of their harassers tossed a hand grenade into the passage, which offered an open doorway to either side, one a little farther down the hall than the other. Chase dove to the right.

Cordova fell behind. The blast blew him from Chase's supporting arm and beyond the investigator's reach from the doorway. Shrapnel perforated his left arm and leg, as well as the side of his torso.

Chase had taken refuge in a living quarters with no other doors, save that to the lavatory, and no windows. He was alone. Mike and Gloria had been in front and sought cover in the room across the hall. But he didn't know if they'd made it, so he readied his rifle, now nearly empty, and watched what he could see of the corridor.

A flurry of shots erupted. Gloria's pistol fired twice, the sound distinctly different from that of the rifles. And when the gunfire stopped, the terrorists lay dead.

Chase raced Mike and Gloria to Cordova. The chief's chest heaved and blood trickled from the corners of his mouth.

Footsteps echoed down the hall from the direction in which Chase's team had come and several men took up defensive positions there. All wore pressure suits that would protect them from rubber bullets. Worse, the enemy could now use live ammunition safely near the exterior windows.

"We got to get out of this hall," Gloria said.

"Leave me." Cordova's voice shook. Blood flecks appeared on his faceplate as he spoke. "I'll buy you as much time as I can."

"No." Chase bent to help him stand.

"You must." He swatted Chase's hand away. "I'll never make it anyway."

"He's right." Gloria handed the dying man her pistol. "It's got six rounds left. Make 'em count." Then she bounded down the hall toward safety.

When Chase hesitated, Mike grabbed his arm. "Come on, let's go find Brower."

Chase took a long look down the passage before following.

They had no time to recover the enemies' weapons, and their own were useless under the circumstances. So Chase led them farther from the fallen security chief, even when gunfire erupted behind them.

For many minutes, they found no one. The gunshots died out and the base went silent except for the sound of their own footfalls. Chase's breathing was labored, but he had more fight left than he'd have believed himself capable. It was amazing what adrenaline could do.

The three progressed carefully now, room by room and corridor by corridor, until they found a narrow stairway plunging into the ground. Dimly lit, it extended for several flights with a short landing that broke the descent every twenty or so steps. Cautiously they approached an open doorway at the bottom.

The room beyond looked like some sort of command bunker, with electronics consoles and telnet monitors lining the walls. It wasn't apparent that the room was occupied, but Chase couldn't imagine that it was vacant.

With only a few steps remaining between Chase and the room, Brower's familiar voice came over the speaker in Chase's helmet. "Don't be shy, Colonel. Go on in."

The traitor stood at the top of the stairs with an Asian man, each wearing a pressure suit and pointing an automatic rifle. There was nowhere to run and nothing to use for cover.

CHAPTER 27

Brower and his companion began walking down the stairs, each with a hand braced against the wall to ensure their footing in the lunar g. "Place your weapons slowly on the steps and walk inside. I'll introduce you to what's left of the gang."

Reluctantly, Chase set down his rifle and motioned for the others to follow suit. Then he walked toward the control bunker.

"Keep your hands where I can see them. All of you," Brower said.

With their hands raised as high over their heads as their pressure suits would allow, the three remaining members of Chase's party moved into the bunker. It was shaped like an octagon with a ceiling at least two standard lunar stories high, yet still well below the Moon's surface. A large conference table dominated the center of the room. The display monitors that ringed the ground floor showed rooms and corridors throughout the stronghold. Some displayed places that they'd come through during their violent passage. The mess hall was recognizable, for instance. Six men had died there, their bodies gathered at the base of the safety doors that had literally sealed their fate.

Brower didn't seem to be in any hurry, so Chase took time to review the image on each screen, a few of which were dark or showed only static. As well as he could determine, no one was left alive in the building except those in the control room.

It was no consolation that, with the possible exception of one man in the entry hall, Chase hadn't killed any of the militants himself, or that his team members had only done what they must. Chase had brought them here, and the destruction they had wrought in their passing was complete.

He paused on the image of Cordova. The chief was dead, along with four of the enemy. He'd made a good accounting of himself in his final moments. It was a shame that it was all for nothing. None of them would leave the stronghold alive.

A catwalk surrounded the room above the array of security displays at about the height that a second floor would have been. On it stood three Asian men in full body armor. Each carried an automatic rifle. The men stood apart from one another. The one on the right, with a military-style cloth cap, scowled more fiercely than the rest.

"The one in the hat is General Chang Lei, the leader of the movement," Brower said.

"The movement?" Chase had heard Chang's name somewhere before.

"The China Dominion." He seemed about to say more, but General Chang launched into an incomprehensible harangue of Chinese.

Brower activated the external speaker on his suit's collar and responded in the same language, though in a more reasonable tone.

The general spat another tirade.

He was a small man. His mustache was gray, but otherwise his face was ageless. The hardness in his eyes and repeated violent gestures with his rifle portrayed him as a ruthless tyrant — the kind of man who'd commit murder, the kind of man who would welcome, no, instigate war. Where had Chase heard his name before?

When Chang finished, Brower addressed Chase once more. "He says it was a mistake to bring you here." He looked purposefully at the more notable security displays. "Perhaps he was right. But I had to make sure your conclusions died with you."

There it was. Chase had known the men would kill them, of course, but the fact seemed more imminent when the words were spoken aloud. He needed time. "This General Lei, he's Chinese military?"

"Ex. He moved from there to intelligence."

Intelligence. General Chang Lei. It all sounded too familiar.

"So all this — " Chase waved his hand at the entire complex — "was built by the Chinese government, put here to support the attacks on the United States?"

"By the Chinese, yes. But not by the government. As the head of intelligence, General Chang was aware of China's treaty violations. He also knows that the United States and other countries are ill-prepared for a war in the cosmos. 'They are lulled into weakness by the Outer Space Treaty,' he's fond of saying." Brower pronounced the quote with a fake Chinese accent, shaking his fist in the air as he spoke. "'But not China. We are ready. We are strong.' For years, he urged the Chinese leadership to assert itself, to flex its muscles, to show its might. He thinks China's in a position to claim the worlds beyond Earth for its own."

Chase allowed himself a moment of silent absolution. He was right. He'd abandoned Erin to play a hunch, and he was right. If he survived the next few minutes, he might yet stop the madness.

Then the moment was gone and the reality of the present returned.

"But the leaders were deaf to his arguments," Brower continued. "They feared that the world would band against China and bring it to defeat. So Chang left. He founded the China Dominion and pursued other means to start his war."

Chang left. *That's it.* Chang resigned as head of China's Ministry for State Security after he'd ordered the UN assassinations. Chase's eyes widened. This man was *that* General Chang Lei. "What does he have to gain from such a conflict?"

Brower shrugged. "A place in China's history. He wants nothing for himself, but he wants everything for his country. And he realizes that a war for Earth would cost millions, even billions of lives. But space, that's another matter. Space is sparsely populated. By conducting the conflict there, the ground gained would be measured in worlds — not in meters, kilometers, or even countries — and human casualties could be kept to a minimum."

"Very noble," Gloria spat.

"Enough!" Chang called in thickly-accented English.

Brower's features hardened. "I guess it's time to go. But first, empty your pockets onto the table. One at a time. It wouldn't do for me to start shooting in here, and frankly, I don't trust any of you."

Chase glanced at the others. Mike looked resolute, his body poised, ready to go down fighting if necessary. Gloria, however, gave Chase a questioning look. She wasn't asking what to do so much as requesting permission for something. Knowing what she carried, it wasn't hard to guess her intent.

Chase nodded slowly, the gesture hidden from Brower by the back of his bubble helmet. Then he waited for the tempest to strike. One way or another, it would all be over in the next few seconds.

~(O)~

Gloria reached into her pocket.

"Left hand only," Brower demanded.

She stopped, switched hands, and pulled a flash-bang from her suit. She placed it on the table, then reached across her body to unstrap her knife.

Brower took a precautionary step back. He didn't seem to notice that the flash-bang's pin was missing.

Gloria closed her eyes and prepared for the blast. Her suit would mitigate the sound and the stunning pressure wave, but the flash could still be blinding.

When the blast came, she whirled with her knife in hand. The blade connected with something firm, then broke through the resistance and sank into flesh. Her vision was spotted around the edges as she stared into the blind eyes of the man who'd entered with Brower, her knife hilt deep in his chest.

Yet he was alive.

He raised his gun, so Gloria grabbed the barrel and pressed it aside. His hand convulsed on the trigger and a spray of bullets took out a wide swath in the monitors on one side of the bunker.

Gloria hooked her leg behind his and shoved him to the ground. She went down with him, taking herself out of the line of fire as a burst of gunshots erupted from the balcony, muffled and indistinct beyond the ringing in her ears. A chip of concrete from the floor pinged her faceplate.

Once down, the enemy struggled fiercely. He rolled her off him and yanked his weapon from her grip.

Gloria kicked the man's faceplate, which snapped back into his forehead. Then she kicked his gun hand, knocked the weapon away, and clocked him in the helmet again.

The man spat blood into his helmet as he tried to stand.

She let him. He was weaponless and blind, and he rose between her and the men on the catwalk. But she stood with him.

He squinted as though trying to make her out in the gloom, but he couldn't stop her from reaching to his chest, pulling the blade free, and plunging it back in to greater effect.

When he fell away, Gloria reached down to retrieve his weapon for herself.

⁓(O)⁓

When Gloria set the charge on the table, Chase recognized its armed state. He squeezed his eyes shut to protect his vision from the flash and waited. When it came, he stepped to the side and shoved Mike to the floor — and, he hoped, out of the line of fire. Then he opened his eyes.

The room was dimmer, or at least seemed so, but he could make out the figures on the catwalk. The man in the middle fired a blind burst into the center of the room. Chase couldn't reach him, so he went for the man on the end instead. With a tremendous push of his legs, he sprang to the balcony handrail.

The man that stood on the walk before him stared sightlessly, unmoving as a statue. By the time Chase clambered over the railing, the man was in motion, crouching down for cover from those on the floor below. But he took no notice of Chase's presence beside him, as though he could neither see nor hear. Chase kicked the man's rifle and sent it skidding over the balcony's edge.

In response, the terrorist pulled a pistol from a holster at his waist. Chase grabbed the gun and wrestled the man for a dominant position on their perch. The man was small by comparison but younger by far and stronger than he looked. It took every bit of Chase's strength to maintain his footing as they staggered back and forth.

Then the man blinked as though his vision was beginning to return. Chase threw his head forward, impacting his faceplate against the bridge of the terrorist's nose. The handgun fell from the man's limp grasp, his eyes glazed over, and blood streamed freely from his nostrils, soaking the front of his uniform. His knees buckled and Chase caught the man's weight in his arms. The terrorist was out cold.

General Chang stood at the far end of the catwalk, across the room from Chase. The other militant was along the balcony to Chase's left. Both seemed to have recovered from the blast.

A burst of gunfire erupted and the man on the left toppled. Sparks from the mesh walk revealed Mike's position beneath.

Chang brought his rifle to bear on Chase and stared at him with an unspoken threat in his eye. "Stop!" The word was almost unrecognizable through his thick accent. Everything in the room went still.

Chase stared down the gun's barrel as he raised the unconscious body in his arms to produce a human shield and hostage. Gloria straddled her dead opponent with her rifle pointed at the head of the Dominion leader. Brower was nowhere in sight.

Determined to stand fast as long as Gloria held the trump card, Chase met the general's gaze with equal determination and waited for his decision.

After a moment, Chang put a bullet into the head of Chase's hostage. An instant later, the general's skull exploded into a spray of gore. The pair of reports echoed through the chamber, then died away into silence.

Chase heaved a long sigh, gave thanks to whoever might be listening, and made his way to the ladder. He found both his friends uninjured, then turned to the video monitors in search of his missing quarry.

Brower was easy to spot — he was the only moving thing in any of the displays — but Chase didn't know the layout of the base well enough to determine the fugitive's location based on the video images.

But as Chase saw it, Brower had three options: fight, hide, or run. He'd already chosen not to fight. And if he hid, Chase would find him eventually. So he had to run, which he couldn't do without a vehicle. And there was only one place on the base to get one.

Before they left the command center, Gloria stopped Chase and handed him a rifle. "We use live rounds this time."

Though he regretted the necessity, he took the weapon without comment.

The only familiar route to the equipment bay was blocked by pressure doors in a number of places, so it took them several minutes to find their way back. When they got to the airlock between the base and the ruined garage, Brower stood inside, holding a crate of dehydrated meals and waiting for the outer door to open. As it did, Chase spoke into the comm link. "Going somewhere, Stan?"

The man turned to face him, his hands full and his weapon slung across his back.

Chase stood just inside the inner door with his rifle pointed at Brower's face.

The traitor watched him, measuring him. Chase and his friends still wore their environmental suits and had nothing to lose if Chase put a bullet through the pane. After a few moments of internal deliberation, Brower's expression changed from contemplation to resignation.

Chase reached out to the control panel, closed the outer door, and re-pressurized the airlock. Somehow, he must convince Brower to help stop the madness. Because he was the only witness left, Chase couldn't do it without him.

CHAPTER 28

Chase confiscated Brower's rifle, emptied the man's outside pockets, stripped off his pressure suit, and searched the rest of his clothing. Then Chase made him put the pressure suit back on. It would encumber Brower's movements and, without a helmet, it would provide no protection from vacuum if he tried to flee the base.

That done, Chase ushered him into one of the living quarters. "How're your odds looking now?"

"Not so good, I'm afraid."

"Then perhaps we can discuss a leniency deal."

"Why? What's in it for you?"

"Stan, in large measure, you're responsible for the US-China conflict. And you have the power to stop it, or at least try. Testify to the existence and objectives of the China Dominion and maybe both countries will stand down."

Brower snorted. "Good luck."

Chase settled himself into a chair, facing Brower. "Maybe they won't, but I've got to try. And you can significantly strengthen my case. Victoria Powers seems like a reasonable woman. She might withdraw the US fighters. Then it's up to China."

Brower was silent for a long time as he sat and stared at the floor.

Meanwhile, Mike and Gloria were in the garage, clearing debris from a cargo truck for their trip back to Lunar Alpha. Once it was cleared, they'd have to check it for damage before committing themselves to it for the two-day journey. It wouldn't take long, they'd said, so Chase guarded Brower while he waited.

"You were the agent, weren't you," Chase continued. It was a statement more than a question.

Brower looked up, his expression blank.

"The CIA agent who reported the Chinese nanochip technology," Chase added.

Brower put his head down and gave an almost imperceptible nod of affirmation.

"Why, Stan? You were just finishing your career. You could have retired."

Brower's head shot up. "That's bullshit! And you know it! You had a distinguished career in the air force. You know what a government pension amounts to. And it ain't shit. Could you live off yours? No! Why else would you work for another twenty years in NASA? Well, congratulations. Now you can retire with two pension checks."

Brower spat in contempt. "You'll be living high on the hog now. Hell, you might even be able to afford your own place. Well, not me. I refuse to work for forty years for just enough to get by. No, thanks."

"What'd they offer you?"

"That's none of your business. More money than you'll ever see, I'll tell you that."

"Enough to sell out your own country?"

Brower seemed to have vented his rage. His shoulders slumped and he looked beaten once more. "I didn't see it that way."

"How did you see it?"

"General Chang wanted a war to dissolve the Outer Space Treaty. Then China could lay claim to any asset they could control. But he assumed China would win. I've got more faith in America than that.

"And there was something else." Brower paused, hesitant to continue. "I spent the last ten years of my life trying to uncover China's treaty violations. I knew they were doing something, but I could never get at what it was. It was my job, damn it. And in ten years, I couldn't figure it out. I was running out of time."

"Jesus, Stan, why not ask the agency for more resources?"

"It's not that simple. We put these things together from bits of information gathered over years, and even then we can only make inferences. You put too many people in the field and the adversary gets nervous.

Then you can't learn anything."

Brower raised his hand in a gesture of resignation. "I figured a conflict would reveal their assets before they became insurmountable."

Chase almost pitied the man, fearing to retire as a failure. It was a specter that had haunted Chase for four years. But no more. The events of the past days had done much to banish that wraith before it had undone him. "Did you intend for Europe and Russia to get involved?"

"I assumed they would. But I thought they'd both take our side. China should have been seen as the instigator."

"What about O'Leary? Is he involved?"

Brower shook his head.

"Snider?"

No, again.

"What about Lesperance?" The man was dead, but the matter of his guilt or innocence weighed heavily on Chase. He'd have to tell Frank's family something.

Brower chuckled. "Serendipity at its finest. You were making me nervous, asking too many of the right questions. I needed a red herring. You gave me Frank Lesperance."

"He didn't know why you requested the ship's manifest?"

"Of course he didn't know."

Because he needed more information, Chase played to Brower's pride. "Well, I'm impressed. You got it all done. The device planted, the war started, everything. But there's something I haven't been able to figure out. How did you get your fingerprints out of the ISC database?"

Brower laughed. "I asked."

"Simple as that?"

"Sure. When you're a CIA field agent, all you've got to do is make up some flimsy justification and the agency'll suppress just about anything. Bureaucracies are stupid."

"Tell me about the bombing," Chase asked.

Brower waved his hand in dismissal. "We were prepared to carry out as many such missions as necessary to ensure that the war got off the ground."

"So you have more people out there?"

"A few. They're scattered now."

"How did you know I was on to you?"

"Oh, that? I placed a flag on my file. I'm notified any time somebody accesses it. It's always helpful to know when people are checking up on you. When I found out it was you doing the checking, I assumed the worst."

"What about Lu Chin?"

"What about him?"

"I didn't kill him, did I?"

Brower shook his head again. "He was a loose end."

"And he didn't steal my thinpad or delete the data."

"No. I did that."

Just then, Mike came in. "You guys ready?"

Chase nodded. They'd have more time to talk on the way back. He handed Brower a helmet and ushered him into the hall.

Brower walked slowly, mechanically, head hanging, in apparent disregard for his surroundings. He was the perfect picture of a thoroughly defeated man.

Brower picked his way through the rubble-strewn garage, a few steps in front of his captors, relieved that the space sickness hadn't hit him yet. That would come when he stepped into the open, but he was ready. This time, he vowed, it wouldn't overwhelm him.

Halfway across the bay, he stumbled over a body and went down, face first, onto another. By their pressure suits, these had been two of Chang's men. Though they appeared unarmed, they should have been carrying a standard allotment of Dominion gear. He felt several of the dead man's pockets as he pretended to try to stand.

The woman, one of Cottington's National Guards, kicked him. "Get up."

Brower was in luck: he found a hand grenade in one pocket and a pistol in another. He couldn't pick either up without being seen, so he just slipped the pin from the grenade and left it in the pocket.

He began a slow count in his head as he struggled to his feet and continued toward the waiting truck. At the count of seven, he dove for the cover of a shattered core-sampling rig.

When the booby trap exploded, it sent a wave of shrapnel into the bodies of those behind him.

Chapter 29

Brower and his captors had stopped at the airlock leading to the equipment bay. The lock could accommodate only three, so Chase stayed inside while Mike and Gloria escorted the prisoner through.

Chase was still in the chamber, waiting for it to pump to vacuum, when Brower's grenade exploded.

Before the dirt settled, Brower recovered the pistol he'd found on the body. His first shot put a hole in the airlock window but missed Chase as he ducked below the sill.

Mike lay nearby, gasping in his perforated pressure suit. Brower picked up the man's rifle and prepared to put him out of his misery.

"Here, you bastard!" The woman sprang up and launched herself toward cover before Brower could bring the rifle to bear.

He let her go. Her rifle lay where the blast had left it. Chase was still armed.

"Morgan, you arrogant ass," he said into the comm, approaching the airlock where Chase was trapped. "You should have gone home when you had the chance." *Crack!* He punctuated his words with shots from his pistol. The sound vibrated through the atmosphere in his pressure suit. "I even had your son-in-law killed to force you back to Earth. They missed Erin, though. Too bad. That would have done it, I think."

The woman tried to circle around, over the debris, in a futile effort to cut off Brower's only exit.

He ignored her. *Crack!* The bullet shattered the window on the inner airlock door and brought down the first row of pressure barriers inside. "The investigation was going well. I'd have framed some poor cuss to take the fall. It didn't matter who, as long as he was Chinese.

"But no, you had to come back and screw things up." *Crack!* "Couldn't leave it alone." *Crack!*

Chase shot blindly into the garage.

Brower scrambled for cover. When the barrage stopped, he fired a few rounds to force the woman back, then left the bay.

The world began to spin as he stepped beyond the confines of the garage. He took a few slow breaths and focused his eyes and thoughts on the truck ahead. It was close, he told himself, just a few meters. The ground canted and he staggered forward, grabbed the truck's fender for support, worked his way along the side, and pulled himself into the driver's compartment. When he finally climbed in, he sealed the source of his vertigo behind the solid walls of the cab, engaged the ignition, and sped away.

"Colonel!"

Chase peered into the bay.

Gloria had Mike by a handful of his loose pressure suit and was dragging him toward the airlock. "He's alive."

Chase scrambled to his feet and snatched a roll of vacuum tape from a first aid kit on the wall. Together, they patched the half-dozen holes in Mike's suit. When it began to swell from the oxygen in Mike's tank, Chase turned his attention to Gloria. She'd been behind Mike when the grenade exploded. Her suit appeared to be intact.

He shoved the tape at her and grabbed his rifle. "Do what you can for him."

She moved quickly. In moments she and Mike were inside, waiting for the pressure doors to cycle open.

Brower was gone, but still in comm range.

"Stan," Chase said between clenched teeth. "You can't run. That truck will get you back to Alpha, but that's about it. You'll find no refuge there."

"Not true, old pal," came Brower's reply. "This thing's got twice as much fuel as I'd need for Alpha. And your guys were nice enough to pack food, water, and air for four. It's not fast, but I can make Mare Serenitatis or even Alexander."

"The cost is too high," Chase screamed. "Don't you see that?"

Brower's reply was calm, passionless. "Don't bother to try the base communications — I've disabled them."

Chase cursed Chang for the whole of the China Dominion, for everything the organization had done. Then he cursed Brower.

There were no usable vehicles in the Dominion garage that Chase could exhume from the collapsed roof by himself, but he did find a pair of jet packs of the type he'd used to maneuver on space walks during his astronaut years.

He picked one up, inspected it for damage, and strapped it on. It had sufficient thrust to overcome lunar gravity and was easy enough to use, so he launched himself from the ground and steered toward the ATV they'd left behind the maintenance shed. He rode that back to the main building, refueled it from the Dominion supply, and then grabbed his rifle and rode to catch Brower.

By then the fugitive had a twenty-minute head start.

Chase pursued, knowing that he'd capture Brower or kill him, or die trying. He wouldn't have enough oxygen and fuel to return without resupplying from the stores on the truck. But none of that mattered. The son-of-a-bitch had gone after his family. It was far too late to back out now.

Brower came into view thirty minutes later. Chase approached from behind, unsure of how to stop the truck once he got there. He could disable it, of course, but then he'd have no way to return to Lunar Alpha. So he pulled up alongside and activated the jet pack, which lifted him off the cycle and propelled him toward the bed of the truck. Brower swerved from side to side as Chase maneuvered to place himself between the side rails. The ATV slowed and fell behind.

When Chase finally managed to center himself over his target and plant his feet firmly on the flatbed, Brower stepped on the brake. Chase flew forward, twisting to prevent an impact on his faceplate. He slammed into the rear of the pressurized cab, leading with the O_2 bottle and jet pack that were fastened to his back, then fell to the floor of the bed and lay still. An alarm wailed in his helmet and his O_2 level dropped rapidly.

The truck leapt forward and Chase slid off the back, but he managed to get a hand on the rear bumper as he fell. His feet, dragging in the soft sand, frustrated his effort to climb back in.

He tried the jet pack with his free hand while Brower taunted him with a constant monologue over the intercom. "Having a nice ride? Still don't know when to quit?"

The jet pack was dead, so Chase popped the harness straps and let it fall away. Then he gripped the side railing and heaved himself onto the cargo platform.

His O_2 light flashed from green to yellow.

Brower steered over a rough patch of ground and the truck began to bounce wildly. The movement rattled Chase's teeth and challenged his grip. But it did have one virtue: it created such a racket with his gear that it drowned out Brower's voice on the speaker. When the terrain smoothed once more, he eased his way toward the cab.

Then Brower slammed the brake again. This time, Chase flew face-first into the back window. His collar ring bruised his shoulders and a small crack appeared in his faceplate. It was no more than a finger's width long, but the weakness in the durapane could easily spread.

Chase's vision narrowed to that tiny fracture, his leaking O_2 tank suddenly minor compared to the threat of an immediate loss of pressure. The truck lurched forward and Chase rolled off into the dirt. When he hit the ground, the crack in his faceplate grew several centimeters in length. With Chase in a near-panic, his sight flew to his suit's pressure gauge. It was holding, but his air was almost gone.

Acting purely on instinct, he brought the rifle to his shoulder, forced his focus past his cracked faceplate, and squeezed the trigger. His target was a vague shape through a swirling cloud of dust. Two rounds. Three. The truck continued.

The O_2 alarm sounding in his ear fragmented his concentration. He forced it out of his mind and squeezed the trigger again.

The left side of the truck sagged as a bullet ripped through the rear tire. The dust screen thickened as the wheel began to drag.

Chase shifted his aim to the other side and fired again. The right rear popped three shots later and the truck ground to a halt.

"Damn it!" Brower tried to free the truck by rocking it forward and back. When that failed, he depressurized the cabin and climbed out.

Chase, who'd begun walking toward the truck, stopped when he saw the door open. Brower held Mike's rifle and Chase had precious little cover nearby.

"You fucking ass!" Brower shouted. "Are you satisfied? Now we'll both die out here. Is that what you wanted?"

No, but at this point, it was better than dying out here alone.

Brower stepped from the cab and aimed his weapon. It took him several seconds to stabilize the rifle, as if he were disoriented or off balance. Grateful for the time, Chase dove into a shallow depression in the sand, careful to keep his faceplate from striking the ground.

Just then, his O_2 light changed from yellow to red and the siren became a steady, mournful tone. The tank was empty. All he had left was the air in the suit. A few minutes, no more.

Brower continued toward him, his stride slow and deliberate. He took a few steps, fired, then took a few more.

A halting diatribe of profanity rang in Chase's ears. He knew his cover was incomplete, the depression too shallow to hide his body, so he lay flat and willed himself into the ground. But Brower was so crazed with anger that his aim was erratic.

Bits of dust and dirt flew as the traitor fired long barrages of ammunition into the small hummock that was Chase's only protection.

Chase didn't dare raise his head to look, but he sensed Brower moving closer.

Then the stream of profanity and shells stopped and Chase looked up. Brower stood halfway between him and the abandoned truck. The rifle had gone empty and Brower stared at it as though he couldn't comprehend. So Chase stood and aimed his own rifle, prepared to capture the traitor once more.

But as he stepped forward, Brower pulled a grenade from his pocket and dropped the pin into the sand. He eyed Chase with a wicked grin as he brought his arm back to throw.

Chase fired a single round into Brower's chest. The man fell backward and dropped the grenade in the dirt. On reflex, Chase crouched and turned from the blast, but he was far enough away that he needn't have bothered.

When the dust settled, Chase inspected Brower's gear. The two things he needed most were still in working order. First, he removed the man's O_2 tank and plugged it into his own regulator. Oxygen flooded his EVA and he took a deep, rejuvenating breath. The fresh air smelled sweet in his nostrils and he indulged in a moment to savor his salvation.

Then he pulled off Brower's helmet, climbed into the truck, and waited for the cabin to pressurize. When it did, he removed his own damaged headgear and replaced it with Brower's, thanking the designers for developing a standard-sized collar ring.

That done, he hiked the kilometer or so back to the abandoned ATV and returned to the Dominion base.

When he arrived, a figure was approaching the compound on foot. The man, obviously injured, appeared to be unarmed. Chase steered the ATV in his direction.

CHAPTER 30

Chase and Gloria helped Clark into one of the undamaged living quarters of the Dominion outpost.

"How's Mike?" Chase asked her.

"Full of morphine. He'll live." She gave Clark enough of the painkiller to put him out and began to work on his wounds. His right leg was broken and his left arm shattered. He'd made it back to the base with the help of a crutch and an oxygen canister he'd apparently salvaged from the wreckage of the ERT transport.

"It was all for nothing," Gloria said when she finished setting and splinting the bones.

"Why do you say that?" Chase asked.

"We can't prove anything. All this — "she waved her arm, indicating the Dominion base — "might as well be Chinese military. Without proof of conspiracy, you'll never stop the war."

Chase pulled out the thinpad he'd kept in a pocket of his pressure suit. "I set it to record before we entered the stronghold. It's captured everything that's happened — the audio, anyway — including my conversations with our friend Brower."

She looked dubious. "You think that's enough?"

"I don't know." He slipped it back into his pocket. "I hope so."

Gloria looked around the Spartan interior of their new home. "You're assuming we'll get out of here sometime soon."

"Count on it. The captain of the *Snow Leopard* knows we're here and she knows both transports were destroyed in the battle. She'll send help. I figure we've got three days at the most." He grunted, unable to bring himself to laugh. "They'll probably send every security guard and National Guardsmen on the base."

⁂

Six days later, the four returned to Lunar Alpha. As soon as Clark and Mike were settled in the base infirmary, Chase contacted Tom O'Leary and insisted on speaking to the president.

"Not a chance," O'Leary said. "I want to review the data and hear your arguments before I request any of the president's time." Nevertheless, O'Leary did promise that Tony Mariano and Dan Norton would be there when they discussed the evidence.

In the middle of that meeting now, Chase sat in a small room provided by the Lunar Alpha intelligence office. Alone with a secure telnet terminal, a hot cup of coffee, and a keyboard, he viewed the others on the display before him. "You have my report. The evidence is overwhelming. There's only one scenario that's consistent with all of the physical evidence found in the wreckage, the later findings of the investigation team, and the series of events that have occurred since the initial incident. That scenario is confirmed by the audio file that I sent with the report." He spoke with the authority of a more youthful man, sure of himself and of his facts. "Stan Brower was instrumental in the China Dominion's pursuit of their objective."

Chase spent the next two hours going through a detailed account of the findings in the investigation report, which had been signed by Jack Snider, building his case step-by-step, piece-by-piece. He didn't rely on the unique nature of the sabotage device that Michelle had brought to light, other than the fact that knowledge of it had come to the CIA through then-agent Stan Brower. Anything else about the technology was too speculative when it came to connecting it to the war-inciting conspiracy. Instead, he relied on the physical evidence of Brower's fingerprints, the lack of any verifiable involvement of the Chinese government, and the existence of the China Dominion base. Then he pointed out that its leader was the retired head of Chinese intelligence who was responsible for the UN assassinations a decade earlier, and presented the wealth of documented evidence that he and Gloria had discovered during their three-day stay at the militant stronghold. He played the audio file as a confirmation of his conclusions only after the physical evidence had already made a solid case.

"The recording said there're additional terrorists at large, did it not?" O'Leary asked when Chase finished his presentation.

"It did. I sent a Dominion membership roster with my report. Our military personnel are still at the stronghold, scouring the base for additional information. By now, a forensics team is attempting to make a positive identification of each of the bodies. You can use the list as a starting point to track down the rest."

"You make an excellent case, Colonel Morgan. I'll take this to the president, though I can't guarantee that she'll respond in the way you expect. Political events have a way of getting out of the control of any one person."

"I, also, will speak with the president," Mariano said, "and urge her to approach President Li with a conciliatory tone."

Dan Norton said nothing.

"That's all I can ask. Thank you, gentlemen, for your time and consideration." Chase disconnected the link and sat back in his chair. Would it be enough? He drained the last of his coffee. Time would tell.

He activated the comm again and keyed the terminal for an outside line.

"Dad!" Erin exclaimed with a smile when she picked up the link. "Dad, it's great to see you."

"I'm coming home, honey. My shuttle leaves tonight."

~(O)~

Victoria Powers walked into the meeting chamber in Le Meridien Luxor Hotel in El Quseir, in neutral Egypt, with Tony Mariano and Dan Norton. She leaned heavily on her cane, the weight of what she must do seemingly too much for her legs alone to bear. The Chinese delegation of President Li and two other men entered simultaneously from the far end of the room. In addition to the people present, each president was permitted an interpreter as a hedge against misunderstanding or false translation.

To begin, Secretary Mariano gave an abbreviated presentation of the data Chase had compiled. He wasn't trying to convince the Chinese leader of the truth of Chase's conclusions, only to provide a basis for the misunderstanding by the United States of the source of the attacks. He omitted any specific reference to Stan Brower by name and avoided stating why the US believed that the computer chip originated in China.

When Mariano finished, President Powers got slowly to her feet, still leaning on her cane, and apologized for accusing China of perpetrating the *Phoenix* attack.

"This is all?" The deep wrinkles that covered Li's face hid all expression. "What of the willful destruction of Chinese property?"

"You're alluding to the Mingyun satellites?"

Li nodded. His eyes never left those of his adversary. "Do you offer apology for this unprovoked attack?"

"Mr. President." Powers spoke clearly and deliberately. "The provisions of the Outer Space Treaty specifically prohibit the deployment of such spacecraft — "

Li shot to his feet. "*Réngrán*!"

Powers waited for the translation as Li continued to speak.

"Nevertheless," her interpreter said, "they were the property of the People's Republic of China. And as such, I demand not only an apology, but financial restitution as well."

Powers began shaking her head and continued until the monologue of the Chinese leader died into silence. "You were in violation of international treaty." Powers forced a calm tone that Li would hear even before he received the translation. "The only attack we made against China was in direct response to that violation. The attack was justified by the violation, even without the other incidents."

"You offer no apology?" The translator made it a question, but there was no inflection or uncertainty in Li's voice.

"Not for a justified response to an act of war."

Li Muyou met Powers' stare for several seconds. "We have nothing further to discuss." With that, he turned and his delegation rose to follow.

"Wait," President Powers said as Li reached for the door. She couldn't leave here without a cease-fire. Ultimately, she was responsible for the commencement of hostilities, which was precipitated, at least in part, by her own erroneous conclusion that China had attacked the lunar targets. If the war continued, it would be her own doing — and perhaps humankind's undoing. That was a burden her conscience couldn't bear.

On the other hand, she couldn't afford to weaken her country's international standing by offering any form of leniency for violating a treaty as fundamental to interplanetary peace as the Outer Space Treaty.

Li paused at the door.

"You have a satellite orbiting the Moon," Powers continued. "We have warships stationed there that are capable of destroying it. We are resolved to do so, along with any others that you deploy, even at the risk of prolonged interplanetary war." Li didn't reply, so Powers motioned to the chair across from her. "Sit, please, and let's talk."

Ultimately, cooler attitudes prevailed and the leaders agreed that the United States would withdraw its remaining warship from lunar deployment, and that China would allow it to depart safely. Once it returned to Earth, China would recover, and then dismantle, the lunar Mingyun satellite.

Bill Ryan woke to the flickering glow and muted sounds of the telnet terminal in the far corner of his one-room flat at Lunar Alpha. Regular injections of bone stimulator had healed his shattered appendages. He'd been released from the infirmary and no longer required constant medical observation. But he was still weak and endured his rehabilitation therapy for several hours each day. In time, he expected to make a full recovery.

He propped himself up on the elbow of his good arm. A dim lamp on the far side of the room lit the austere apartment, with a bed and nightstand in one corner; a small dining table and kitchenette along the opposite wall; and reclining chair, short sofa, and a miniature coffee table in the middle. The latest newsblips played on the telnet monitor.

He and Dana were the last vestiges of a military force that had now returned to Earth. When the *Snow Leopard* was recalled, Dana was granted leave to remain at Alpha until Bill was strong enough to go home as well. The National Guard troops left a week or two later, after they'd completed their work at the Dominion stronghold.

"What time is it?" Bill asked.

"Eight-thirty." Dana rose from the recliner, wearing Bill's robe, and turned to face him, holding a glass of juice. "How'd you sleep?"

"Late, if it's eight-thirty already."

"You have someplace you need to be?" She sat beside him on the bed, set her glass on the nightstand, and helped him rearrange the pillows. When he was propped comfortably against the headboard in an inclined position, she handed him the glass.

He took a long drink of the cold, refreshing fluid. With it, he washed the foul taste of the night's sleep from his mouth.

"They caught another one," Dana said, alluding to the newsblip.

"How many is that now?"

"Four, I think." She looked down at the bedding. "Tell me, Major. What have you got on under there?"

He flushed. "Same thing I had on when we went to bed last night."

"I know." She smiled as though she was proud of herself for something, then pulled back the covers to expose him. "They sure caused a lot of trouble."

"Who?"

"The China Dominion."

"Oh. Yeah, they did. But one good thing came out of it."

"What's that?" She scrutinized his face.

"I got you."

Dana laughed. "What can I say? It put my priorities in proper order." She kissed him passionately on the mouth.

Bill returned the gesture with equal fervor.

When she was ready, Dana took the glass and set it on the bedside table. Then she swung her leg over him.

"I'll never let you go," she promised.

Chase arrived at Erin's Seattle home by taxi. He flung his carry-on bag over his shoulder, lifted Penny's carrier in one hand and a bag of groceries he'd picked up in the other, then headed up the driveway.

The debris from the explosion had been stripped away and the entrance from what once had been the garage was boarded up until the insurance company and construction contractors could come to some sort of settlement on Erin's behalf. Chase could help expedite the process now that he was finally home.

His legs, just beginning to adjust to full gravity, ached by the time he got to the front door.

Erin answered quickly, her smile broad. "Come in." She led him into the den. "Put your stuff down."

"Gramp!" Laura and Katie yelled in unison as they barreled toward him.

He barely had time to set down his bags before the girls bowled him over in a pair of baby bear-hugs.

"Easy, girls," Erin scolded. Penny barked excitedly from within her carrier.

Chase laughed and wrestled with his granddaughters for a minute before saying, "Okay, okay. That's enough. I need to talk to your mother."

Laura, the older girl, stepped away. Chase sat up against Katie's weight. "Ugh. I'm not as young as you girls are. You'll have to go easy on me." He held Katie, now four, at bay by her shoulders. "I'll play with you in a little bit. Okay?"

She stuck out her bottom lip. "That's not nice," Erin told her.

"It's okay," Chase said. The girl's pout lasted only until he released Penny. Immediately, the dog took off across the room, her tongue and tail wagging, both girls in pursuit.

Chase retrieved the groceries and led Erin into the kitchen. "How are they doing?"

Erin glanced over her shoulder. "All right, most of the time. Laura cries herself to sleep most nights. Katie won't sleep at all unless she's in bed with me. Even so, I don't think they fully comprehend that they'll never see him again."

"And how's their mother?"

Erin slumped into a seat at the table. "It's so hard, Dad. I don't know how I'm going to do it. The girls are my strength. Their resilience keeps me going most of the time. But they wear me out, too."

She took an unsteady breath. "I've never had to do this alone."

"You don't have to, sweetheart."

She stood and hugged him for a long time. The sounds of laughter and barking reached them from the other room.

Erin took a deep breath and released him. "Will you stay with us? At least until I get things figured out, until I feel I can stand on my own? You can have the guest room."

Originally they'd talked about his staying for only a couple of weeks, but that was before Erin's life fell apart. He took her hands in his own. "I'll stay until the girls are grown, if that's what you need." Even then, he planned to buy a house in the neighborhood so he would always be nearby.

Her hands relaxed in his.

"But right now — " he displayed the grocery bag — "I'm going to cook dinner."

"Don't be silly. I still have a freezer full of casseroles. I won't have to cook for a year."

"You're probably sick of casseroles."

She sighed "You have no idea."

"Okay then, point me to the pot cabinet. I'm a pretty fair cook, for a bachelor."

EPILOGUE

European President Peter Hunt sat in his private study in the Executive Mansion in Brussels.

Arthur van Arsdel came in, greeted him, and took the offered seat across from the president. They were alone.

"*Centurion*'s in flight," van Arsdel declared.

"Excellent. When does the next one launch?"

"Three weeks." Van Arsdel was silent for a time. "It's a dangerous thing we're doing. It's been a month since the cease-fire was signed."

"Arthur, the Americans were nice enough to bring down the Mingyun satellites for us, and they're too timid to do something like this themselves." He leaned forward in his chair. "This is an opportunity to increase the preparedness of the European Union over that of even the United States. No such opportunity has ever occurred in the past, and it may never do so again. We can make Europe the leading force of capitalism and democracy in the world."

"I see."

"God willing," the president continued, "we'll never have to make them known to the worlds, let alone use the things, but I'll sleep better at night knowing they're there."

THE END

About the Author

Kirt Hickman was born in 1966 in Albuquerque, New Mexico. He earned a Bachelor's degree in electrical engineering in 1989 and a Master's degree in opto-electronics in 1991, both from the University of New Mexico. Since then, he has worked in research and manufacturing fields related to high-energy lasers, microelectronics, and micro-machines, fields that he leverages to enrich his science fiction. Kirt makes his publishing debut with *Worlds Asunder*.

CPSIA information can be obtained at www.ICGtesting.com
Printed in the USA
LVOW110727091011

249680LV00004B/2/P